Spanish Li€s
Mark Harrison

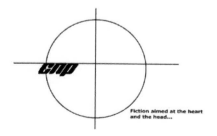

Fiction aimed at the heart
and the head...

Published by Caffeine Nights Publishing 2010

Published in Great Britain by Caffeine Nights Publishing
www.cnpublishing.co.uk
British Library Cataloguing in Publication Data.
A CIP catalogue record for this book is available from the British Library
ISBN: 978-1-907565-00-7

Cover design by
Mark (Wills) Williams
Everything else by
Default, Luck and Accident

Also by Mark Harrison

I Want to Live in Spain
Published by UKA Press 2007
ISBN 978-1-905796-07-6

Missing
Published by UKA Press 2006
ISBN 978-1-905796-02-1

Available from:
vimark@inicia.es
www.ukapress.com
www.amazon.co.uk

In loving memory of Jessie.

PROLOGUE

Shadows ebbed as twilight deepened and stars emerged, flickering in a moonless sky. He was strolling home feeling smug and self-satisfied at the end of another eventful day, juggling the affairs of his burgeoning empire. Life was good, recent problems behind him. His conscience should have been burdened with the weight of his recent exploits, yet he felt not the slightest twinge of guilt and for the first time in months he began to contemplate the future.

He looked down at the unguarded precipice to the jagged pile of rocks and rubble lying on the ground thirty feet below. The scene hadn't changed for as long as he could remember, ever since the old house crumbled and collapsed. Someone could fall from the edge, he thought. Yes, he really must do something about it.

That was last week. Now it was too late. His balance was lost. For a brief moment he clung to something with his right hand, desperately trying to hold on. His grip failed, his hand slipped and only his fingers grasped his last remaining hope until finally they weakened and detached.

He toppled forward, arms and legs flailing, tugging at thin air in a futile attempt to slow his descent. He swivelled his body to cushion the impact, instinctively pushing out his arms to break his fall. A searing pain shot through his right forearm as bones shattered and collapsed. His left shoulder took the full force of the next jolt, followed by his left hip. His head rocked backwards uncontrollably, overpowering taught neck muscles, and crashed against the sharp corner of an ancient piece of masonry. A crimson cloud drifted across his eyes as he tumbled backwards until, at last, he came to rest.

1

In the silence that followed he was gripped by fear. He wasn't afraid of death; he had cheated that particular fate before. What concerned him more was that all his successful, scheming subterfuge might be wasted were his life to end now with so many unexploited opportunities available to him. Most of all he feared that, finally, he might be forced to atone for a life spent in rapacious pursuit of his own vainglory, oblivious to the consequences for others whom he had abused to satisfy his craving for power, wealth and self-indulgence.

Later, a hand touched him and a blurred shadow hovered before fading into obscurity.

CHAPTER ONE

A single spotlight focussed attention on the corpulent figure seated at the expansive mahogany desk. Behind the silhouette, the portrait of King Juan Carlos, illuminated by a small brass library light, still hung at an awkward angle, just as I remembered it from my last visit three months before.

'Well Captain Fernandez, how are you adapting to life in the Guardia Civil? It's all rather strange, I expect.' Colonel Antonio Cardells remained seated and stroked his greying moustache, following the folds of his flabby cheeks down to his chin.

Rather strange was no exaggeration. It was very strange. 'I feel uncomfortable carrying a gun.'

'But I thought you did firearms training when you were with the Nottinghamshire Constabulary.'

'That's true, sir, but it's very different carrying this lump of lethal metal all the time.'

'You don't have to sleep with it, you know, not unless you want to.'

'Are you sure? I wouldn't want to break regulations, not whilst I'm still on probation.'

Cardells almost smiled. 'You can keep it under your pillow, with your handcuffs. You're fixed up with somewhere to live, I gather.'

'Yes, I'm moving into the town house I inherited from my father in Parcent… if it's ready.'

'Good move. You still have family there, I understand.'

I wondered what else Cardells knew of my past and my links with the tiny inland village I had only recently and reluctantly discovered.

'It's a pleasant village and very well placed for the northern Costa Blanca. We've assigned you to that area, for now at least, and your HQ will be at Jalon, ten minutes away. I bet you're itching to get started.'

'*Itching.* Yes.'

The cluster of mosquito bites on my inner thigh suddenly flared up. I resisted the impulse to scratch them and crossed my legs hoping that would remove the temptation.

'There are a couple of cases for you to get stuck into. The first is a suspicious death in Beniforell, not far from Parcent. The local Mayor in fact. He fell over a precipice and cracked his skull. Here's the file, you can read it later. It may come to nothing, but we need to take a look.'

'You said he fell off a precipice. What's suspicious about that?'

'You'll see when you read the file.'

'But I thought I was supposed to deal with the British ex-patriot community. What's the death of a local Mayor got to do with me?'

'As I said, you'll see when you read the file.'

'You said there were a couple of cases.'

'Ah, yes.' Another file edged in my direction, this one much bulkier than the last. 'This is much more up your street. A missing seventeen year old boy, English, well at least his parents are English; the boy's spent all his life in Spain. He's not been in contact for more than four months now.'

'Four months!'

'I know, I know. It sounds like a cold case. The lad has probably run away, but the parents are refusing to let it drop. They've been on to the British Consulate in Alicante and the Consul's asking questions. It's a PR job really. I'd like you to take a look, talk to the parents, reassure them and tell them everything possible is being done. You know the form, I'm sure.'

Great, just what I wanted, a local Mayor, probably drunk at the time, falls off a ledge and some teenage kid has a row with his mum and dad then does a runner and I'm expected to placate them with platitudes. Not exactly cutting edge detective work. I wondered if I was being

4

deliberately sidelined to keep me from meddling in anything more complex or sensitive.

'Is there anything else, Colonel?'

'No, that's all for now. Sergeant Poquet has been assigned to work with you. She knows the area well. In fact she's billeted in quarters at the *comisaría* in Jalon, so you'll almost be neighbours.'

I had worked with Mariela Poquet on my last case in Spain. A British couple had disappeared here on the Costa Blanca and since I was fluent in Spanish (courtesy of my father and my now ex-wife) the Nottingham Constabulary thought it a good idea to second me to the Guardia Civil to investigate. The truth was they were glad to be rid of their aberrant Detective Inspector, for a while at least. The outcome, two dead and the culprit sentenced to life in Alicante prison, was not entirely satisfactory, well not for the two deceased at any rate, but Colonel Cardells had been sufficiently impressed with my detective skills (and presumably my Spanish) to offer me a probationary job with the rank of Captain. I was still not sure why I had accepted the offer, but there were forces at work that made it seem like a good idea at the time.

An image of long blonde hair, dark glasses and perfect white teeth flashed before my eyes followed by a pair of slender hips wriggling in a short denim skirt and long legs teetering on stiletto heels. '*Sergeant* Poquet you say?'

'Yes, she's been promoted since you last worked together. It seems your commendation after the Harrington murder case did her prospects no harm at all. In fact I'd say she has a lot to thank you for.'

I thought I detected a wink, but it might have been an involuntary twitch or a nervous tic. Whatever, Cardells' face quickly returned to its normal stern scowl and his eyes drifted downward to a blue-covered folder in front of him.

'She's a good officer, Michael,' Cardells said as he opened the folder. 'You are still using Michael are you? Only I've been looking through your file – did I mention that Nottingham Constabulary have been good enough to forward your personnel records?'

No you didn't bloody mention it and nor did anyone in Nottingham.

'Just routine you understand. And I couldn't help but notice that your birth name is Miguel-Ángel Fernandez. Of course I understand you preferred Michael in the UK, but I just thought…'

I had ditched Miguel-Ángel years ago; about the same time I ditched my Spanish ancestry. I had my reasons, very good reasons, and I would have ditched Fernandez as well, only changing my name by deed poll seemed a step too far even for someone like me who hated Spain and everything it stood for. Besides, I was fed up of people calling me Migwell. Oh, and by the way, it's Ángel with a soft 'A' and a hard 'G', not Angel as in Gabriel.

'It's still Michael,' I said, realising how brusque I sounded. 'Unless that causes a problem.'

'No problem at all, Michael. As I was saying, Sergeant Poquet is a very good officer — solid, reliable, astute. She lacks a bit of experience as a detective, but under your expert tutelage I'm sure she will come on. And… now how can I put this, Michael? You're an excellent detective, your record speaks for itself and we know that from your last case, but… well, you are still new to Spain and the way we do things here might be a little different from what you are used to. Look, what I'm trying to say is that Mariela knows the way we work here and you might find it useful to ask her advice from time to time.' Cardells raised his eyes to gauge my reaction.

'Of course,' I said through a forced half-smile. What I really meant to say was, 'So she'll be keeping an eye on me then?'

'What do you think?' said my uncle Pepito as he climbed the narrow stairs, clinging to the heavy rope spiralling around the wall.

'It looks great. I can't believe the transformation. Last time I was here the place was a ruin. I still can't accept it's really mine.'

'It's a shame your father isn't here to see the old place again, and you moving in,' said Pepito.

I paused, imagining what it would be like to be climbing the stairs with my father; sharing his trepidation at being

6

back in Parcent. But that could never happen because my father was dead.

Three months after I had first visited Parcent during my secondment, I was still trying to come to terms with the fact that I had inherited a house in the village where my father was born; the village that rejected my father as a teenager when he was diagnosed with leprosy; the village that led my father to live in self-imposed exile in Britain with his English nurse, Susan, my mother. These were the events that had shaped my life; that had led me to believe, mistakenly as it turned out, that my father hated his homeland and hated the family that had seemingly acquiesced in the collective cruelty of a whole village. This is why, until three months ago, I had never even set foot in Spain and certainly never wanted to acquaint myself with a part of my family I had studiously ignored. Deep down, I still wanted to perpetuate that myth and feed my own perceived hatred of Spain and of Parcent. But the discovery that my perception was wrong; that my father had grown to understand and forgive the fear and prejudice induced by ignorance, had caused me to attempt some kind of atonement for my own convenient rejection, to this stage in my life, of my Spanish ancestry. In truth, I had not discovered these facts for myself; rather they had been placed before me by someone who had made it their personal mission to disabuse me of the feelings, beliefs and attitudes that had, to that point, ruled my life.

'I'm sorry, I didn't mean to...'

'It's all right, Pepito.' I stepped out onto the roof terrace and clenched the wrought iron balustrade, marvelling again at the magnificent view of the Carrascal mountain range filling the skyline like the backdrop to a painting.

What was it she said? Paradise in the mountains.

'How's Rosana,' I asked.

'Ah.'

'Is something wrong?'

'You could say that.'

'Well are you going to tell me?'

'Her mother died last week.'

'Last week! Why did nobody tell me?'

'You'll have to ask Rosana.'

I had not seen Rosana Ferrando Moll since deciding to take up the offer of a transfer to the Guardia Civil. I'd only known her for a few months and we'd only spent a few hours together, but there was something about her. Rosana was one of the reasons I fought my initial trepidation about staying in Spain. But I wasn't sure if I was trying to please her or appease her by moving into the house in Parcent.

'I never imagined the place could turn out like this,' I said. 'It's much bigger than I remember. You've kept all the old features, I see. The fireplace in the lounge is wonderful and I'm impressed with the new kitchen. It must have cost a few euros. I'll have to settle-up with someone, I guess.'

'There's no need.'

'No, I must pay. I've rented out my old flat in Nottingham until it's sold, so I have a little extra cash and I can take out a loan if need be.'

'There's really no need. Julio did the work.'

'Julio?'

Pepito's eldest son had not exactly been pleased when I turned up out of the blue. I don't suppose I could blame him really. Before his long lost (and best forgotten) cousin arrived on the scene, Julio was sitting pretty, expecting one day to inherit the house I was about to occupy and a serious chunk of land dotted around the village. Julio ran a small building company, but had ambitions to join the speculators and become a property developer. His younger brother, my other cousin, Emelio, was a simple lad content to fashion a meagre living from the family land and Julio knew he could easily manoeuvre Emelio into seeing the benefits of selling-up to take advantage of the burgeoning market for holiday homes. However, under Spanish inheritance law, when my grandfather died eleven years ago, the house and land had come to Pepito and my father, Antonio, Pepito's brother. And my father's share now belonged to me. In law, Pepito and I were joint owners and that meant none of the land could be sold without my approval. Pepito was happy to accept the situation and happy to let me decide the future of the estate. It was perhaps fanciful on my part, but I somehow imagined my father wanting to keep the land in agricultural use and so I

8

had rejected Julio's speculative offer to share the proceeds of his ambitious development plans. Besides, I liked my cousin Emelio, which is more than I could say for Julio.

'Don't sound so surprised,' Pepito said.

'The last time I was here, Julio and I didn't exactly see eye to eye. I really must pay him.'

'As I said, there's no need.'

'I insist.'

'Well, if you must know, your grandmother has paid.'

'Oh.' I said, hoping my lack of gratitude was not obvious. Now, not only was I bound to Parcent by virtue of my inheritance, I was indebted to my grandmother. Already I could feel the reactionary forces of small village life creeping like tentacles to ensnare me.

'Rosana, I'm so sorry,' I said as the door opened, allowing a shaft of light to enter the gloomy hallway. 'I've only just heard.'

Her eyes were moist, set in dark hollows, and there wasn't even a flicker of emotion as she met my anxious stare. 'Come in,' she said routinely, as if she had become used to greeting sympathetic visitors.

I wanted to reach out to her, hold her, comfort her, but she turned and retreated into the gloom of a hallway denied light by shuttered windows.

'How are you?' I realised the stupidity of the question. 'I mean... I don't know what I mean. I... I'm just so sorry. How's your grandmother?'

'It's all right, Michael. No one knows what to say. It's good of you to come. Grandmother is not very well I'm afraid. She's taken it badly. I suppose we all expect our children to outlive us, but when you are 85 and your daughter dies, it's hard to accept. Have you seen your grandmother?'

'No, I came straight here as soon as I heard the news.'

'Then you'd better go and see her. I know she's been wondering about you. A phone call wouldn't have been asking too much would it?'

Here she goes again, pushing, prodding, prompting; acting like the big sister I never had.

'It's just that... I... I wasn't sure I would be staying – in Spain I mean. So I...'

Rosana had turned her head away, staring at the worn tapestry chair her mother had occupied the last time I saw her. I read the gesture and thought better than to contrive an excuse. 'I'm on my way to see her now.'

Rosana remained silent, motionless.

'I'll go now if... if you're sure there's nothing I can do.' I paused. 'I'll be at the funeral, of course.'

'Thank you,' Rosana said quietly, her gaze still fixed on her mother's chair.

This place, I thought, I wish I'd never come here. Never found this family. Never discovered the truth about my father. Never met Rosana. Actually that wasn't quite true. I was attracted to Rosana, but I wasn't sure the feeling was mutual. Sometimes I felt she had simply seen it as her mission in life to bring the long-lost grandson back into the bosom of the family I had studiously avoided. Family meant everything to Rosana; it was what defined you as a person; more important than wealth or possessions or work or career. That was one reason why she had forsaken a successful banking job in Barcelona and returned to Parcent leaving behind the trappings of wealth and the husband who had helped her acquire them in the first place.

CHAPTER TWO

'Well, Sergeant Poquet, you drew the short straw then?'

'Please, call me Mariela... if that's all right with you, Captain Fernandez?'

'Fine, and you can call me Michael... unless that offends some form of protocol in the Guardia Civil.'

'Not that I'm aware of... Michael, but *Jefe* would be more normal.'

'Anything, but not *Jefe*.'

'The answer's no, by the way.'

'No?'

'I didn't draw the short straw. I asked for this assignment.' Mariela stepped over to the smaller of two desks in the drab, featureless room and eased herself into the swivel chair, leaning backwards with her hands clasped behind her head. The buttons of her blouse stretched and I could see the dark outline of her bra beneath the pale blue silk. She sat forward, flicking her blond hair behind her shoulders and adjusting the sunglasses that lifted it from her brow.

'I guess this one's mine,' she said, opening one of the empty drawers and then closing it. She picked up the black plastic telephone and untangled the cord then placed the receiver to her ear. 'At least the phones are working. The computers will be here tomorrow according to the desk sergeant. Where do you want to start?'

'Coffee would be nice. Is there a canteen or something?'

'A canteen? This isn't England you know. There's a bar across the road.'

'A bar?'

'Yes, a bar. You know? Where they serve food and drinks.'

'The bar it is then. Let's go... and bring those files with you. Should we tell anyone where we're going?'

'Michael, you're a Captain in the Guardia Civil with a special brief to liaise with the British community. You don't need to account for your movements to anyone... except of course Colonel Cardells, and he's in Alicante.'

Inside Bar Juan the odour of tobacco smoke mingled with the aroma of fresh coffee. Shrill voices from a wall-mounted television competed at full volume with the grating of a coffee grinder and the hissing steam pipe frothing hot milk. A group of workmen filed out after *almuerzo*, leaving tables cluttered with empty beer and wine bottles, saucers full of olive stones and plates of half-eaten *bocadillos*.

I was heading for the counter when Mariela steered me in the direction of a corner table, freshly wiped, but still streaked and sticky. The waitress shuffled towards us in a pair of greasy bedroom slippers, and shuffled away with an order for a *café solo* and a *cortado*. For a brief moment, I made eye contact with Mariela, noticing the vivid green colour of her pupils and thinking they now looked less frosty than the first time I had seen them.

'Are you sure you need the jacket?' Mariela asked.

A jacket and tie, had been my normal "uniform" for the last ten years in Nottingham CID. Stupid really when I think about it, since most of the rest of the British population only wear a tie for weddings and funerals. I undid the brass buttons of my navy blue, double-breasted blazer. 'It's not so warm.' I loosened my tie.

'No... I wasn't suggesting... it's just that I always thought the idea of being a plain-clothes detective was to be inconspicuous.'

The coffees arrived with a grimy ashtray. Such things had disappeared from British bars years ago when the smoking ban consigned them to the outdoor terraces where smokers huddled together for a furtive fag in the freezing cold. I pushed it to one side.

'I thought I'd read somewhere they'd banned smoking in bars and restaurants.'

'Sort of, but small bars like this were given the choice. Juan banned smoking at first, but it lasted less than a week when most of his customers deserted him.'

This, I was beginning to realise, was a typically Spanish approach – good intentions are fine, but not when they get in the way of practicality.

'Have you read the files?' I asked.

'Of course. Where do you want to start?'

'The missing kid's a waste of time. We'll pay the parents a visit later this week. It's the Mayor of Beniforell that interests me.' I stirred the sachet of sugar into the tiny coffee cup and emptied it in one gulp. 'What do you make of this Walter Wilkinson chap?'

Mariela sipped the *cortado* and replaced the glass on the saucer, slowly licking a fine trace of milky coffee from her top lip and glancing in my direction. I was sure the gesture was intentionally provocative and lowered my eyes so as not to stare.

'He's lived in Beniforell for almost five years. Retired anaesthetist and local magistrate in south London. He seems to have lived a quiet life until eighteen months ago, when the trouble started.'

'The development plans you mean?'

'Yes, it's been in all the papers. The council in Beniforell wants to build fifteen hundred new houses on his doorstep and he and his neighbours stand to lose a large chunk of their land and a pick up huge infrastructure charges in the process. The Mayor of Beniforell, Juan-Jose Mora, is – was – the driving force behind the scheme.'

'Can that happen?' I asked.

'It can and it is. All over the Costa Blanca, small councils are trying to cash in on the boom in demand for holiday and retirement homes. The coastal towns are over-developed, so the focus has switched inland.'

'Yes, but losing land and having to pay for infrastructure?'

Mariela looked bemused. 'I thought this was an inquiry into a suspicious death, not a study of Valencian land laws.'

I smiled benignly. 'Humour me for a while.'

'There is, or was, a controversial law in Valencia governing new development. It's called *Ley Regulador de*

Actividades Urbanisticos – LRAU for short or the "land-grab" law as it is commonly called. It means town halls can re-designate rustic land as urbanisable. Then a developer submits a plan to build more houses and if the town hall approves the plan, the landowners have to forfeit some of their land to the developer and pay a proportion of the costs of building new roads, sewers, water, street lighting – all that kind of thing.'

'But surely, the developer has to buy the land first or compensate the owners.'

'You've a lot to learn about Spain, Michael. Ever since the days of Franco, it's been an accepted principle that the owners of land who stand to gain from development must contribute to the social benefits which enhance the prosperity of the community as a whole.'

'You sound as if you're quoting a political manifesto,' I said, standing to remove my blazer and placing it on the back of the chair, lifting the sleeves to prevent them from dangling on the floor. Something else I had noticed about Spain – ash trays were for collecting olive pips; the floor was where you flicked your ash and stubbed out your fags.

'I guess it does sound that way,' said Mariela, 'but LRAU has been hugely controversial recently so there have been hundreds of articles in the papers. It's hard not to be aware of the arguments. The Generalitat de Valencia supports the law stridently. It's been hugely successful in freeing up land for development quickly and cheaply, and it's one of the key factors in the boom in the construction industry.'

'Even if it means other people have to pay?'

'Exactly!' Mariela sat back, shrugging her shoulders. 'But remember this. It's mainly Spanish landowners who get caught up in the law. It's not as if the Generalitat is targeting the foreign community. Many other parts of Spain are looking with envy at the explosion in development in the Valencia region and some are planning to adopt a similar approach.'

'You sound like a supporter.'

'You asked for an explanation, I've given you one.' Mariela folded her arms across her chest and shifted her gaze to the bar.

'I thought I read somewhere they'd scrapped LRAU.'

14

Mariela pursed her lips peevishly, unfolded her arms and leant forward, resting her elbows on the table and her chin on her intertwined fingers. 'So you're not as ignorant of this matter as you make out.'

'I read the papers like everyone else. Has LRAU been scrapped?'

'Yes, at the end of last year. The European Parliament adopted a fiercely critical report saying LRAU was in breach of several aspects of the European Convention on Human Rights. Valencia was forced to act. So they replaced LRAU with a new law – *Ley Urbanistica Valenciana* – LUV.'

'So what's the problem?'

'The problem is that the Generalitat announced it was going to change the law one month before it happened. And hundreds of plans were rushed through and approved by town halls in the meantime.'

'Is that what happened in Beniforell?'

'Precisely. It made some people very angry.'

'Angry enough to want to kill the Mayor?'

'You might want Mr Wilkinson to answer that.'

'All in good time. What do you make of the pathologist's report?'

'Haven't you read it?'

I didn't answer, but narrowed my eyes in rebuke – a gesture Mariela was quick to interpret.

'Do you want the science or the summary?'

'Spare me the science.'

'It's only preliminary at this stage. Time of death has been established at between 11.00pm and 1.00am on 20th June. The suspected cause of death was a hefty blow to the head, or should I say a hefty blow by the head, against a sharp rock which caused a fracture to the base of the skull. The right wrist and forearm were fractured in several places, almost certainly the result of trying to cushion a fall from the road above. There was bruising to the left shoulder and hip consistent with the body having rolled over several times after the initial impact.'

Mariela paused. I was distracted by the weather map on the television screen – from Asturias to Andalucía, coast to coast sunshine – *escorchio* you might say, except there is no such word in Spanish.

'Is that it?' I asked, without looking away.

'For now, yes. We're still waiting for a more detailed report from the pathologist, and the forensics team are still analysing material from the scene.'

'Anything else?'

'No, that's it for now, I think.'

I turned from the television to face her. 'Have you looked at the photographs of the body?'

Mariela turned a page and shuffled through six large photographs taken at the scene. 'I've seen them, yes.'

'Anything strike you as unusual?'

She thought for a moment. 'Not that I can see. They look like routine scene of crime shots.'

'Seen one dead body, seen them all, is that what you mean?'

'Is there a point to all this?' She folded her arms and sat back in her chair.

'You've seen photographs of victims before; don't you think these are just a bit too neat? The position of the body, I mean. Mora is lying on his back, perfectly flat with his arms by his side. If he died as a result of a fall, it's hard to believe he would have ended up like that.'

Mariela sat forward and studied the photographs again. 'I see what you mean.'

'You'd better ask the pathologist to take a look at lividity.'

'Lividity?'

'Yes, lividity. It will show us...'

'I know what lividity is.' She gave me a peevish glance. 'I'll get onto it straight away.'

I nodded. 'And the other thing... in the post mortem report?'

Mariela frowned.

'The kidney transplant; recent, according to the pathologist.'

'Do you think that's relevant?'

'There's something you need to learn, Mariela, about criminal investigation, I mean. Everything is relevant until we know it's irrelevant.'

'What does that mean?'

16

'It means, Mariela, I don't know what it means until I know what it means. When are we seeing Wilkinson?'

'This morning at eleven-thirty. We've got time to see Mr and Mrs Robinson before then if you want, you know, the missing son.'

Mr and Mrs Robinson and their runaway teenage son were a waste of time. I'd seen hundreds of similar cases in the UK. The boy was seventeen for God's sake, if he wanted to come back he would, but if he didn't want to be found he wouldn't be. London was the magnet for runaways in the UK and I wondered where that might be in Spain – Madrid, Barcelona, or perhaps more local, Valencia.

'Oh, I think that can wait. It's not as if there's any urgency. The boy's been missing for months now.'

'Mr and Mrs Robinson might see things differently.'

I recognised the tone of mild rebuke. For a moment I was inclined to reinforce my superiority. Instead I replied, 'Fix an appointment for later this week and make sure you read the file before we see them.'

'I've already read it.'

'I'm sure you have. So read it again. Make sure there's nothing we've missed.'

'We've missed?'

'How long will it take us to get to Wilkinson's place?'

'About half an hour. Why?'

'Then you've got time to talk to the pathologist.'

I let Mariela drive. No point in having a dog and barking yourself, I thought, smiling to myself at the idea of anyone calling Mariela a dog. Clouds were forming, rolling down the mountain, evaporating as they descended and encountered the warmer air rising from the base of the valley. We approached a confluence of sunlight and mist as we followed the twists and turns of a narrow asphalt road leading to a group of houses dotted between groves of almonds and olives. The air chilled noticeably as we moved from sunlight to shade. Not everywhere was *escorchio* it seemed.

Walter Wilkinson's villa nestled at the end of a small cul-de-sac behind a hedge of oleanders with pink and red flowers withering to brown. From the far corner of the garden a dense cloud of wood-smoke billowed from a bonfire. A nameplate composed of blue and yellow ceramic tiles cemented to a gatepost read: *Casa Buena Suerte*.

'Tempting fate, don't you think?' I said to Mariela as she pulled the chain that caused a small brass bell to jangle.

Walter Wilkinson crunched across a gravel driveway looking like an English farmer in beige corduroy trousers and a thick checked shirt with sleeves rolled up high above his elbows. But it was the green Wellington boots that most attracted my attention. A small buckled strap at the calf of the boots made them instantly recognisable, as a pair of Hunters – de rigueur with the English county set when attending pony club gymkhanas or sipping malt whisky from silver hip flasks at the local point to point races. Wilkinson took a bundle of keys from his pocket and unlocked a padlock connecting the ends of a heavy metal chain twice wrapped around the adjoining sections of a pair of wrought iron gates. Uneven stubble, ginger turning grey, contrasted with his wiry, shoulder length brown hair. Mid-fifties, I surmised.

'I'd say, "Welcome to Good Luck House," but it doesn't seem appropriate in the circumstances does it?' said Wilkinson, opening the gates.

Introductions over, we sat at a hardwood table on a quadrant shaped terrace adjoining the house and overlooking a small grove of recently pruned olive trees. Refreshments, it seemed, were not on offer.

Mariela, oversized dark glasses shielding her eyes and masking her face, placed a folder on the table and began turning pages as if looking for something specific.

I looked at Wilkinson for signs of nervousness, but couldn't detect any, so I started the questions. 'You know why we're here, Mr Wilkinson?'

'I could take a guess, but why don't you tell me.' There was an arrogance about the man which made him instantly dislikeable, to me at least.

'The Mayor, Juan-Jose Mora. You've heard about his unfortunate accident.'

'Ah, yes, his accident.' The sarcasm in Wilkinson's voice was meant to be detected. 'Very unfortunate.'

'But not disappointing?'

Wilkinson didn't respond.

'In fact, some might say you'd be relieved.'

'Relieved?'

'Pleased, even?'

'I'm not grief-stricken if that's what you mean.'

'And why is that, Mr Wilkinson?'

'It's no secret. I hated the man. And with good cause.'

'The development plans you mean?'

'No, not the development plans. We can fight the developers. We can fight the town hall. What we can't fight is a lying, cheating bastard motivated by greed and corruption who smiles to your face while he stabs you in the back.'

I resisted the temptation to point out that doing the two things simultaneously would be near impossible. 'Would you care to explain?'

'With pleasure. Eighteen months ago my wife and I were settled and happy here. Then I went to the town hall to ask for permission to build a carport. "Sorry, no," was the answer, "We're going to put a road through your garden. Oh, and by the way, we're going to build one thousand five hundred new houses on your doorstep. But don't worry because it's all for the good of the community so you and your neighbours will only have to pay a modest contribution to the cost of all the new roads and infrastructure." A modest contribution? That's a laugh, only 50,000 euros, and, no, I won't get any compensation for the losing half my land.'

'I can understand why you might be a little upset.' It was my turn to be sarcastic.

'Your sympathy is appreciated, Captain Fernandez. You did say "Captain" didn't you?'

'You were saying?'

'Was I?'

'Something about a lying, cheating bastard, I think.'

'Our friendly *Alcalde* you mean? For the past year and a half he has constantly assured us not to worry. The plans won't be approved, he said. They're only provisional, he said. Of course we don't want thousands of concrete boxes in the countryside, he said. Only last month he told us the

19

plans were paralysed, "until we take a proper look at the future of the whole village." Consultation, he promised, "with full transparency." And then the law was changed, or rather was about to be changed, and the bastard calls an emergency meeting of the council and approves the plans just two days before the deadline expires. Now we find out he's been having secret meetings with the developers for months. It was all cut and dried. He's sold out. Everyone in the village will tell you what it's all about – money – not for the village, but for our greedy Mayor to feather his own nest and sod the rest of us.'

'But you can't prove that, can you, Mr Wilkinson?'

'I don't need to. Ask anyone, they'll tell you. He must be getting thousands, hundreds of thousands.'

'Don't you mean he would have got thousands?'

'My heart bleeds.'

'And that's why you threatened him, is it Mr Wilkinson?' I looked for signs of surprise in Wilkinson's reaction, but saw nothing. Instead Wilkinson continued almost boastfully.

'The incident in Bar Mica, you mean? I don't deny it. Yes, we argued.'

I turned to Mariela. 'What were the exact words, Sergeant Poquet?'

Mariela didn't need to search the file. '"You won't get away it, you corrupt son of a bitch. I'll kill you first,"' she said, reading in her best monotone police voice.

'And that wasn't the only occasion you threatened him, was it? Remind me, Sergeant Poquet.'

Mariela looked down again at the file, but before she could answer, Wilkinson intervened.

'Okay. It's no secret. I hated the man. I'm glad he's dead. But if you're looking for suspects, you'll need to interview half the village. It's not just a few foreigners who stand to lose out; dozens of local farmers will face disaster if they have to pay these ridiculous bills. Do you know that Mora's brother is going round offering to buy them out, but for a pittance – a fraction of what the land is worth to a developer – if it ever gets developed? And some of them have been frightened into signing.'

'That may be so, Mr Wilkinson, but so far you're the only one known to have threatened to kill him. Where were you at ten o'clock last Wednesday evening, 20th June?'

'Well, Captain, now you have a problem.' His face twisted to a conceited smirk. 'I was in the UK. In fact, I was there all that week. I came back on Saturday.' Wilkinson sat back, his face crinkling with an artificial smile.

'You can prove that, I suppose?'

'I have the print-out from the computer confirming the flights, if you'd like to see it.'

'And the purpose of your visit?'

'I was visiting my mother. She had a stroke six weeks ago and she's recently moved into a nursing home in Greenwich. You can confirm that with her if you like, only she's a little confused at the moment and she's lost her power of speech. The doctors say it may return, but for now, all she can do is mumble. But don't let that stop you if you really feel it's necessary.' Wilkinson's hard stare seemed to be issuing a challenge.

'If you can give us the address that would be helpful.'

Wilkinson scowled.

'Your wife, Mr Wilkinson, it might be helpful if we could talk to her as well.'

'Well that might be difficult at the moment.'

'Oh?'

'She's in England.'

'Visiting your mother?'

Wilkinson looked irritated. 'No. If you must know, she's returned to the UK for a while. She's staying with her sister in Leeds.'

'Will she be coming back – soon, I mean?'

'I'm not sure that's any of your business, Captain Fernandez, but no, I don't think she has any immediate plans to return to Spain.'

I raised an eyebrow, but left it at that. 'Is there anything else you can think of that might help us?'

Wilkinson thought for a moment, or looked like he was thinking. 'If I knew what this was all about, I might be able to help. But if it was simply an accident; if old Mora just happened to topple over the edge in the dark, then I don't see how I can help. Of course, if you want to know about how that crooked bastard hoodwinked the whole village then I could talk to you all day. I've got a fat file with all the papers if you want to see it. Then you can see just what he's been up to and how he lied through his teeth to get the development plans through.'

'Thank you, but that won't be necessary at this stage. I'll be talking to the other councillors and the staff at the town hall later this week. If I need to know more I'll come back to you.'

Mariela asked the next question. 'What happens now, Mr Wilkinson? I mean to the development plans?'

'Your guess is as good as mine. Your Captain says he is going to talk to the other councillors so perhaps he should put that question to them. I expect Mora wasn't the only one on the take. He needed three other votes to get the plans approved and one of them was his deputy, Paco Santos, whose brother is an agent for the developers.'

Wilkinson's protestations were becoming tedious. I feigned indifference, restraining a yawn. 'Thank you Mr Wilkinson. You've been very helpful. Now, if we could have the computer confirmation of your flights to and from England. And it would be useful to have a contact number for your wife… And the number of the nursing home where your mother is staying.'

'Of course,' he said nonchalantly, rising from his chair to enter the house.

'So what do you think?' I asked as we returned to the anonymous silver Seat provided by the Guardia Civil.

Mariela started the engine. 'About Wilkinson? He's a suspect, of course, but he didn't try to hide his dislike for Mora, or the fact that he had threatened to kill him. But I'm not sure he's capable of murder – if there is a murder, that is.'

I thought for a moment. 'Well someone moved the body. Perhaps that someone wanted to check the extent of Mora's injuries; perhaps they wanted to check he was dead; perhaps they wanted to make sure he was dead. Get the pathologist to take another look at the cause of death. It's clear that the fractured skull could have caused death, but I want to be absolutely sure it was the actual cause of death. As for Wilkinson, you're right, he didn't try to hide his feelings about Mora, but then there wouldn't have been much point in that, would there, given what everyone knows about the history between the two of them?'

'I guess you're right,' Mariela said.

'There's something that puzzles me though – about the development plans. If the owners of the land have to pay those huge infrastructure charges before the land can be developed, why would Mora or anybody else want to buy the land even if it was cheap?'

'Ah.' Mariela cleared her throat. 'I can see why you ask. Under LRAU, once a development plan is finally approved the developer assumes responsibility for building the entire infrastructure, but they also take on public powers to re-charge the landowners, even the power to confiscate property if it comes to that. There are claims – only rumours though – that developers deliberately inflate the price to some landowners in order to reduce the cost to themselves and their chums.'

'But does no one check the costs – someone in the town hall for example?' I realised the naivety of the question. 'There's no need to answer that.'

'Where to now?' Mariela asked.

'You need to get back to Jalon and chase the pathologist. And check those flight details as well. And speak to Wilkinson's wife and the nursing home.'

'And you?'

'Drop me off in the village, will you? I want to poke around for a while. Oh, and I want you to talk to the doctors at Denia hospital about Mora's kidney transplant. I'd like to know more. He must have been on anti-rejection drugs or something. I'd like to know if they were working, if Mora was fully recovered or if something might have caused him to fall – a blackout or something. Just see what you can find out.'

'Anything else,' Mariela asked, 'while you're poking around in Beniforell?'

'Yes, when you're finished you can come and pick me up. I'll be in Bar Mica. No rush, after lunch will be fine, let's say about three o'clock.'

23

Lunch was *puchero*, a local speciality, so I was told by the cheerful barman whose wife was cooking it. A greasy broth with noodles was the first course, made from the stock in which the stew had, apparently, simmered all morning. It was followed by meatballs wrapped in cabbage leaves and, apparently, steamed on top of the stew that had simmered all morning. The main course was the stew of mixed rough-cuts of meat and sausages served with an assortment of vegetables and chickpeas that had, apparently, simmered together all morning.

Despite my initial misgivings, I enjoyed the rustic fare. Far better, I thought, than the tasteless cottage pie served up every Wednesday in the canteen of Nottingham Police HQ. I did, however, discard a lump of pork fat, pushing it to one side of the plate, and I declined the offer of ice cream which, I had been assured, was included in the price of the meal.

Mariela's entrance, causing the chain fly screen to jangle, was followed by a noticeable reduction in the level of conversation as heads turned. She paused for a moment, lifting dark glasses to the top of her head. She saw me in the far corner, beyond a group of tables occupied by workmen who were enjoying the view. Her high heeled, ankle-strap shoes clipped across the tiled floor and I thought I detected a touch of catwalk training as she strutted towards me with giant strides. She was clearly enjoying the attention provoked by her short denim skirt.

'You've changed – your clothes, I mean.'

'It's getting too hot for trousers.'

'And this is your idea of plain clothes?' I said with more than a hint of sarcasm as she sat at the table, now cleared of leftover *puchero*.

'You sound as if you don't approve,' she said, crossing her legs and lifting a hand to attract the attention of the barman whose attention she already had. 'No one would think I was an officer in the Guardia Civil, would they? In fact we could be a couple meeting for lunch, a clandestine meeting perhaps, between two secret lovers.'

I wondered if there was an invitation in her comment, but dismissed the thought. She was a beautiful woman and any red-blooded male, especially one with Spanish blood in his veins, would find her attractive. And she knew it. But what I couldn't figure out was whether her flirting was a genuine attempt to attract attention or part of a strategy to make me feel uneasy.

'I doubt it.' I said.

'Why do you say that, it's plausible isn't it?' Her eyebrows rose as she cocked her head, ever so slightly, to one side.

'I very much doubt it.'

'Oh, why?' A look of disappointment crossed her face, but I couldn't tell if it was genuine or feigned.

'Because I've flashed my badge to just about everyone I've spoken to since I arrived.'

'Ah.'

The barman hovered.

'There's ice cream if you want it,' I said. 'It's included in the price, so I'm told.'

'Tea, please.'

The barman was still hovering.

'Nothing for me, thank you,' I said, and the barman finally moved away.

The pathologist, Mariela reported, had been instructed to examine lividity in the body and re-examine her findings as to the exact cause of Mora's death. She had reluctantly acquiesced. Doctor Ernesto Alvarez, the chief renal surgeon at Denia's general hospital had, likewise, been reluctant to pass on too much information.

'Mora had a kidney transplant twelve weeks ago,' said Mariela, now reading from a notebook. 'He was diagnosed with acute renal failure just over six months ago and had been undergoing dialysis three times a week. The transplant was successful according to Alvarez. He was seeing Mora every couple of weeks and he seemed to be making good progress. Mora was taking anti rejection drugs – immuno-suppressants, cyclosporine and prednisone – they can cause side effects, including trembling and dizziness.'

'Blackouts?' I interrupted.

'I asked that specifically. Alvarez says it's possible, but unlikely. However he didn't rule out the possibility of a blackout if the kidney was beginning to be rejected – the drugs aren't always successful. But Mora last visited the hospital a week before he died and everything seemed fine.'

'So Mora might simply have blacked out and fallen.' I was still thinking. 'Did you ask Alvarez if it would be possible to tell from a post mortem if the new kidney was showing signs of rejection?'

'I thought of that, yes, and Alvarez's answer was that it would be possible if you were looking for it at the time.'

'At the time?'

'At the time, yes, but it may be more difficult now because...'

'Spare me the details. You need to...'

'Talk to the pathologist, yes, I already have done and she's going to take another look at that as well. It's unlikely, however, that Mora's new kidney was being rejected because, according to Alvarez, there was a good tissue match with the donor kidney and nowadays, with modern drugs, rejection is unusual in these cases.'

The barman returned, delivering a small glass of hot water containing a tea bag attached by a string to a Twinings label. Mariela dunked it twice and set it on the saucer.

'No lemon?' I said.

'I didn't ask for lemon.'

An argument erupted at the bar as a gnarled old man in a sweat-stained shirt shouted at the barman then slammed an empty glass on the stainless steel counter before stomping towards the exit.

'Seems he doesn't want to pay,' Mariela said.

'He's the owner,' I replied. 'And it seems he doesn't expect to pay.'

'You have been busy. What else did you find out?'

'When did General Franco die?' I asked.

'1975, why?'

'Someone needs to tell the people of this village, that's why.'

'Are you going to enlighten me?'

I pulled my chair closer to the table and looked around sheepishly then spoke in a hushed voice. 'I chatted with several people over lunch about the Mayor and about the development plans. They all know what's going on. Without

26

exception they said they don't want to see more holiday homes built in the village. So I asked why it was happening. Most of them just shrugged, but a couple said it's all about money. So I asked – money for the village? One of them laughed and the other one tapped his back pocket and winked. "Money for Mora," he told me.'

The strange thing about these conversations was that they were devoid of anger. In the UK I could imagine the outrage that would have accompanied such comments. Petitions would be signed, protest marches organised and banners unfurled. The great unwashed of the environmental lobby would doubtless jump on the bandwagon in the hope of causing a riot and Swampy would have dug himself into a hole somewhere. I looked at Mariela whose facial expression was unchanged. 'You don't seem surprised.'

'Surprised by what?' she asked.

'By the fact that Mora was on the take and everyone seems to know about it, but no one seems to give a damn.'

Now Mariela smiled. 'Michael, you've a lot to learn about village politics in these parts. Any Mayor worth his salt is expected to line his pockets – it's always been that way.'

'But it gets worse. The Mayor's brother, Victor Mora, is one of the major landowners in the area covered by the plans and he's done a deal with the developers. That's why he's busy pressurising the local farmers to sell their land at knock-down prices.'

'So?'

'So it's doubly corrupt. The Mayor is, or was, taking a bribe from the developers and his brother stands to gain as well.'

'So?'

'So if the people don't want it, why don't they oppose it – sign a petition, organise a protest? Spain's a democracy after all.'

'Democracy, there's a word.' Mariela sipped her tea. 'All things to all men. Yes, Spain's a democracy, but in these villages that means they have an election every four years. In between times, everyone's expected to do as they are told.'

'So why vote for these people in the first place?'

'There's a kind of ruling class in many of these villages – a handful of rich and powerful families. They've handed out favours over the years and people tend to get reminded of that when it comes to elections. People vote along family lines and it doesn't do to express opposition openly – bad for business, jobs are lost, work dries up or worse.'

'Worse?'

'Friends can shun you or problems suddenly arise.'

'What kind of problems?'

'Well, if you own a shop, your customers might stop coming. Or your electricity supply might develop a fault and you might find it hard to get the electrician to fix it. Or your allocation of water for irrigation might be cut, that kind of thing.'

'Jesus. It sounds like the Mafia.'

Mariela looked round the room and put a finger across her lips. 'Careful what you say,' she whispered.

I emulated Mariela's tone. 'And this still goes on today?'

'To a degree, yes. But people are used to that. In Franco's days he had his henchmen in all these villages; loyal supporters, the eyes and ears of the regime. It was their job to sniff out dissent, however insignificant, and report it. You know Franco banned the Valencian language, don't you? Everyone had to speak Castellano. It was Franco's way of trying to unite the county after the Civil War. It failed of course; opposition simply went underground. And there's something else you should know.'

I raised an eyebrow.

'The Guardia Civil were Franco's enforcers in these parts and some rough justice was meted out. It was not unknown for *rojos* or *izquierdas* to disappear for a while – some never came back.'

'That must have made the Guardia Civil popular.'

'Things have changed, but some people have long memories. In any event, people round here have more important things to worry about. There are vines to cut, orange trees to tend and olives to harvest. That's what really matters to most people.'

'Even if they lose their land to the speculators?'

'There's not much of a living to be made from the land these days, and the young people aren't interested in farming anymore.'

'So the politicians sell out to the speculators, the speculators rob the people of their land and the developers take the gains.'

'In a nutshell.'

'Except if you're British and get caught up in all this, you tend not to take it lying down.'

'Walter Wilkinson, you mean?'

'And many others, I'm sure.'

'But they don't all resort to murder.'

I sat back and folded my arms. 'More's the pity, perhaps.'

Mariela leaned forward, still whispering. 'There's something else you should know about Mora.'

I moved closer; close enough to pick up a hint of Mariela's fragrant perfume which permeated through the overriding odour of food and tobacco smoke.

'I've been looking through our records and Mora has a history. He was linked with drug dealing and money laundering in the nineties, but nothing was ever proved. He ran a couple of clubs, you know, those places you see on the N332, the old coast road. You must have seen them; there are about a dozen between Calpe and Denia. Well, they call them clubs, but actually they're brothels.'

'And the police know about them?'

'Of course we do. But so long as they aren't involved in anything more serious, we tend to leave them alone. You look as if you don't approve,' said Mariela, returning my frown.

'Well, it's just... I thought they were night-clubs, discos, that kind of thing.'

Mariela smiled. 'With names like "Club Erotica". Michael, you are naïve.' Her smile broadened to a grin. 'This isn't prudish England, you know, where people pretend this kind of thing doesn't go on. And it's not just sad old perverts who take advantage of the facilities on offer. Perhaps you should try one yourself some time?'

I felt myself blushing. 'You were telling me about Mora. You say he owned a couple of these places?'

'Still does, we think, though ownership is hard to trace. It's usually well hidden through companies, leases, sub leases, that kind of thing.'

'So, if you turn a blind eye to these... brothels, as you call them, why the interest in Mora?'

'In the early nineties he was suspected of people trafficking. Mainly young girls from Eastern Europe. It was alleged that some were being forced into prostitution in his clubs.'

'Alleged, you say?'

'Yes, we never made it stick. The Guardia raided the places on three occasions. According to the records, they pulled in more than a dozen women, some were Spanish but there were also some from Latvia, Estonia and Romania. But none of them lodged a complaint. It seems they were happy at their work, or too frightened to talk more likely.'

'The eminent Mayor of Beniforell certainly has a colourful history, or should I say had? I wonder what else we might find in the closet if we dig deep enough.'

CHAPTER THREE

Most of the older citizens of Parcent attended Tuesday's funeral of Isobel Moll, Rosana's mother. The women outnumbered the men by two to one. Even the Mayor of Parcent was present, discreetly keeping in the background surrounded by her entourage.

Rosana steadied her grandmother, Asunción, as they left the church and entered the cobbled square, grey and glossy from an early morning spruce up. Pepito took my grandmother's right arm and I thought of supporting her left, but Carmen Maria appeared stubbornly steadfast as she stepped towards the car waiting to follow the hearse to the cemetery on the outskirts of the village.

The wake was in Bar Casino. The majority of women mourners had stayed on, but the number of men had dwindled to a handful of close friends. I felt uncomfortable, and wondered if protocol required my presence. But I needed to speak to Rosana who flitted between elderly mourners, touching hands, exchanging commiserative pecks on cheeks and smiling dutifully.

'Seems a strange place for a wake,' I said to Pepito who had distanced himself from the women to join me at the side of the bar. 'Bar Casino, I mean.'

Pepito divided the last of a bottle of red wine between our glasses. 'Ah, I see what you mean. It's never been a casino – at least not officially. In Franco's time gambling was strictly prohibited, but there's a cellar underneath this place and the men used to gather illicitly to play cards. It soon became known as the Casino, at least to the locals, though I expect the authorities knew about the place and turned a blind eye. It changed hands recently and the new owners decided to change the name to Casino – a kind of belated one in the eye for the *Generalísimo*.'

'Do people still harbour memories of those days? It's seventy years since the end of the Civil War and Franco's been dead for more than thirty years.'

'You'd need to have lived through those times to understand, Michael. The war caused massive divisions between families and even within families. Brother against brother, father against son in some cases, and people have long memories. Even in this village there are people who could tell you who fought with the republicans, who joined the Falange and who sided with the nationalists. There are even a few old communist supporters who survived the aftermath of the war, though they were lucky to have done so.'

I looked around the room, noticing a large majority of elderly people, a few looking to be in their nineties. I realised they would have lived through the Civil War and the forty years of virtual dictatorship that followed until the monarchy and democracy were eventually restored.

Rosana joined us at the bar, though it was difficult to determine whether she had sought us out or had merely gravitated in our direction in the course of doing the rounds. Her long, wavy auburn hair was pulled back from her face in a ponytail, curled under and tied with a black ribbon beneath a pill-box hat fronted with black netting that covered her brow and eyes. Her face was pale and drawn; bloodshot eyes framed with dark rings, the result of tiredness beyond a lack of sleep. A hint of rose coloured lipstick was the only exception to her otherwise wan appearance.

'Thank you for coming, Pepito.' She kissed both his cheeks. 'And you too, Michael.' She repeated the gesture.

I had expected her to call me Miguel-Ángel, as she had stubbornly done since we first met just a few months before. I hated the name, but somehow, from Rosana, I found it bearable. I suspected it was part of her plan to force me to acknowledge my Spanish ancestry and, perhaps fancifully, I imagined it implied a degree of affection. Now, by using my English pseudonym it was as if she was trying to distance herself from whatever relationship we had previously established.

She seemed to have aged; an effect exaggerated by a shapeless black coat, too large for the slender frame I had admired in a khaki button–through dress when we dined together at restaurant La Tasca four months ago. I remembered the dainty black leather belt that pinched her waist and the matching high-heeled shoes that gave her poise and elegance.

'No need for thanks,' Pepito said. 'We will all miss your mother. It must be hard for Asunción.'

'Very hard. She is going to need all the time I can give her.'

'If we can be of any help…' Pepito said.

'Thank you, it's appreciated.' She kissed Pepito again, hugging him briefly before pulling away.

She turned towards me and I felt obliged to speak, but not really knowing what to say. 'I… I feel rather out of place. I hardly knew your mother, but I just wanted to…'

'Pay your respects, I know. It's kind of you.'

'No… I mean, yes. I mean, well, I just wanted to be here… with you… for you. I mean…'

She leant forward and kissed me again on the cheek. Her warm lips made just the faintest of contact with my skin, but it was enough to stir memories of a more meaningful kiss; memories that had never been far from my mind.

I met her eyes. 'Perhaps… when things have settled down… I could see you.'

I looked for a sign of interest in her expression, but found only indifference.

'I have a lot to do at the moment and my time is taken up with my grandmother. But we're neighbours now, so I expect we'll bump into each other. I must go… my grandmother.'

Pepito tapped me on the shoulder. 'Rosana's taken it quite badly. Ever since she returned to Parcent, after the divorce, she's thrown herself into her family. It's as if she is trying to compensate for the years she spent away, making up for lost time. My fear is she'll blame herself and atone by taking on the burden of caring for her grandmother alone.

It's understandable, but she's young and she needs to find a life. There are people who can help, but only if she wants it.'

I watched Rosana return to her grandmother who sat awkwardly in a wheelchair by a table in the corner, her back arched and her head bowed. Two elderly friends sat with her, like Asunción, dressed entirely in black. Rosana fussed dutifully, inching the wheelchair closer to the table and repositioning Asunción's left foot on the base-plate from which it had slipped. I thought about joining the group, offering my help, but I had exhausted my supply of sympathetic remarks. I also sensed, again, that feeling of alienation from the village that rejected my father; a feeling reinforced when the young village priest, bespectacled, portly and prematurely bald, joined the elderly women and hovered at the side of the table with a carefully practised funereal expression.

Ever since I had first learned about my father's leprosy, I had found it convenient to believe that the villagers of Parcent had forced my father away. In my mind, the whole village of Parcent shared a collective guilt for their inhuman behaviour in rejecting a young teenager whose only crime was to suffer the stigma of a disease that provoked fear and hostility born out of ignorance. My grandmother, Carmen Maria, had explained that the villagers' fears had been exploited by the old priest, Father Ramon, who upheld the creed that leprosy was a punishment imposed by God. This wasn't in the Dark Ages; this was in 1951 and leprosy was curable. Father Ramon knew Antonio had spent some time in the leprosy sanatorium at Fontilles just a few kilometres away, and it was Father Ramon who made sure Antonio was never allowed to return to the village, even after he had been treated and cured. Despite this, I still found it hard to accept that no one in the village had found it in their heart to challenge the view of the old priest that lepers must be shunned and cast out. The only person to have shown compassion to Antonio was my mother, Susan, an English nurse who worked in Fontilles at the time. When it became clear that Antonio could never return to Parcent, Susan and Antonio had left Spain in 1952 to live in England where they later married. I was born

34

some years later and I was thirteen years old before I discovered the secret they had tried to hide.

'There's someone I'd like you to meet,' said Pepito, 'or rather someone who wants to meet you.' He grabbed my elbow and led me towards the far end of the bar. A tap on the shoulder caused a head to turn.

'Pepito,' she said, 'I was hoping you'd come over.'

I wasn't sure if the young woman who faced me was here for the wake. She was in her early twenties, dressed in a very un-funeral-like bright yellow top over a green knee-length skirt. She teetered on high-heeled ankle boots that caused me to look up at her sharp-featured face, framed in a mass of crimped blond hair.

'Michael, this is Vicenta Sendra, a distant cousin of yours, but then you are probably a distant relative to half this village. Parcent is like that, you know. Vicenta is the *policia local* officer for Parcent. I suppose you could call her the village bobby.'

Bobby-dazzler, I thought, noticing the unsubtle purple eye shadow and pale peach lip-gloss.

'She's wanted to meet you for a while. It's not every day we have a Captain in the Guardia Civil in Parcent, and a famous one at that.'

I cringed, but took the hand Vicenta offered.

'Pleased to meet you, Captain Fernandez.'

The hand was small and cold, clammy.

'Please, call me Michael... since we appear to be related.'

'Vicenta wants your advice on something,' said Pepito. 'A small problem she has.'

'Well, it's not really important... perhaps now is not the time.' Her face flushed.

'No, it's quite all right.' I said. 'I'm all out of funeral talk. How can I help?'

'If you're sure. It's just that there's been an outbreak of vandalism in the village over the last two months. Most unusual for Parcent, and I'm getting nowhere in trying to catch the culprits.'

I perked up. Even if it wasn't crime of the century, it was better than mingling with the morbid. 'Let me buy you a drink.'

Without her notebook it was difficult for Vicenta to be precise, but over the last eight weeks there had been nine cases of wing mirrors broken from cars parked in village roads. Broken mirrors were not uncommon in the narrow village streets, but in seven of the nine cases the broken mirrors were on the inside, pavement, side of the parked cars, suggesting that they were deliberate acts of vandalism. All the cars were British registered. Vicenta explained there was a group of young Valencian nationalists in the village who actively campaigned for Valencia's independence from the rest of Spain. They were opposed to what they saw as the colonisation of the Costa Blanca by retired foreigners or rich Europeans buying houses in the village to use for a few weeks' holiday each year. She had talked to some of this group, but her enquiries had come to nothing.

'I thought you might be able to help.' Vicenta said. 'Suggest a line of enquiry perhaps? I know it's not serious enough to involve the Guardia Civil officially. I've done all the obvious things, fingerprints, interviews – I've even done a few night patrols and kept watch over a couple of foreign registered cars.'

'It sounds to me like you're doing all the right things,' I said, trying to imagine Vicenta in her official policia local uniform – epauletted blue shirt, military-style cargo pants with slots for everything including a baton and handcuffs, peaked cap and army-style jackboots laced to the ankles. 'Have you plotted the incidents on a map?'

'Well, I have all the details, but I haven't exactly plotted them, no.'

'Let's start with that then and see if it takes us anywhere. We can talk again in a few days. I take it you have other crimes to solve in the meantime.'

'Actually, no. There's not much of a crime wave in Parcent. Most of the time I'm helping kids and mums across the road or on the lookout for illegal building work.'

'What made you join the local police?' I asked, still picturing the uniform. 'It seems an unusual career choice for an attractive young woman.'

Vicenta scowled, her initial shyness overcome. 'You're not suggesting it's a career only for unattractive women are you?'

I squirmed. I really should have paid more attention at those compulsory equal opportunities training courses I had been put through in Nottingham.

'No, not at all,' I said, trying to hide my embarrassment. 'Still, I expect the uniform helps you pull the boys.' I raised an eyebrow.

'Actually, no. I'm gay and my partner hates to see me in uniform.'

I definitely should have paid more attention. 'Ah... well... anyway, plot those incidents on a map and we'll talk again soon. I'd better circulate now, offer condolences you know, that sort of thing.'

I chatted with Pepito for a few minutes longer, slowly overcoming my embarrassment, sipping the rough red wine until, thankfully, my glass was empty. I was preparing to leave when a group of four old men entered the bar. Seemingly oblivious to the gathering of mourners, one of the men spread a sheet of green baize over one of the glass-topped wicker tables. Another man emptied a box of dominoes onto the cloth, turning them face down for one of the others to shuffle. The fourth man limped towards the bar and spat out the standard Spanish imperative, devoid of civility: *'Pongame cuatro cañas.'*

Pepito looked across and greeted the man. 'Rafael, how are you? I haven't seen you for ages.'

The old man appeared unmoved by the greeting. He nudged the black beret from his forehead and squinted at Pepito through milky eyes.

'As well as God permits,' he answered, adjusting his focus beyond Pepito and screwing up his deeply lined face as he fixed his view on me with an inquisitive glare.

'I don't think you've met Michael,' Pepito said. 'Antonio's son. Michael, this is Rafael Fernandez, your grandfather's brother, your great uncle.'

Pepito stepped away from the bar to clear the space between the two of us and I moved over to offer my hand.

The old man glowered at me then turned away and moved towards his friends, yelling over his shoulder at the barman who was filling four tiny glasses from the Mahou Cerveza pump.

'Bring the beers to the table,' Rafael said.

'You'll have to excuse him,' Pepito said apologetically. 'I'll explain later, but now is not the time.'

'There's no need.' I replied, imagining again what my father might have felt had he ever set foot again in Parcent.

I had discharged my duty to be seen at the funeral and it was time to leave. I wanted to talk to Rosana, but it didn't seem the right time, so I used work as an excuse to get away. Walking through the quiet streets of Parcent my route took me through the Placa del Poble, along Carrer de Dalt and down Avenida de la Constitución to Carrer de L'Era where I had parked. As I walked, I noticed several foreign-registered cars, four British, one Dutch and two German. They all had their wing mirrors intact – for now at least.

CHAPTER FOUR

Seventeen year old Anthony Robinson had lived all his life in Spain with his parents, Graham and Eileen, who moved to Spain nearly eighteen years ago, after Mr Robinson had been medically retired from the Fire Service in South East London. Anthony was last seen on Friday 15th February when he had left home at around 7.00pm saying he was going out to spend the evening with friends – a routine event.

There were photographs on the file as well a list of all his friends and a detailed description of the clothes he was wearing when he disappeared. "Missing" posters had been pinned up at police stations throughout Alicante Province and leaflets circulated to local schools and night-clubs.

A sheath of press cuttings and cassette recordings of radio and TV bulletins showed no lack of interest from both the Spanish and English media. There had been four reported sightings of Anthony in the two weeks after he disappeared, two in Alicante, one in Calpe and one in Javea. They had each been followed up by the investigating officers, but had come to nothing.

The previous investigation, I concluded, had been handled proficiently, if routinely, given the circumstances and the pressures imposed by other more serious crimes. There was no evidence of foul play and brief background checks of both parents – always the first suspects in this type of investigation – had revealed nothing out of the ordinary, at least nothing on police files. Interviews with neighbours suggested the Robinsons were an ordinary, respectable family and Anthony himself had been described as quiet and unassuming; a description confirmed by the head teacher of his school who had added that Anthony was a studious boy, popular with other pupils.

Despite reassurances that everything was being done to find Anthony, Mrs Robinson had pestered the British Consulate with phone calls expressing dissatisfaction with the investigation. She had also written to the British Ambassador in Madrid, who had forwarded the letter to the Commander of the Guardia Civil in Alicante.

The village of Lliber was just five minutes drive from the Guardia Civil HQ in Jalon. I knew it well having passed through the linear settlement several times on the way to Parcent and grown used to the chaos caused by the one-way system through the town centre that usually brought traffic to a standstill. No such problems on this occasion as Mariela jumped the queue at the traffic lights, hung a right and wound her way through the narrow back streets, joining the main road again on the far side of the village before taking the road signposted to Gata de Gorgos.

'Almost there,' Mariela said, turning into a dusty, pot-holed track flanked by vineyards.

The Robinson's house was the last in a staggered row of twenty identical bungalows shoehorned into a narrow strip of land between the access road and a dried up riverbed at the rear. They reminded me of the post-war prefabs I had seen on the outskirts of Nottingham, most of them now demolished. Faded and flaking paintwork on rough, pebble dashed walls and terracotta roof tiles pock-marked with scaly lichen gave the development an air of neglect.

There was nowhere to park on the narrow road outside the house so Mariela left the car at the entrance to La Solana and we walked to the Robinson's front gate.

I had already reached the conclusion that my visit would be a waste of time. There were more important things to be doing than interviewing a couple of over-anxious parents who could not accept the fact that their teenage son had left home. But Colonel Cardells wanted a PR job so that is what I planned. A quick chat, assure the Robinson's that the case was still active and then back to more important issues.

'Nice flowers,' Mariela commented as we approached the front door.

I was distracted by a giant, 2.5 metre satellite TV dish anchored in concrete and secured by metal cables fanning out at angles. 'What? Yes. They must have fertilised this one on a regular basis to reach that size.'

I noted the logo stencil-painted in the centre of the dish: "Javea Satellite TV Systems – BBC, ITV, Sky TV." I marvelled at the ingenuity of the entrepreneurs who managed to find ways for ex-pats to receive British television, even when it meant installing a mini Jodrell Bank in the garden.

Eileen Robinson welcomed us at the door. Floral print frock, brown sandals with buckled fastenings, reddish brown hair, grey at the roots.

'Mrs Robinson, I'm Sergeant Poquet, we spoke on the telephone. This is Captain Fernandez.'

'Thank you for coming, please come through. My husband is on the terrace.'

A glimpse at the interior gave me the same impression of neglect I had formed from the outside. A worn rug in the lounge was centred by a white melamine coffee table. MFI, I concluded, definitely pre-IKEA. A gold-coloured velour sofa and matching arm chair were positioned at angles and focussed on an oversized flat-screen television stationed in the corner of the room. An electric, coal-effect fire filled the hearth and a layer of dust on the red and amber "coals" suggested it was more for show than for any practical purpose.

'Would you like tea?' Mrs Robinson asked.

I conjured up thoughts of tea bags in mugs with creamy long-life milk. 'No thank you Mrs Robinson, we can't stay long,' I replied before Mariela could answer.

'Graham, it's that police lady I told you about and Captain Fernando.'

I couldn't be bothered to correct her as I had heard this particular misinterpretation of my surname many times before and put it down to that song by Abba.

On the terrace, already shimmering in the mid-morning heat, Mr Robinson rose from a collapsible director's chair. A thick mane of grey-brown hair flopped over his brow with side strands hanging over his ears where they had escaped from a ponytail at the back held in place with a rubber band.

'Please, sit down,' Mr Robinson said, ushering us to one side.

I opted for a white plastic picnic chair rather than the folding canvas which I left for Mariela in the belief that it was less likely to collapse under her weight than my own.

'If I could just explain, Mr and Mrs Robinson, Captain Fernandez is new to the Guardia Civil. His brief is to work with the foreign, mainly English, community on the Costa Blanca.'

I cast Mariela a glance that said, just get on with it, there's no need to explain and followed this with: 'Sergeant Poquet is more familiar with the case than I am, so I'll leave it to her to ask the questions.'

Mariela narrowed her eyes and frowned, then opened the folder she had placed on her lap. 'We've been through all the case notes, Mr and Mrs Robinson, and I have to say that the previous officers did a very thorough job. But I – we – would just like to reassure you that the case is still active and everything possible is being done to trace your son – Anthony, isn't it?'

'Tony,' Mr Robinson replied.

'Tony... We've circulated Tony's photograph to all our offices and the press have been given it as well. We'll be issuing a fresh statement to the press and the TV later this week. And we'll be contacting all Tony's friends again, but there are a few things I'd like to go over.'

'Of course,' said Eileen Robinson. 'It's so good to know that you are still looking for him. We've been so worried. I know people think he's probably another runaway teenager, but we know him better than anyone and he's just not like that. He wouldn't just run away, not Tony. We're at our wit's end with worry.' She sniffled into a handkerchief and lifted tortoise-shell framed spectacles to wipe her eyes.

I sensed there was little to be gained from listening to a distraught mother who wanted only to demonstrate what a good boy Tony was. A distraction was needed and perhaps Mariela might get more useful information from Mr

Robinson who, to this point, had seemed quite calm about the situation.

'Mrs Robinson,' I said, 'why don't you show me Tony's bedroom, perhaps I could have a look around. Sergeant Poquet can run through a few details with your husband.'

The distraction worked. Now Mrs Robinson had something else to do, and more importantly, something else to talk about as she led me towards the back of the house.

'Yes of course, Captain. It's just as he left it, we haven't touched a thing. Well, I've dusted of course... and made the bed. Oh, I hope that wasn't the wrong the thing to do. I haven't disturbed evidence or anything like that, have I?'

'No, that's quite alright.' I entered the room at the end of a short corridor. 'Actually, Mrs Robinson, that cup of tea might be a good idea after all, if it's not too much trouble. I'll join you on the terrace when it's ready.'

I closed the door and slowly moved my focus around the room, trying to form an impression of the person who slept – or used to sleep – there. A single divan bed filled the space beneath the widow on the far wall. It was covered with a crisp plain blue duvet with pressed creases running down and across. Mrs Robinson had clearly done more than make the bed; she had changed the duvet cover as well. A glimpse at the matching sheet below, confirmed this.

Zigzag patterned curtains framed the window with matching tie-backs holding them at each side, exposing a set of yellowing net curtains that obscured the view. There was a faint smell of tobacco smoke in the room and I wondered if this had caused the discolouration. I knelt on the bed and lifted the nets, sniffing them to confirm my first thought. The wooden frame housed two side-hinged windows that locked with a central metal strut operated by a twisting handle. Open, they were certainly large enough for anyone to climb out to the small garden below, which was separated from the dry riverbed beyond by a low, wood-panel fence – easy enough to scale.

I dropped the nets and smoothed out the duvet cover before turning my attention to the narrow built-in wardrobe on the side wall. I opened the panelled wooden doors and flicked through a collection of clothes on hangers tightly pressed together on a metal rail. A shelf below contained a collection of precisely folded and neatly stored pullovers and T-shirts. Either Tony Robinson was tidier than the average teenager or Mrs Robinson had done more than simply change the bed. Next, I turned my attention to the base of the wardrobe, lifting in turn a pair of nearly-new Nike Pro trainers, some scuffed plain black leather shoes with well-worn rubber heels, a pair of two-tone brown bowling-type shoes with Velcro fastenings and a pair of backless, open-toed brown leather sandals. Pretty well equipped in the shoe department, I surmised, together with whatever he was wearing when he left. I closed the doors and turned the small key.

On the top of a pine dresser, a circular tilting mirror caught my attention. I bent forward and couldn't resist a casual glance. I needed a haircut. I resisted the temptation to make use of the plastic hairbrush lying at the side of a small square dish that contained a few copper coins and a pair of nail clippers. A rummage through the drawers revealed an unremarkable collection of socks and underwear and a deeper rummage through the items revealed nothing of interest beyond an old wristwatch (stopped), a rolled-up school tie and a half-empty pack of foil-wrapped extra strong mints – good for disguising the smell of smoke on one's breath?

The corner of the room behind the door was taken up with a basic, metal and Formica computer console which held, on its lower shelf, a computer tower emitting a low hum indicating it was turned on. I withdrew the seat from beneath the knee-hole and sat down before tapping the space bar on the keyboard to bring the flat-screen VDU into life. The desktop revealed a set of icons floating on the standard Microsoft Windows background of blue sky and white clouds.

'Tea's ready, Mr Fernandez.'

I returned the chair to its original position and moved towards the door. I paused for a moment and took in the whole scene; putting together the individual components I had examined to form a composite impression. Something was wrong. Even accounting for Mrs Robinson's dusting and tidying, this simply wasn't the bedroom of a seventeen-year-old. Something was missing. There were no books or magazines, no scraps of paper, no games, no clutter whatsoever. I thought for a moment, shifting my gaze around the walls. Then it came to me. No pictures. No posters. I walked to the far wall to the right of the computer console and examined the surface, painted in pale blue emulsion. I could just make out the vague outline of a square of slightly deeper blue where the paint had been protected from fading. I traced my finger round the edge of the outline – about 50 centimetres wide by 75 centimetres high. I looked further to the left and traced another, slightly smaller, outline within which I detected tiny particles of what looked like Blue-Tack.

The door opened and I turned to see Eileen Robinson with a steaming mug in her hand. 'Would you like it here, Captain Fernandez?'

'No… no, I'll join you on the terrace, thank you.'

Mariela was busy scribbling notes as Graham Robinson spoke. She stopped as I returned to the plastic chair.

'Please, carry on,' I said, placing the mug on the table in front of me as Mrs Robinson joined us, sitting in a matching chair and sipping her tea.

'Mr Robinson has been telling me about the night Tony left. Apparently he received a phone call that afternoon from a friend. Mr Robinson took the call himself, but didn't recognise the voice, except that it was male, and the caller didn't give a name. Later that evening – a Friday – Tony left and said he was going to meet some friends in the village. He went to school in Lliber and had quite a few friends in the area, so there was nothing unusual about that. But he never came home.'

'That's right,' Mrs Robinson said. 'He was usually home by eleven. That was his normal curfew. In fact I reminded him as he left and he promised to be home on time. He's never even been late before, well, give or take a few minutes and then he always rang us to say where he was and what time he'd be home.'

'He had a mobile phone, then?' Mariela asked.

'No… Well, he wanted one of course.' Mrs Robinson glanced at her husband. 'But Graham said…'

'Look, Eileen, it doesn't matter now, phone or no phone the fact is he didn't come home and we haven't heard anything from him since he left – no one has.'

Mrs Robinson began to sniffle once more and I felt, again, that a diversion was needed if we were to avoid witnessing a full flood of tears. 'Mrs Robinson, how did Tony get to the village?' I asked.

'He walked; it's only a few minutes.'

'And where would he have met this friend or friends?'

'They'd usually meet in the village square, next to the town hall.'

'Are any of his clothes missing – apart from what he was wearing, of course?'

'No, everything else is here as far as I can tell.'

'Did Tony have much money with him?'

She screwed the handkerchief in her fist. 'Not much, no, perhaps twenty or twenty-five euros. He had more, over two hundred and fifty euros, in a savings account at the CAM Bank, but we've checked and it's never been touched.'

I lifted my mug off the table, took one look at the pale creamy liquid and put it down again.

Mariela picked up the thread. 'The school Tony went to, Mrs Robinson, it was the private school in Lliber, the Lady Teresa School I think it's called, is that right?'

'Yes that's right. We wanted him to go there because... well, it's an English school and we wanted him to have an English education. They teach Spanish of course and Tony was very good, fluent I'd say. He's lived here all his life, so you would expect that.'

'And his friends,' Mariela continued, 'were they mainly English or Spanish?'

'Mainly English, I'd say – at school at least, but he had a lot of Spanish friends; local boys and girls from the area. He used to mix with them at weekends and in the holidays because most of his school chums weren't around. They came from all over, you see – Javea, Moraira, places on the coast and so he didn't see much of them outside school.'

46

'I see,' said Mariela, turning again to Mr Robinson, 'and the person who telephoned that last Friday night. Was he Spanish or English, do you recall?'

'Spanish. He only spoke a couple of words, in English, to ask for Tony, but he was definitely Spanish, I could tell by the accent.'

I was still thinking about the bedroom, or rather what was missing from the bedroom. I wanted to broach the subject, but without sounding abrasive or accusatorial. I turned to Mrs Robinson.

'I'm sorry, this is going to sound rather rude of me, but I believe there may have been some posters on the wall in Tony's bedroom, but they're not there now. Is there any reason for that?'

Mrs Robinson's face showed signs of guilt and she twisted the handkerchief in her hand. 'There were some posters, yes.' Her eyes dropped down to her lap. 'We didn't much like them; they were rather weird and gaudy. They were drawings depicting a kind of occult figure. They were just a passing phase, nothing serious, and we didn't want anyone to think Tony had any real interest in such things because we know he didn't. So we thought it best to take them down.'

'I see,' I said. 'Do you still have them?'

'Yes, we've kept them.'

'Then I think we need to have them, if you don't mind.'

Graham Robinson interjected. 'You can have them, if you feel you need them, but I don't want this to divert your enquiries in any way. Eileen's already told you they were just a fad, a fashion; they should have no bearing on your investigation.'

'I think you'll have to leave us to be the judge of that, Mr Robinson. I hear what you say, but in this kind of investigation we cannot afford to ignore any piece of information, whether it turns out to be relevant or not. If we could have the posters? We'll get them back to you of course.'

Mrs Robinson rose from her chair and went back into the house. An awkward silence reigned until she returned a few moments later with a rolled up tube of stiff paper.

I unrolled the paper to reveal a print of a wild boar baying on it hind legs, evil eyes flashing, blood seeping from the short tusks on its snout and trickling down the coarse black fur on its chest. The other poster contained a similar image. I passed them to Mariela who studied them briefly before rolling them up again.

'You're sure these posters have no significance?' I asked.

Mr Robinson scowled. 'I've already told you, no.'

Eileen Robinson looked inquisitive. 'Why do you ask, Captain Fernandez? Do they mean something to you?'

'No, I've never seen anything like them before. It's just that posters of pop stars, fast cars or footballers would quite normal, but you have to admit these posters are quite... different.' I resisted the temptation to say weird, sinister even grotesque. I could see Mrs Robinson fretting, so I decided to change the subject. 'I noticed the computer in Tony's bedroom. Did he use it much?'

'Quite a lot, yes.' Mr Robinson replied. 'He used it for homework and that kind of thing.'

'And did he surf the internet?' Mariela asked, suddenly taking a renewed interest in the conversation. 'Chat rooms, that kind of thing?'

'Yes, he did use the internet, but not very much. We don't have a broadband connection and the call costs soon mount up if you spend hours on-line. So we made sure he didn't use it for long. And I don't think he used those chat room things. We've always warned him about them.'

'And do you use it as well, Mr Robinson?' I asked. 'Only I noticed the computer is still switched on.'

'I use it, yes, but not very often. I look up the weather forecast sometimes and I have an interest in classic cars, not that I can afford one, but it was a hobby of mine when I was younger.'

'I see.' I wondered how to frame the next remark but decided there was no point in pussyfooting around. 'I'm afraid we'll have to take the computer away. There may be something useful that could help us with our enquiries.'

'Mr Robinson sat upright in his chair. 'Is that really necessary?'

'If you want us to be thorough then I'm afraid it is. Sergeant Poquet can disconnect it for you and I'm sure we can get it back to you within a couple of days. I promise we won't damage it or destroy any of your files. It's just routine, as I have said, but we never know where we might find a hidden clue that could help us find out what has happened to Tony. That's what we all want, I'm sure.'

Mr Robinson looked uneasy, but didn't protest further.

'Mr Robinson, does Tony have any friends in the UK?' I asked.

A slight shiftiness crossed Robinson's face; an unexpected reaction to a seemingly innocent, but pertinent question, I thought.

'No he doesn't.'

'Or family?'

'No.'

I waited for a further comment or explanation, but none was forthcoming. 'Does Tony have a passport?'

'No he doesn't.'

This was not the answer I had expected. I waited again.

'He's never been abroad so there was no need.' Graham Robinson flashed his eyes in my direction as if trying to gauge my reaction to the previous answer. I made a determined effort to appear unmoved even though the answer struck me as curious.

'Thank you, Mr and Mrs Robinson. I think that's all for now. If Sergeant Poquet could just get the computer. Oh, and I noticed a hairbrush in Tony's bedroom. I'd like to take that as well so we can obtain a DNA sample. It might be useful at some stage.'

I should have realised the panic this would cause as Mrs Robinson's eyes widened in fright.

'You don't think Tony's dead, do you? Why do you need a DNA sample?'

I didn't have a clue if Tony Robinson was dead or not, but I felt the need to offer reassurance. 'No, Mrs Robinson, I don't think he is dead. DNA may be useful in all sorts of ways. It's just routine and I'm sure you want us to be thorough. Now, we really must be going.'

The abrupt end to the interview seemed to catch the others off guard and there was a moment's silence as no

49

one seemed sure what to do next. I filled the void with my next, and final, question, focussing on Mrs Robinson as I asked it.

'You're quite sure there's nothing more you can tell us about Tony? Nothing further that might give us a clue to what has happened?'

Mrs Robinson lifted her head and flashed her eyes towards her husband. By the time I shifted my focus all I saw was Mr Robinson's eyes dart back from the direction of his wife before meeting my stare.

'We've told you all we know,' Mr Robinson said. 'Now it's up to you to find Tony – and not before time. Now, I'll get you that computer.'

'And the hairbrush,' I reminded him.

'You think they're hiding something, don't you?' Mariela said as we strode back to the car.

'You saw that look, didn't you? Damn right, they're hiding something. Why the hell should we waste our time trying to find some runaway teenager when his parents won't even be frank with us? For two pins I'd...' I reached the car and waited for Mariela to unlock the door. 'How old would you say they are?' I asked. 'The Robinsons.'

Mariela placed the computer in the back of the car along with the posters and the hairbrush, now enclosed in a polythene evidence bag. She slid into the driver's seat and started the motor. 'Difficult to say, late fifties perhaps. Why do you ask?'

'No reason. People tend to have kids late these days, I guess.'

'You mean there's hope for you yet?' She smiled wryly, but I was in no mood to be teased.

'Just get that computer back to HQ and get someone to take a look at it. And get that DNA sample. And find out what those weird posters are all about.'

'Quite a delicacy round here, you know,' Mariela said.

'What?'

'Wild boar. They still roam in herds around the mountains and the villagers hunt them occasionally. In fact, if you're interested, I know a little restaurant not far from here that specialises in all kinds of game, wild boar included. I could book a table for tonight if you like.'

The thought of spending time with Mariela was not unappealing. She was stunningly beautiful and intelligent, too. I realised I knew very little about her; her age, her family, her boyfriends. Surely she must have a boyfriend. And then another thought occurred to me. She couldn't possibly be gay, could she? I dismissed the idea immediately and wondered if the invitation to dinner had an ulterior motive. She wasn't asking me on a date, was she? I dismissed that idea as well. At thirty-six years old, I was much older than Mariela. What might she be? Twenty-seven or twenty-eight? Not that much older come to think of it.

'Some other time, perhaps,' I said, unconvincingly. 'I've had enough bores for one day,' I added, causing Mariela's hopeful smile to twist into a grimace.

CHAPTER FIVE

I wondered which would break first – the day-old dry bread roll or my teeth. Perhaps the bakers of Spain were in league with the dentists. I gave up in the end, slammed the *bocadillo* on the plate and almost broke that instead. At least the coffee was good – hot, strong and syrupy – my usual kick-start to the day. For the first time in as long as I could remember I craved a cigarette – I must have been spending too much time in smoky Spanish bars.

Much as I had tried, I couldn't stop thinking about the Robinson boy. I had laid awake most of the night churning over the previous day's interview. Time and again I had told myself it was a waste of time – an adolescent teenager pissed off with his parents and striking a blow for freedom. I had done the same thing myself when I was thirteen and first learned of my father's leprosy. My parents had kept the secret well hidden, but one of the neighbours found out and it wasn't long before I was being taunted at school. I was unprepared and confused when the other kids started calling me a leper. Bewildered, I ran home demanding an explanation and when it came I was full of anger and hatred.

My parents tried to reassure me that the leprosy was cured and could not be inherited or passed on through contact. But the very mention of the word leprosy stirred in me feelings of revulsion and disgust. I was in tears and when my father tried to comfort me, I recoiled, realising only later how much pain this must have caused him. That night I ran from home, though I only stayed away for a couple of nights until I ran out of money for food and my clothes began to stink. But things were never the same with my father after that.

My parents later explained how they had met at Fontilles and left Spain to avoid the fear and prejudice they knew they would have faced had they remained. I accepted the explanation, but used it to blame Spain for my own misfortune at being born the son of a leper.

A sharp rap on the front door roused me from my reflections and I shuffled along the hallway in my baggy slippers, tightening the belt on my Marks and Spencer knee-length silk dressing gown as I moved to answer.

'Polka dots, very fetching,' Mariela said. 'All you need is a cravat and you'd pass for that old English actor – what's his name?'

I ignored the question, focussing my bleary eyes on the vision before me – a skin tight T-shirt, emblazoned with the logo FCUK tucked in skin tight jeans, tucked in black leather boots. Glossy blond hair, gelled in clumps and carefully flicked in all directions gave the impression of organised chaos.

'Coffee smells good.' She moved inside, heading for the kitchen.

'Help yourself, there's plenty in the pot on the stove. Sorry, there's no milk, I'm still getting straight and I haven't found the village shops yet. There's bread if you want it, but I wouldn't recommend it, unless you have a good dentist.' I glanced at my watch – 8.15. 'What's so pressing anyway?'

'Noel Coward.'

'What?'

'That English actor with the cravat.'

I tugged at the dressing gown to cover my exposed chest and sat down at the kitchen table, tugging again to cover my knees.

'Couldn't you have phoned?'

'I tried. Your mobile seems to be switched off and I don't have a number for your land line.'

'I don't have one yet. It's ordered, but there seems to be a problem – no spare lines in Parcent apparently.'

'You should pull rank with Telefonica. Tell them you're a Captain with the Guardia Civil and they'll jump to it, otherwise you'll wait forever.'

'As I said, what's the emergency?'

'Oh, you're needed at the office. We've had an overnight guest in the cells and he's dying to meet you. Paco Santos, the deputy Mayor of Beniforell, remember? Mora's right hand man; the one whose brother is an agent for the developers.'

The fog in my brain suddenly cleared as the caffeine kicked in and my curiosity was aroused.

'In the cells you say, but why?'

'You can thank the *policia local* in Beniforell for that – Sergeant Benitez. He was out and about late last night when he spotted a light on in Mora's house and the door was open. He knew the house was empty so he took a look inside. That's where he found Santos, in the main bedroom. He was levering up the base of a wardrobe with a screwdriver.' Mariela paused, teasing to provoke a response.

'And?'

'And he found a briefcase full of five hundred euro notes. About a quarter of a million euros, in fact.' Her face stretched to a beaming smile. 'Interesting don't you think? Worth an early start.'

'I'll get dressed – five minutes.'

I left Mariela pouring the last of the sludgy coffee. 'You should try *fartons*,' she yelled.

'What?' I shouted from halfway up the stairs.

'*Fartons*.' she yelled back. 'Sugary sponge fingers – a speciality in these parts. People dip them in their coffee for breakfast.'

Paco Santos looked tired, forlorn and rather ridiculous in his would-be burglar's outfit of black jeans, black shoes and a black crew neck sweater. There was even a pair of black leather gloves resting on the table in front of us when we entered the interview room at the *comisaría* in Jalon.

'About time,' Santos said, scrutinising us as we sat on the opposite side of a badly scratched metal-topped table.

We had discussed the interview on the journey to Jalon. I wanted to go on the offensive and link the attempted burglary with Mora's murder. The money was an obvious motive in my view. Mariela preferred a more cautious approach. Perhaps, she had suggested, we should simply let Santos talk, explain what had happened and see where that led. There was still nothing to prove that Mora had been murdered, but we could keep this in reserve and spring it as a surprise if Santos was uncooperative. I decided to go along with Mariela's suggestion, though I was convinced of two things: Mora's death was murder and Santos had something to do with it.

Mariela made the introductions then placed two cassettes in a tape machine and set them in motion. 'Mr Santos, for the purpose of the tape, would you please confirm that you have been advised of your rights and that, at this time, you have declined the services of a lawyer.'

Santos sat straight-backed, his arms folded tight across his chest, doing his best to look confident, though the constant flickering of his eyes between the two of us suggested nervousness beneath the veneer of defiance.

'Yes,' Santos replied.

Mariela pressed on, leading the questions as we had agreed. 'Perhaps you could start by explaining what you were doing in Mr Mora's house at 2.30 this morning.'

Santos shifted his gaze to the far wall and maintained his focus without blinking. The silence that ensued was disturbed only by the faint hum of the tape machine and Mariela allowed the awkward quietude to linger for several seconds before interrupting. 'For the purpose of the tape, the prisoner declined to answer the question.'

Santos unfolded his arms and sat forward. 'Prisoner? What do you mean prisoner? I've done nothing wrong.'

'Then perhaps you would answer the question.'

Santos ran a hand through his thick black hair, momentarily straightening the wiry curls which immediately snapped back into place, scattering flecks of dandruff to add to the drift that had already built up on the shoulders of his sweater. 'I was merely recovering something that belonged to me.'

'The money, you mean. A quarter of a million euros.'

Santos said nothing.

'And to recover this property of yours, you entered Mora's house in the middle of the night, dressed all in black, then proceeded to lift the base of the wardrobe in

Mora's bedroom and remove a briefcase containing the money. And there was nothing suspicious about this because the money belonged to you. Is that your story?'

I had to admire the way Mariela put this scenario to Santos without even a trace of sarcasm in her voice.

'Not all of it.' Santos sat back in his chair and re-folded his arms.

'Just some of it was yours then?' Mariela said. 'A third? A half? A hundred thousand? Just how much?'

'Half, I suppose.'

'I see, so you were going to take one hundred and twenty-five thousand and put the rest back in the wardrobe?' Now her sarcasm showed.

'Something like that. Look, do you realise who I am? You've no right to question me like this.'

'We can halt the interview whenever you want. You'll be returned to your cell and we can come back again later, if that's what you want.'

Santos sighed. 'Juan-Jose Mora was the Mayor of Beniforell and I'm his deputy. This is council business and you've no right to go poking your noses into this matter.'

'I think you'll find we have every right, Mr Santos. When someone, even the esteemed deputy Mayor of Beniforell, is caught red-handed trespassing on someone else's property and helping himself to a briefcase containing a quarter of a million euros, we have every right to be suspicious. Don't you agree? After all, we only have your word to say that the money, or some of it, was yours.'

Santos looked across at me, as I raised an eyebrow and offered the faintest hint of a smile as if to indicate I was enjoying his discomfort.

Mariela continued. 'You say this is council business, Mr Santos. Would you care to explain?'

'No I wouldn't.'

'When you say, "Council business" do you mean the money belongs to the council? Perhaps you were simply collecting the money on behalf of the council. Is that it? We can have a word with the Secretary to the council if you like or the Chief Accountant. That should clear things up don't you think?'

Santos bit his bottom lip to stop it quivering. Defiance had clearly been replaced by anxiety. 'I've told you, the money was ours, Mora's and mine. It has nothing to do with the council.'

'I see,' Mariela said, intentionally adopting a puzzled expression. 'It's council business, but it has nothing to do with the council?' She paused momentarily then pressed on. 'What do you do for a living Mr Santos?'

'I'm a postman, not that it's any of your business.'

'A postman, I see. Which makes me wonder. How does a postman come into a half share of a quarter of a million euros?'

Santos returned to the offensive. 'That's none of your business. You've no right to question me like this. I've had enough. I've told you I was simply collecting money that belongs to me. Mora was holding on to it for us. When he died I couldn't leave it in his house, so I decided to collect it. I've explained what happened. I've committed no crime. Now, are you going to release me?'

I sensed it was time to turn up the pressure. 'There's another explanation,' I said, leaning forward and looking straight into Santos's eyes. 'The money was Mora's. He's a wealthy man after all, and you knew he had a large amount of cash in his house. So you murdered him and then broke into his house to take the money.'

The expression on Santos's face suddenly changed as a combination of confusion and panic left his mouth agape and his eyes bulging in their sockets. 'Murder! Who the hell said anything about murder? Mora died when he fell from the road. It was an accident. No one's said anything about murder.'

'Or he was pushed.' I said, still staring directly at Santos. 'Where were you on the evening of June 20th?'

'What? I was at home.'

'Was anyone with you?'

'No. I live alone. There was no one else with me. This is ridiculous. You can stop now. I'm saying nothing more until I have a lawyer.'

I sat back casually. 'Fine. Interview suspended at...' I glanced at my watch, '...10.22 a.m. Turn off the tape machine, Sergeant Poquet, and return the prisoner to the cells.'

Santos banged his fists on the table. 'You can't do this. I have friends in the Guardia Civil. I'll have you thrown off the case. I'll have you sacked. You don't know what you're meddling with here. If I were you, I'd tread very carefully, Captain Fernandez.'

'The tape's still running Mr Santos and that sounded very much like a threat to me. I think it's you who should tread carefully. You need to see your lawyer and explain to him how you came by all that money if, as you say, half of it is yours and why, after Mora died, you thought you could just break into his house and help yourself.'

I rose from my chair. 'Now you can turn off the tape machine, Sergeant Poquet. We have finished with Mr Santos for the time being.'

'Santos was right, Michael, you need to be careful.' We had returned to the office and Mariela seemed anxious.

'Careful of what, Mariela? Of some jumped up politician from a toy town hall?'

'I'm sorry, Michael, if this sounds condescending, but some of these toy town politicians, as you call them, have links with influential people.'

'You're suggesting I should back off when we have someone caught red-handed with a great deal of money, the source of which is dubious to say the least?'

'No, I'm not saying that, but just be careful. You told Santos that Mora had been murdered and we've no clear evidence to prove that at this stage.'

'Trust me, Mariela, Mora was murdered and Santos has something to do with it. Now, I suggest you get someone to search Mora's house. Let's see what else we can turn up. Perhaps there's something to explain where that money came from.'

'I'm on my way,' Mariela said, lifting her denim jacket off the back of the chair. 'Where will you be?'

'I'm going to see the pathologist to chase up the results of that lividity test and see if they've determined the exact cause of death. Mora's body had been moved before he was found; moved by someone who didn't just stumble across him in the dark; someone who knew he was there because they pushed him.'

'I'll see you later then.' She placed the Wrangler jacket around her shoulders and scooped up a black leather clutch bag from her desk.

I took my blazer from the coat stand. 'And if you have a moment to spare, see if the computer whiz-kids have found anything on the Robinson's computer and find out what you can about those weird posters from the boy's bedroom.'

'Anything else?'

'Yes. Book somewhere for dinner tonight... if you've nothing better to do. I want to know more about how these tin-pot town halls work.'

Mariela looked surprised. 'Yes, I mean... no. I've nothing better to do tonight. Do you like pizza?'

'I think we can do better than pizza. My treat, book somewhere nice; somewhere local. There must be at least one decent restaurant in the Jalon Valley.'

'I know just the place.'

CHAPTER SIX

I hate mortuaries. It isn't just the antiseptic smell or the echo of hard surfaces; it's the chill I found in every one I had ever entered. Like the chill of a fresh meat counter at the supermarket, designed to prolong the shelf-life of the products. Except there was a soullessness about these places, which, I had often rationalised, was to be expected in buildings devoid of life; a temporary stopover between this world and the next.

'Captain Fernandez, pleased to meet you. I wondered how long it would be before our paths crossed. I might have hoped it would be in happier circumstances, but perhaps this was inevitable given what we do for a living.'

Dr Pilar Vidal, Chief Pathologist for the Province of Alicante, had the cheery air of someone happy at her work, unaffected by her morbid surroundings. Her grey-flecked auburn hair was drawn up tight in a bun; that and her crumpled tweed suit reminded me of a middle-aged librarian I had once encountered in Nottingham. But I could never have visualised the librarian in a heavy rubber apron and white rubber boots − even if I had tried.

'I'd say it's nice to meet you, too,' I said, 'but it doesn't seem appropriate in the circumstances.'

'There's no need to be reverential here, Captain Fernandez. There's no fear of upsetting the customers.'

Like most forensic pathologists I had met, Pilar Vidal made light of death. It was, I surmised, a defence mechanism to avoid dwelling on the sadness and tragedy that lay behind the cases that came her way, each one uniquely painful to friends and family. It was, I supposed, necessary to set aside feelings of sadness and remorse for fear of being engulfed by them. Even so, the casual, cold-hearted formality of most pathologists left me wondering if they ever felt sorrow or pity; wondering why anyone would choose this as a profession.

'If you come with me, Captain Fernandez, Mora's body is on the table waiting for us.' Pilar Vidal led the way down a long corridor, apron swishing and rubber boots squeaking on the polished marble floor. 'I'm intrigued about why you asked us to re-examine the cause of death.'

I trotted behind, matching her brisk pace. 'Intuition, at least in part. In my job you learn to question everything. I never believe the obvious, at least not until all the other possibilities have been ruled out. But in this case there was more to it than that. The position of the body was too perfect to believe Mora had come to rest like that. You've seen the photographs?'

'Yes, and I understand what you mean. You're sure no one moved the body after it was discovered – the officers first on the scene perhaps?'

'We've checked and they are certain that nothing was touched.'

We approached a set of heavy-duty clear plastic curtains at the end of the corridor. Pilar Vidal brushed them to one side and entered a long narrow room lined on each side with sliding cabinets stacked three high. The chill sent a shiver down my spine and I felt the thump of my pulse in my throat. No matter how many times I had been required to view the dead bodies of victims, I could never shake off my revulsion. Necrophobia, I think they call it, and over the years, immersion therapy hadn't helped.

'You might want to put this on,' Pilar said, passing me a thin disposable plastic apron which I placed over my head to cover the front of my jacket and trousers.

We reached a stainless steel trolley-table in the centre of the room and Pilar peeled back a plastic shroud to reveal Mora's head and shoulders.

My pulse raced faster and I almost gagged as I looked down at Mora's face. The flesh was mostly milky white, flaccid, devoid of muscle tone. There was a hint of colour in the cheeks where a few threadlike veins were visible just beneath the surface of the skin. Mora's mouth gaped open

61

to show crooked yellow teeth behind lips that had a faint tinge of blue. Greasy black hair lay ruffled against his scalp in haphazard fashion and I noticed a trace of dried blood at the back of his head. I was transfixed as my gaze settled on Mora's open eyes; dull, opaque eyes with dilated pupils staring into infinity. I swallowed hard.

Pilar moved to the other side of the table. 'On first examination it seemed clear that the likely cause of death was the blow to the back of the skull. The skull is severely fractured and there was heavy internal bleeding in the brain. We found tiny grains of chalky rock in the wound, consistent with the reports from the scene that the deceased had fallen some distance from above and had struck his head on a rock. There are several fractures to the right wrist and forearm suggesting he tried to cushion the fall before hitting his head. The left hip is also fractured and there's bruising to the buttocks and chest. I can show you if you like.'

I felt a slight giddiness. 'No, that won't be necessary. Please, carry on.'

'Are you all right?' she asked.

'I'll be fine. Please... continue.'

'So, without evidence to the contrary, death was initially presumed to be the result of the fracture to the skull. The fracture was compressed and it was certainly severe enough to have been fatal. I'll go further and say that it would certainly have resulted in death – eventually.'

I looked up. 'Eventually?'

'When you asked us to look again, we found some clear inconsistencies in our initial conclusions. The lividity tests you asked for show that at the time the heart stopped pumping, causing the blood to gravitate to the lowest point, Mora's body was in the exact position depicted in the photographs taken at the scene.'

She paused and looked across at me as if checking that I was not about to faint. I took a deep breath and held it for a moment before speaking.

'So, if I understand you correctly, Dr Vidal, if I am right and Mora was moved after the fall, the lividity tests show that he was not dead when he initially came to rest, but that death occurred after he was moved.'

'Correct.' Dr Vidal said, moving to a side bench to pick up a magnifying glass. 'Which led me to question whether the fracture to the skull was indeed the cause of death.' She handed me the magnifying glass. 'Take a close look at his eyes – pay particular attention to the eyelids.'

I gripped the handle of the magnifying glass and leant forward holding it above Mora's face, raising and lowering it until the right eye came into focus, ten times magnified. My face was so close to Mora's that I detected a faint odour of disinfectant mingling with Mora's own bad breath – or at least an odour from his open mouth since he had long since stopped breathing. I gagged and swallowed hard before refocusing on the magnifying glass. A myriad of tiny blood vessels criss-crossed the white of the eye, some of them bundled into knots.

'What am I looking for?' I asked.

'If you look closely, you can see two or three distinct areas where the tiny capillaries in the conjunctiva have haemorrhaged.'

I didn't understand "conjunctiva", but I could clearly see two small areas to the left of the pupil where the blood vessels had ruptured and blood had spread like ink on blotting paper.

'I see them, yes.'

'You'll find the same marks in the left eye if you take a look and if you pull down the bottom eyelid, you will see similar marks there. They are more difficult to find than the ones in the conjunctiva, but they are there, tiny pin pricks just beneath the surface of the skin.'

I straightened and handed the magnifying glass back to Dr Vidal. 'I'll take your word for it. I assume these marks have some significance.'

'Indeed they do.' She picked up the shroud and pulled it back over Mora's face then wheeled the trolley to the far wall where she pushed the button on an intercom. It was answered with an indistinct crackle to which she responded. 'We've finished with Mr Mora now, you can return him to the filing system.' She walked back towards me. 'We like to keep things tidy in here, everything in its place.' She smiled for the first time since we met. 'We can talk in my office.'

'Those tiny pinpoint marks you saw are called petechial haemorrhages. They occur when blood leaks from the tiny capillaries in the eyes which can rupture due to increased pressure on the veins in the head when the airways are obstructed. Their presence is a strong indication of asphyxia.'

'You're saying Mora was strangled?'

'Now, now, Captain, you know better than to jump to conclusions like that. I said the presence of petechiae was an indication of asphyxiation, nothing more.'

'A strong indication, you said.'

'Yes. So we took a closer look. There was no sign of bruising to the neck or throat, so we ruled out strangulation. Then we examined the nose and mouth.'

She pulled out the top drawer of her desk and removed a set of glass slides set in a plastic sleeve. 'We found these.'

I examined the sleeve, but all I could see was a few minute specks sandwiched between the small pieces of glass.

'They're fibre of some kind, cotton would be my guess, but we need to do more tests. We found several filaments in Mora's nasal passage, not an unusual occurrence by itself – people might easily inhale particles of fibre, they are present in almost any dusty atmosphere. But we also found more identical particles in Mora's mouth – some on his tongue and a few between the lips and teeth. Now that is unusual. You see, even if someone inhaled particles of fibre through the mouth, they would be unlikely to remain there for long – they would cling to saliva and almost certainly be swallowed. But we found no further such particles in Mora's oesophagus.'

I quickly realised the significance of what Dr Vidal was suggesting. 'You're saying Mora was asphyxiated by smothering?'

'Almost certainly. And the irony is that whoever did it needn't have bothered because Mora was as good as dead in any event.'

'Is there any evidence of a struggle? It takes time for someone to suffocate.'

'You're right of course. But remember Mora's right arm was smashed and he was probably only semi-conscious after the fall. It wouldn't have taken much effort to hold on to his left arm and maintain sufficient pressure with a cloth of some sort over his nose and mouth.'

Amongst the many questions now racing through my mind, I allowed myself the quiet satisfaction of knowing that my first instincts had been correct. Mora had been murdered.

'Thank you, Dr Vidal.'

'No need for thanks, and please, call me Pilar. Besides, it's me who should thank you for pointing us in the right direction.'

'It's called teamwork, I think.'

'Well, thank you all the same. Now is there anything else?'

'Just one thing. Those fibres in Mora's nose and mouth, I don't suppose you can be more specific – wool, cotton, synthetic, that kind of thing.'

'You've done this kind of thing before, I think, either that or you watch too many American crime shows. The sample will be in the lab this afternoon, but the analysis might take a few days if we are to be exact. I expect we will be able to tell you a little more than natural of synthetic – colour perhaps, even a type of dye, or a source country for the material itself.'

'That would be very helpful, thanks.'

'It will cost you lunch,' the pathologist said with a smile.

Lunch with the librarian, I thought. 'Fine. What do pathologists like to eat?'

'Anything but offal.'

CHAPTER SEVEN

Reluctantly I had to concede that Mariela's knowledge of Spain and Spaniards was something I couldn't do without. Speaking the language was one thing, understanding the way things worked was quite another, I realised. It wasn't simply a matter of appreciating police methodology or the way the law worked in Spain – it was the nuances of personal interactions with Spaniards that confused me. Years of experience as a detective in Britain enabled me to "read" the people I encountered whether as witnesses or suspects. And this insight allowed me to manoeuvre, even manipulate people to get what I wanted. Now, however, I was all at sea, struggling to interpret the subtle mannerisms of speech, facial expressions and body language that usually fed my intuition.

So I needed Mariela. She had the makings of a good detective and she had shown enthusiasm and initiative. But did she have the insight to make the linkages between pieces of seemingly insignificant information, to find the inconsistencies and flaws in evidence or to see through the mire of useless information to find the real clues? More importantly, could she be trusted? Could I rely on her discretion if, as I was apt to do, I bent the rules a little, or would she go running to Colonel Cardells? I wasn't sure, but for now, I had no option but to rely on her. And that in itself was something I wasn't used to. And to make matters worse, I liked Mariela; I might even be attracted to her, though I dismissed the thought, knowing it could not be mutual.

'You look pleased with yourself,' she said as she entered the office where I was leaning back in my chair, hands linked behind my head.

'Mora was murdered – suffocated by smothering.' I said with an air of satisfaction. 'Dr Vidal confirmed it and there's enough forensics to hold up in court. Now all we have to do is find out who did it.'

'And that may not be as easy as we thought. Here, take a look at these.' She placed a plastic folder on the desk. 'We found these at Mora's house this afternoon.'

I removed a series of grainy monochrome photographs from the folder and thumbed through them quickly. They all showed men walking towards the camera, obviously unaware they were being photographed. They had been taken at night and the background to the photographs was the same in every case – a painted brick wall with a shuttered window.

'Is there something I'm missing here?' I asked.

Mariela smiled and moved around the desk to lean at my side. Her blond hair fell forward almost brushing my face until she combed it with her fingers, lifting it behind her ear. A faint waft of almond scented shampoo caught my nostrils. She spread the first three photographs side by side across the desk.

'The background is the same in every case – you see?'

'That much I noticed.'

'But did you notice this part here?' She pointed to the top left hand corner of one of the photographs – to part of an illuminated sign and the letters CA formed in italic script.

I studied this part of each of the photographs, concluding that they were all stills taken from a precisely the same position, probably, I thought, from a fixed video surveillance camera. 'And the significance is?'

'This is one of the clubs we believe Mora owns – CLUB EROTICA – it's on the N332 near Gata de Gorgos.'

'Well, well, well,' I said, grinning. 'This is interesting.'

'More interesting than you think, Michael. We're trying to identify the men in the photos – there are twelve of them in all. But take a look at the last two.'

I shuffled through to the bottom of the pile, reaching the penultimate photo then leaning forward to study it in more detail. 'Is that who I think it is?'

'The very same – Walter Wilkinson, resident of the municipality of Beniforell, arch opponent of Mora's plans to urbanise half of the parish. Now take a look at the last one.'

The face of the man in the photograph meant nothing to me.

'That, Michael, is none other than Salvador Guardiola,' There was a note of caution in her voice.

'You'll have to enlighten me.'

Mariela moved to her desk and placed the photographs in front of her. 'Salvador Guardiola is the owner of Guardiola Property S.A., parent company of Tierra Nueva S.L. whose plan for the redevelopment of Beniforell was approved by Mora and his fellow councillors, in January.'

'Jesus.' I allowed the information to sink in before I spoke again. 'So let's get all this in perspective. Juan-Jose Mora, we now know, was murdered. We find his deputy Mayor, Paco Santos in the process of recovering a quarter of a million euros from Mora's house. Now we discover that Mora had in his possession photos of this Salvador Guardiola, the man behind the development plans for Beniforell, as well as a photo of Walter Wilkinson, the man who more than anyone has led opposition to those plans – photos that are embarrassing to say the least. What the hell have we got here – murder, theft, extortion, bribery, corruption? This is turning into something big, really big, Mariela, and it's fallen into our lap.' I could barely hide my excitement.

Mariela was not quite so enthusiastic about the prospect. 'There's something you need to understand, Michael,' she said in a guarded tone. 'Salvador Guardiola is one of the richest men in Valencia and one of the most powerful and influential as well. He has some very important connections at all levels of Valencian society.'

I frowned. 'What sort of connections?'

'Well, for a start, he's a major contributor to the Partido Progresivo, the party that controls the regional government, so he has the ear of some very senior politicians.'

'So what? He wouldn't be the first grandee I've crossed swords with.'

'I said, "for a start." His influence reputedly extends beyond politics.'

'So what are we talking about? The national government, the judiciary... the police?'

'I'm not saying that, I am just pointing out that this case has taken on a whole new dimension.'

'You can say that again,' I said with enthusiasm, before noticing a degree of exasperation in Mariela's facial expression. 'You're not suggesting we should go easy here, are you?'

'No, of course not... It's just that you – we – need to tread carefully. There are ways of doing things in Spain that you don't understand and... perhaps you need to think about this before doing anything that might...'

'Open up a can of worms, you mean?'

'That's not the term that I would have used, but yes, that kind of thing. Look, perhaps we need to take some advice... consult someone before we do anything else.'

I felt my face redden with anger. 'Colonel Cardells you mean. Is that what you're getting at?' Is that why you're here, Mariela? Is that why you were assigned to work with me – to keep tabs on me? To make sure I don't upset the apple cart?'

It was Mariela's turn to demonstrate her anger as she rose from her chair and flung an arm across her desk, scattering the photos to the floor. 'Damn you, Captain Michael Fernandez. Is that what you really think? That I'm simply here as Cardells' spy? If that's the case then you can find someone else to chaperone you, someone else to stop you digging a great big hole for yourself.'

I wasn't sure whether her outrage was genuine or whether I had simply touched a nerve. Whilst I was making my mind up, Mariela stomped towards the door.

'Have you checked Wilkinson's alibi yet?' I shouted.

Mariela paused in her stride, glared at me and then slammed the door hard as she exited the office.

'I suppose dinner's off.' I muttered to myself as I listened to her footsteps fade into the distance.

Best to get these things out in the open, I thought as I collected the photographs from the floor. Perhaps I had been a little hasty in expressing my suspicion of Mariela's motives. Perhaps she really was trying to be helpful in outlining Guardiola's profile. Perhaps she was on the phone to Colonel Cardells right now.

CHAPTER EIGHT

The outskirts of Parcent were virtually deserted as I cruised around looking for somewhere to park. I had learned from experience that it was not worth the risk of trying to park in the narrow streets in the centre of the village. I found a space at the bottom of the Avenida de la Constitución near to the Cooperativa bar where a few elderly men occupied a small front terrace watching the world go by or perhaps, I thought, keeping an eye out for strangers entering the village – a kind of unofficial passport control. I cut the ignition and paused for a while wondering if the old men were already wagging their tongues about the foreign prodigal grandson who had returned to claim an inheritance he didn't deserve.

I was thinking about Rosana and wondering whether to call at her house. I wasn't sure what kind of welcome I would get if I did. Once before I had called at her house expecting to take her for lunch. Instead she had whisked me off to Fontilles, the sanatorium where my father had been briefly confined. The purpose of the visit was to show me that, far from being a place of dungeon-like incarceration I had imagined, it was a warm and friendly place, renowned world-wide for the excellence of its facilities and its expertise in curing leprosy. Worse still, during the course of the visit it was revealed to me that, instead hating the place as I imagined he must, my father had been an active supporter, sending regular donations amounting to thousands of euros over the last thirty years.

Rosana had taken a kind of satisfaction in further undermining my ill-conceived hatred of Spain and I never really understood why. In most of our encounters, Rosana had behaved like a sister concerned to bring about a family reconciliation. And yet I could not forget the occasion when I left Parcent at the end of my first secondment from Nottingham, when our farewell kiss had lingered just a fraction of a second longer than either of us expected.

Climbing one of the many steep hills that converged on the Placa del Poble at the summit of the village, I was still in two minds about whether to call on Rosana. I turned a corner and was startled to be confronted by a blue-clad figure silhouetted against the sunlight. I squinted to shield my eyes from the brightness and focused on a pair of black jackboots laced to the ankles.

'Oh, Michael, it's you. I was hoping I would bump into you,' the figure said.

I lifted my head and raised a hand across my eyes to bring a face into view, shaded by a peaked baseball cap. 'Vicenta?' I said. 'Is that you?'

'Didn't you recognise me?'

'I wasn't sure. You look quite different in uniform. How are you?'

'Fine thanks. I don't suppose you have a few minutes to talk about those damaged cars do you? There was another one last night. I've just come from the owner's house, Kevin Courtney, and he's very upset at losing a wing mirror from his brand new Peugeot. I gather there are rumblings amongst the English residents and suggestions that the police are not taking the matter seriously. It's not true of course, but I'm no further forward so I could really use your help.'

Rosana would have to wait.

'Of course,' I said. 'How can I help?'

'I've plotted the incidents on a map of the village as you suggested and I was hoping you'd take a look. It's in my office in the town hall, just around the corner.'

I paused for a moment as we crossed the main square, glancing up at the church tower rising against a perfect blue sky. Its outline seemed to have been etched in my mind even before I had viewed it for the first time just a few months before. It was as if the impression had been inborn; inherited from my father.

72

Three flags fluttered from the balcony of an old stone building wedged between two houses – the Spanish national flag, the Valencian flag and the blue and gold circle of stars of the European Union. Beneath the balcony a sturdy wooden door filled an ornate arch. Vicenta pulled a bundle of keys from one of the thigh pockets of her military-style trousers and unlocked the door.

'You have your own key to the seat of power?' I asked.

'Not exactly. The town hall is only open to the public in the mornings, but I work all hours so I need to have access to my office.'

'Who else has keys?'

'Why do you ask?'

'Just curious.'

'The Mayor and all the councillors have keys, and the council secretary of course, and Enrique the clerk. But that's just to the front door. All the offices are locked and I only have a key to my own office on the first floor. The Mayor is the only one with a full set of keys to all the offices.'

'Including your office?'

Vicenta looked puzzled. 'Of course, it's her town hall.'

'Hers in the sense that she owns it or just that she has control of the council?'

'It's pretty much the same thing. Some Mayors treat the town hall as their personal domain during their term of office.'

I wondered whether Juan-Jose Mora was one such Mayor.

'Here we are,' Vicenta said as we entered the small office at the top of the stairs. She rounded a desk and pulled a plan from the top drawer, unfolding it and spreading it across the surface. 'I've marked all the incidents on the plan, as you can see. There are eleven cases including the one last night, all confined to the centre of the village – nothing on the outskirts.' She reached for a second sheet of paper. 'Here's a list of the dates, and the vehicle registration numbers. As you can see they are all British registered cars. I've included the time of the incidents as well, though it's difficult to be precise as most of the vandalism was only noticed by the owners when they returned to their cars in the morning after parking up for the night. There are three, however, where it's possible to be a bit more precise because the owners had parked earlier in the day and returned to their cars late in the evening. I've highlighted them in yellow on the list, as you can see these three cases all occurred between 10.30pm and midnight.'

I studied the plan and the list looking for a pattern of some kind. The plan showed three incidents occurring in Carrer San Lorenzo one of the main streets leading to the main square. There were two more incidents in the plaza itself and the remainder in two side streets leading off the plaza and connecting to Carrer Gabriel Miro, another of the main village streets. There was no discernable pattern to the attacks except, as Vicenta had pointed out, they were all in the centre of the village.

'Why these particular streets, Vicenta?' I asked, still trying to pin point a rationale.

'That's easy to answer,' Vicenta replied. 'They all have parking spaces. Most of the village streets are too narrow to allow parking so it's not surprising the attacks took place there.'

'But they are not the only streets where there is space for parking?'

'That's true, there are a quite a few more in the centre of the village.'

I turned my attention to the list. 'And why only British registered cars? They are not the only foreigners living in the village. I noticed some Dutch and German registered cars only the other day.'

'I've all ready thought about that, but I can't find a reason. The vast majority of foreigners living in the village are British so maybe it's just a coincidence.'

'I don't believe in coincidence.' I said. 'Here's what you need to do next. It will need a bit of leg work I'm afraid.'

I outlined a plan. Vicenta was to contact all the owners of foreign registered cars habitually parked in the village overnight, including the current victims, and find out if they regularly parked in the same place. From this we would be able to see if there were any non-British cars regularly parked overnight on the streets where the incidents had occurred. It would also show if there were any British registered cars regularly parked on other streets which had, so far at least, avoided vandalism.

'Can you do that?' I asked.

'It shouldn't be too difficult, it's a small village and there aren't that many foreigners who live in the centre.'

CHAPTER NINE

I was finishing my second cup of coffee when Mariela burst into the office carrying a bundle of files. Looking business-like in navy blue trousers with a matching bolero jacket, she clipped across the tiled floor in stiletto heels and planted the files on her desk as she sat down without the slightest acknowledgement of my presence. She lifted the top file, opened the cover, and lowered her head to read, allowing her blonde locks to fall forward shielding the sides of her face.

I stayed silent, studying the top of her head to confirm what I already knew – Mariela was a natural blonde; a natural blonde with fine silky hair; fine, silky, shiny hair. I was waiting for eye contact, but the lengthening silence seemed to be developing into a battle of wills. I had been contemplating an apology, or at least a climb-down. Perhaps her advice about Guardiola was wise counsel; a well-meaning attempt to urge me to be cautious. But how did I know I was wrong to be suspicious of her motives? For all I knew she had already reported to Cardells. Only time would tell.

'Coffee?' I said, when the silence became deafening.

'No thanks.' Her head remained lowered to the file.

'Anything interesting?'

Finally she lifted her head and brushed the wayward strands of hair away from her face. Her expression was implacable as she shuffled a batch of papers.

'Wilkinson's alibi seems to hold up. I've checked with Easy Jet and he flew from Alicante to Stansted on Monday 18th June, returning on Saturday 23rd. Mora was killed on the 20th. The nursing home in Greenwich where his mother is staying confirms seeing him on several occasions during that period. I spoke to his wife as well. She's staying in Leeds as Wilkinson said and though they didn't meet during his stay in London, she says she spoke to him by phone on a couple of occasions.'

'Did you ask what she was doing in England or when she might return?'

'She said only that she was visiting an old friend and had no plans to return for the time being.'

'Did you mention that photograph?'

'What do you think?'

She looked for a response, but I said nothing so she pressed on, opening the next file and reading.

'The wild boar depicted in the posters from Tony Robinson's bedroom is a Celtic warrior symbol known as Torc which has spurned various cults across Europe and America. Followers of the Torc cult believe that the animal's spirit will balance out male energy and suppress the more virtuous aspects of the masculine nature by enhancing strength, ferocity, personal power and leadership skills. Some sects actively seek the wild boar pearl believing that the owners of the pearl will absorb wild boar virtues into their lives and be imbued with the spiritual energy and mental prowess of the warrior.'

'Pearls?' I quizzed. 'I thought they came from oysters.'

Mariela adopted a slight air of condescension as she continued. 'Not exclusively. Pearls have been found in fish, snakes, whales and tortoises and in legends they are believed to have been found in serpents, dragons and sea monsters. Chinese tales connecting the dragon and the pearl date from around the middle of the first millennium BC...'

'I thought we were talking about wild boars.'

Mariela looked peeved but quickly recovered her air of superiority. 'Wild boar pearls are found at the base of the tusk of mature male animals. They are more accurately described as stones and are thought to be formed when an impurity becomes lodged in the tusk and gradually grows by layers of calcium and saliva into a small translucent sphere. The most likely cause of the impurity is a crack or chip in the tusk which followers believe is the result of damage sustained in fights between dominant pack males. Hence, only the bravest and most ferocious boars are thought capable of producing a pearl. Of course, the only way to find a wild boar pearl is to kill the most powerful male in a group.'

'Anything else?' I asked, trying not to sound too interested.

'There is as a matter of fact.' Mariela opened the next folder. 'I've checked Anthony Robinson's computer. The internet history had been deleted and so had the temporary internet files. That's relatively easy to do, but deleting internet history and temporary files does not delete the files. Only the index to them is deleted making them inaccessible to most people but I managed to find them.'

'Am I supposed to be impressed?' I interjected.

Mariela sighed. 'I connected to several web sites visited in the last eight months or so. There were several sites associated with the occult and three which covered the Torc, but as far as I can see there had been no email contact with the organisations operating the sites and none of the sites contained the posters we recovered from the Robinsons' house, so he must have got them from somewhere else. I've got Officer Blazquez checking now to see if we can find the source of the posters as they're not the kind of thing you can buy just anywhere.'

I was impressed, but I wasn't going to show it. I had my own thoughts on the information Mariela had uncovered, but I preferred to keep them to myself for the time being and I wanted to find a way to keep Mariela involved. It was the least painful way I could think of to try and move on from yesterday's conflict.

'So where does all this take us?' I said.

Mariela responded as if she had already thought this through. 'Well, for a start, it looks as though we can rule out Walter Wilkinson from any involvement in Mora's murder, at least any direct involvement.'

I raised my eyebrows at this final caveat, but left my query unspoken as Mariela pressed on.

'The cult thing is interesting. It suggests that Tony Robinson had an interest in the occult and in this Torc cult in particular. And the fact that he didn't acquire those posters over the internet, suggests he had contact with another source.'

'This Officer Blazquez, is he any good?'

'*She* is first rate. A real whiz-kid with computers, and not shy of leg work either. If anyone can find the source of those posters it's her.'

I thought for a moment before speaking. 'So that brings us back to Paco Santos. He's still in custody, I trust?'

'He's still with us, yes. His lawyer is kicking up a stink and not just here in Jalon.' Mariela cast me a sideways glance to be sure I had picked up the implication she had deliberately imparted.

'His lawyer?' I asked on cue.

'Eduardo Moreno.' The name was spoken with a sense of deference that was easy to discern.

'Is that supposed to mean something to me?' I asked.

'Eduardo Moreno is one of the most prominent and successful criminal lawyers in Valencia with a string of high profile cases to his name.'

'So how come he's representing an unimportant little rogue like Santos?'

Mariela shrugged and diverted her eyes in a gesture that told me she knew the answer, but would rather not say.

'And he's making noises you say?'

'Apparently he's been on the phone to Alicante demanding Santos's immediate release.'

'Apparently! What does that mean?'

Mariela hesitated before answering and diverted her eyes when she finally spoke. 'Colonel Cardells was on the phone this morning.'

I resisted the obvious temptation to ask why Cardells had called Mariela and not me – or perhaps Mariela had called Cardells. 'And what did Cardells have to say?'

'He just wanted to know why we were holding Santos and what we intended to do with him.'

'And what did you tell him?'

'I just explained why he had been arrested and said we were making checks before interviewing him again.'

I noted the use of *we* in Mariela's replies and wondered if she was deliberately implying a joint sense of responsibility or whether she was simply being diplomatic. I also found it hard to believe that Cardells had left it at that. 'And that was it?' I asked. 'No ranting, no demands, no interference?'

Mariela looked sheepish. 'No, nothing of that sort. He simply asked to be kept informed of progress.'

'He asked to be kept informed or he asked you to keep him informed?'

'He wasn't specific.'

I decided to leave it at that, though I sensed a none-too subtle warning shot had been fired across my bows. For now at least I planned to continue as if nothing had happened. I was used to running my own show, and communication with the powers on high was always a time-wasting chore in my book. Results were what mattered and I preferred to leave the upper ranks to play with strategy and statistics since they rarely offered any real insight into the intricacies of criminal investigation. But that was in Nottingham and I was not sure how far my approach would be tolerated in the ranks of the Guardia Civil especially given its near-military ethos. There was only one way to find out.

'Line up another interview with Santos,' I said brusquely. 'And tell Moreno to be there. Later this morning, 11.30 would be fine.'

Mariela opened her mouth to say something then changed her mind. As she picked up the telephone she said, 'Do you want me to be there as well?'

'Unless you've got something better to do,' I said, almost adding — well Colonel Cardells will expect to be kept informed won't he?

Paco Santos had showered and shaved leaving a small graze on the base of his chin. A change of clothes, discarding the amateur burglar's all black outfit, had transformed him from a sorry-looking buffoon to a respectable citizen, though the ill-fitting suit and open-neck shirt fell short of exuding absolute integrity. Eduardo Moreno, on the other hand, was every inch the sharp suited, sharp shooting lawyer. There was a subtle sheen to his high-buttoned grey suit and a crisp whiteness to his stiff-collared shirt with just the right amount of cuff protruding from the sleeves of his jacket. Everything about the man's appearance was carefully designed to create the right impression, from the scrupulously clipped goatee beard to the precisely knotted paisley silk tie, all culminating, I noticed, in a pair of chisel-toed brown leather shoes, polished to a brilliant shine.

Moreno rose from behind the battered old table as Mariela and I entered the bare interview room and he assumed a casual smile as he offered his hand to the two of us in turn. Clearly at ease, he introduced himself before anyone else could speak, giving the impression that this was his meeting and he was in full control. Santos sat lazily, trying hard to appear unconcerned by examining his fingernails as if looking for dirt.

I reciprocated Moreno's firm grip and completed the introductions placing, I realised, a little too much stress on the word *Captain* as I gave my own name. Mariela moved towards the recording system fixed to the wall at the side of the table and placed two blank cassettes in the open slots. Before she could start them rolling, Moreno interrupted.

'Before we start, Captain Fernandez, perhaps you could assuage my curiosity by explaining why you have kept my client in custody for more than thirty-six hours.'

Assuage, I thought, adding verbosity to arrogance in my initial assessment of Moreno.

'I thought your client might have outlined the circumstances of his arrest.' I retorted, fixing my eyes on Moreno's.

Moreno responded with an almost imperceptible shrug. 'Of course, but I'd like to hear your version.'

Unwilling to give way, I turned to Mariela and said, 'Perhaps Sergeant Poquet can explain.'

Mariela dutifully obliged, consulting the file and making me smile to myself as she spoke in her best monotone police voice. 'In the early hours Wednesday 29th June Mr Santos was discovered by Sergeant Benitez, the local police officer for Beniforell, in the house of Juan-Jose Mora. He had lifted the boards in the base of the wardrobe in the main bedroom of the house and was found in possession of a briefcase containing two hundred and fifty thousand euros in used notes. In a subsequent interview, Mr Santos confirmed that he did not require the services of a lawyer at that time and went on to claim that half the money belonged to him. He later suggested that it was the council's money, and then later stated that the money had nothing to do with the council. At that stage Mr Santos declined to answer further questions, so the interview was suspended and he was returned to custody.'

Moreno listened to Mariela's statement maintaining a fixed expression throughout then turned to me. 'Tell me, Captain Fernandez, was there any sign of forced entry at the house?'

'No,' I replied.

'And was any property actually removed from the house?'

'No.'

'Then perhaps you could explain what charges you have in contemplation in respect of my client.'

Contemplation?

'I am sure you are aware that Juan-Jose Mora was found dead on the night of 20th June.'

'And what has that to do with my client?'

'Murdered, in fact.'

Santos shuffled in his seat, but Moreno was unmoved. 'And have you any evidence to connect my client to this murder?'

I knew I was on thin ice, but I was unwilling to give ground. 'We are still investigating and awaiting the results of forensic and post mortem reports.'

'Then might I ask why he remains in custody?'

'He's helping us with our enquiries.' I almost chuckled on hearing my own punctilious police-speak.

'And how might he do that?'

'He could start by telling us the truth about the money.'

Moreno smiled — a smug, self-satisfied smile — as if he had won some kind of victory.

'I wonder, Captain Fernandez, perhaps I could have a private word with you.'

The unexpected request surprised me. I was not unused to informal approaches from lawyers representing suspects; indeed I had occasionally initiated them myself. But this was blatant, in front of his client and another police officer. I put it down to the Spanish way of doing things and conceded my unfamiliarity with this new territory. I glanced towards Mariela, looking for a sign or a gesture, but she remained impassive.

Curiosity outweighed my unease and I said, 'Sergeant Poquet, would you return Mr Santos to the cells and wait for me in the office.'

A conceited grin formed on Santos's face as he left the room in silence. Mariela gathered her files and followed Santos towards the door, deliberately avoiding eye contact and leaving me to wonder whether this was a routine occurrence or whether she was simply pissed off to be summarily dismissed.

As soon as the door closed, Moreno sat back, unbuttoned his jacket and loosened his tie. Before I had time to compose myself he opened the conversation. 'It's Miguel-Ángel, I believe. My first name is Eduardo.'

Shocked, I stuttered a response. 'Michael,' I said, then thought again. 'Captain Fernandez if you don't mind, Mr Moreno.'

'As you wish. I understand you are new to Spain and the Guardia Civil. Your Spanish is excellent if I may say so, did you study in Britain?'

I bristled, unwilling to enter into small-talk. 'Can we just get on with it? You asked for this meeting and I have an investigation to run.'

'Very well. I'm sure you are an excellent detective, Captain Fernandez, but you may not be entirely familiar with the way things are done here.'

'Things?' I asked, adopting a puzzled expression.

'The legal system, our government, the constitution. You have to remember that Spain is a young democracy. We haven't had four hundred years to get things right as you have had in Britain. We're still developing and evolving. Our economy, too, has been transformed in the last few decades. Fifty years ago people were literally starving in this part of Spain, scratching a living off the land or from the sea and struggling to make ends meet. Then the tourist boom arrived. And more recently the demand from our wealthy northern European neighbours for holiday homes or permanent residences has fuelled a new construction boom. And who can blame Spain for exploiting its sunny climate and relaxed way of life. I'd be the first to admit we haven't always got it right in the rush for progress, but the economic benefits are clear for all to see. There have been social benefits too – better pensions, new hospitals and schools. It's easy to understand why most people welcome this new investment and the new wave of tourists and immigrants that come to Spain in increasing numbers each year.'

My patience was wearing thin. 'I'm grateful for the potted history of modern Spain, but I'm sure that isn't why you wanted to talk to me.'

'Forgive me for going around the houses, but it's important to see things in perspective. There is a point to all of this. Spain is a bureaucratic country; a legacy of Franco's days when the state contrived to control everything, even down to local level. We could teach the world a few things about form-filling and referring decisions from one organ of government to another and back again. We simply weren't equipped to cope with the demands of developers and investors to free up land for building and cut through bureaucratic red tape. So something had to give. Rules were bent, or at least sidestepped, and the most creative and astute politicians reaped the rewards for their communities. And once the doors were opened, others joined the scramble to attract investment to their areas. Our government has tried to keep pace, but they have been reactive not proactive when it comes to finding the balance between the benefits to the community and the rights of individuals. There have been gainers and losers along the way, but no one can deny that the vast growth in the construction sector has brought about substantial benefits for the region as a whole.'

Moreno paused at this point as if he was trying to gauge my reaction, but I remained passive, giving nothing away. I guessed where the conversation was leading, but was happy to feign ignorance and play the part of a naïve plodding policeman. 'I'm still listening, Mr Moreno, but I have yet to see how any of this is relevant to our investigation into the death of Juan-Jose Mora or your client's attempt to recover all that money.'

If Moreno was becoming exasperated, it didn't show as he continued in the same, condescending style. 'It's fair to say that in these tumultuous times a few people may have acted with undue alacrity – developers, speculators, politicians, local officials – none would be exempt from criticism, but their motivation is not always reproachable. True, our government has not been overly censorious of such conduct, but neither has it condoned it.'

I restrained a yawn. *He's swallowed the dictionary.*

'Of course we all wish such things had not occurred, but in an uncertain world, where the bounds of acceptable behaviour are vague it is only human nature to push the boundaries until the limit is found. That limit is gradually becoming defined and the worst abuses have been dealt with, but it would be quixotic to think that a culture that has evolved over decades can be curbed overnight.'

My patience finally snapped. 'We are talking about corruption, are we?'

Moreno adopted a look of distaste, just short of outright shock. 'That's not the word I would use, but sometimes inducements have helped to cut through red tape and scepticism. Usually it's enough to point out the benefits to the community as a whole. Sometimes an offer of a new school or public library acts as an incentive, but occasionally, unscrupulous people have offered, or demanded, more.'

'And is that what occurred in Beniforell with Juan-Jose Mora and your client?'

Moreno twisted in his seat. 'You wouldn't expect me to answer that, I'm sure. I am simply trying to outline a general background that might help you see things in perspective.'

'But this does bring us back to your client, the deputy Mayor of Beniforell, and the matter of two hundred and fifty thousand euros?'

Moreno straightened and fixed his eyes on mine. 'Let's be clear. There was no sign of a forced entry at Mora's house and though a sum of money was discovered, you cannot prove there was any intention to remove it, so a prosecution for theft would seem out of the question. And you have yet to demonstrate any involvement on the part of my client in the death of Mr Mora. In fact, as far as I can see you have no reason to hold my client in custody.'

I paused for a moment and thought. I could hold Santos for a while longer, at least until I was forced to justify his detention before a court. But I knew that would achieve little as Santos would simply remain silent. On balance, I saw an advantage in letting Santos out and watching how things developed. One thing was certain, the money was staying put and I was sure that someone would want to do something about that. As things turned out, I was right.

'You are right, Mr Moreno, there is no reason to hold your client any longer. I'll arrange for his immediate release.'

Moreno smiled, not out of smugness, but as if he had anticipated this outcome all along. 'Good,' he said, remaining fixed in his seat as if to indicate that the meeting was not yet over.

'Anything else?' I said.

'There's just the matter of the money,' Moreno said, studying my reaction.

I obliged with a look of surprise. 'The money? You mean the money recovered from Mora's house? We'll be holding on to that, of course, at least until we determine where it came from and who it belongs to.'

'I might be able to help you there.'

'I'm listening.'

'Suppose, just suppose, I could help you identify the source of the money.'

'So that it might be returned, you mean?'

'Well, not exactly. I'd be interested to know what you would do with that information.'

'That would depend on what you were able to tell me and how the information related to the investigation of Mr Mora's death.'

'That's my point. If I could convince you that the money had nothing to do with Mora's death how would you respond?'

'You mean could it be returned to the owner?'

'That's not what I'm getting at. The money is not important. What's more important is whether you would feel obliged to delve into the source and the reason it was in Mora's possession.'

I understood perfectly the nuance of Moreno's advance and the reason he had been at pains to explain the subtleties of Spain's political processes when it came to oiling the wheels of progress in matters of planning and development. However, it was the statement, "The money's not important" that intrigued me more than anything else.

'I'm not sure I fully understand you,' I said with false naivety. 'A quarter of a million euros is a great deal of money.'

'To some people, yes it is. But to others it's a trifle, far less important than a person's standing and reputation.'

'I can see that, yes.'

'Of course you can, you're an intelligent man, Captain Fernandez. Murder is a heinous crime, far more damnable than any minor transgression of conventional protocols.' Moreno raised an eyebrow as if to check my understanding of the implicit suggestion in his last remark.

'You are right of course,' I said. 'My principal focus is the investigation of Mora's murder, anything else is incidental.'

Moreno's expression hinted at a smile which he quickly suppressed. 'I'm glad we understand each other,' he said. 'I'll see what I can find out about the money and get back to you. In the meantime, thank for agreeing to talk to me. I've taken up a lot of your valuable time and I'm sure you are anxious to get back to your investigation.'

As Moreno closed the door, one question remained. How the hell did he know my full name is Miguel-Ángel?

CHAPTER TEN

'But why release him now?' Mariela said. 'We're still no nearer knowing what Santos was doing in Mora's house and whether he is linked to Mora's murder.'

My frustration showed. I didn't expect to justify my decision to a junior officer. 'We'll get nothing more from him at this stage, especially now Moreno is advising him, so there's no point in keeping him locked up.'

'But what about the money? Surely that needs to be investigated; it could be the motive for getting Mora out of the way.'

'The money's not important.' I snapped, echoing Moreno's words. 'We have no idea where it came from and we can't even prove that Santos intended to steal it. Now, where are we up to with Tony Robinson's disappearance?'

Mariela looked peeved at this sudden change of tack. 'Still waiting for news from Officer Blazquez.'

'Then chase her up, we can't wait forever and the Robinsons will be expecting some answers.'

'I thought you believed it was a waste of time; just another runaway kid.'

'Never jump to conclusions, Sergeant Poquet, because often they will be the wrong conclusions.'

I strode towards the door as Mariela breathed a heavy sigh.

'And where will you be?' she asked before hesitating. '…In case I need to reach you, if something crops up.'

'I'm going to see Ernesto Alvarez, the consultant renal surgeon at Denia General. You can reach me on my mobile if you need to.' I turned as I reached the office door. 'Um… what's the best way to get to Denia?'

Mariela snorted. 'The quickest way from Jalon is through Pedreguer and pick up the coast road from there.' She hesitated for a moment. 'But why don't you take the scenic route through Gata de Gorgos. It's not much longer and there's something on the way you ought to see.'

'And what might that be?'

Mariela smiled. 'I don't want to spoil the surprise.'

'But how will I know what I'm looking for?'

'Don't worry, Michael, you'll know when you see it.'

It was another clear, bright sunny day and I was beginning to wonder if it would ever rain. Perhaps it was true; the rain in Spain did indeed fall mainly on the plain. The parched landscape looked in desperate need of a downpour, but the forecast promised only continuing drought with temperatures remaining in the mid thirties Celsius for at least another month. How I would have welcomed one of those melancholy Nottingham days when daylight struggled to penetrate steel grey clouds and the rain fell in never ending torrents. The Costa Blanca sunshine was great for tourists in search of an express tan but, as I was beginning to discover, working in a permanent hothouse was quite a different thing.

I turned up the car's air conditioning as I left the village of Lliber and followed the sign for Gata de Gorgos. Even the blast of icy air in my face failed to alleviate the clamminess I felt as my shirt stuck to my back and a bead of sweat trickled down my neck.

The road climbed steeply through a series of sharp bends flanked by vineyards with rigid ranks of vines growing in rich red soil. The vines gave way to olives and almonds growing in neglected terraces with crumbling walls and choked by weeds. A few modern villas dotted the landscape each one remote from the others, presumably, I mused, for people who coveted privacy and a quiet life. Rounding another curve, I peered down into a steep ravine strewn with rocks and boulders, noting there was nothing to prevent an inattentive driver from careering over the edge. A line of dry bamboo canes lying horizontally about six metres above the river bed provided evidence of a bygone flood. It was comforting to realise that the rain must fall at some time in these parts, but for now there was not so much as a trickle of water to be seen.

The road followed the gorge for more than two kilometres until I crossed a single-track bridge and the river bed meandered into the distance behind a steep hill dotted with pines and bearing the scars of a recent forest fire. A few moments later civilisation loomed in the distance in the form of the Alicante - Valencia motorway stretching across an elevated concrete viaduct masking the view of the coast in the far distance. I could see a town in the foreground, presumably Gata de Gorgos, and I wondered if I had missed whatever it was Mariela had wanted me to see. Another bend and I was in no doubt I had reached the spectacle to which she had alluded.

An elevated ridge to the left of the road was obliterated with newly built houses identically painted in beige with terracotta roof tiles, each with a tiny chimney stack protruding into the horizon. I pulled over and stopped on a rough piece of ground at the side of the road to get a better view. Row after uniform row of terraced houses tumbled over the ridge forming an avalanche of concrete slowly creeping down the folds in the hillside like a giant glacier devouring the once-green slopes. I made a quick calculation – each row contained twenty blocks of five terraced houses and there were six rows that I could see on this side of the ridge alone and probably more on the far side beyond my view. A tiny space separated the terraces one from the other and there was not a single tree or patch of green to be seen. It reminded me of old photographs I had seen of northern mill towns in England where vast swaths of two-up-two-down houses suffused the landscape – except that there was no smoke emitting from the chimneys, but then this was summer in Spain.

I started the car and moved off, coming to a halt a few moments later opposite a wide entrance road dominated by a vast hoarding announcing, *Bienvenido a Residencia Gata*. At that moment a loud horn sounded behind me and I moved off again to allow a concrete mixing wagon to rumble into the entrance and grind its way up the steep hill to fuel the avalanche.

It was a suit and tie day for Ernesto Alvarez who faced me across a cluttered desk. His hands, I noticed, had a chapped and blotchy pinkness born of frequent scrubbing, a stark contrast to the rest of his tanned complexion.

'It's good of you to see me Dr Alvarez. It is doctor, I presume, only I'm unfamiliar with the protocol in Spain?'

'Doctor is fine, Captain Fernandez. How can I help you?'

'Thank you. I know you spoke with Sergeant Poquet recently, but we are now treating Mr Mora's death as murder which puts things in a different light. There are just a couple of points I'd like to explore, if that's all right with you?'

'Murder you say?' Alvarez stiffened. 'I'll help you all I can, but you'll be aware of the concept of doctor-patient confidentiality.'

'Of course, but hopefully that won't be an issue, my questions are mostly of a general nature. Mr Mora was diagnosed with renal failure about six months ago, I understand.'

Alvarez frowned, suggesting he was already wondering if this was more than a non-specific enquiry. I decided to qualify the question. 'Approximately, that is, I don't need specific dates or anything like that.'

Alvarez opened the buff coloured file in front of him, tilting it towards his body as if to prevent me from prying. 'Around six months, yes.'

'And the transplant operation was twelve weeks ago... approximately?'

'Yes.'

'That's very soon after the initial diagnosis isn't it? I have always understood that donor organs are in short supply and there is usually a waiting list.'

Alvarez raised his eyes from the file. 'That's true, but you have to understand we have a slightly different approach in Spain to that with which you are familiar in Britain. You see when a suitable donor presents himself after a sudden death or an accident, there's a general presumption that the deceased would consent to organ donation unless there is a specific indication to the contrary.'

My eyes widened in surprise, but before I could speak, Alvarez continued.

'Don't be so shocked, Captain Fernandez, that doesn't mean we just whip out organs willy-nilly. We always consult the next of kin, but as the presumption of consent is well established it tends to make the decision easier for the relatives, and because of that we have a much higher level of acceptance than in countries that practice the strict principle of family approval.'

'I see, but even so three months from diagnosis to transplant seems unusual. Is that normal?'

Alvarez returned to the file, turning a page. 'Ah yes,' he said, turning another page. 'The answer to your question is no, that is not normal, but neither is it unusual. Spain operates a strict kidney matching and allocation procedure, but don't get that confused with a waiting list. There are a great many factors that have to be taken into account. Length of time waiting is one criterion, as is the prospective recipient's age and condition. Sometimes location is important, by which I mean that donated organs have a limited useful life and their condition deteriorates rapidly after harvesting.'

Harvesting? It seemed such a strange term to use. I thought of gathering crops, picking ripe fruit, but not collecting body parts for re-use.

Alvarez continued in the same matter-of-fact tone. 'Sometimes it's better to use a donor kidney quickly than to risk deterioration. But the most important criterion is the match between donor and recipient. I can explain if you wish.'

'That would be helpful.'

'I'll spare you the exact science, but basically there are two factors to be taken into account in assessing the likely success of a transplant and minimising the risk of rejection. The first is blood type. Without going into detail, we know from experience and scientific study that certain blood types can be combined in a transplant and others cannot. That is not to say that both donor and recipient must have the same blood type. Are you with me so far?'

'So far, yes.' I said, presuming it made perfect sense that O negative might curdle if mixed with A positive.

'The second factor is tissue type and this is rather more complicated. Everyone has an inherited tissue type made

92

up of many different characteristics only some of which are important in transplantations. To make matters more complicated there are twenty or more different versions of each characteristic, meaning that there are literally millions of different tissue types. Fortunately, a kidney transplant can be successful even if there are differences between the tissue type of the donor and recipient, so the match does not have to be perfect. However, the more of these characteristics that are the same for the patient and the donor, or potential donor, the better the chances are that the transplanted kidney will not be rejected.' Alvarez sat back and folded his arms across his chest.

'I see,' I said, not seeing at all. 'And in Mr Mora's case? I only need the general, not the specific… in terms of how he came to the top of the list. '

Alvarez raised an eyebrow, thinking how to answer. 'It was a combination of all the criteria I have mentioned.'

I felt he was being evasive. 'Can you be more specific?'

'I can say to you that Mr Mora was a lucky man. He was in the right place at the right time when we found a match for his blood and tissue types.'

I noticed that Alvarez had answered this last question without referring to the file in front of him. It was feasible, I supposed, that because Mora's transplant had occurred relatively recently, the details might still be fresh in his mind. Even so, my suspicions were aroused.

'I'm presuming, Dr Alvarez, that the donor's details are confidential.'

'Absolutely,' Alvarez replied with a stony faced expression.

I shuffled in my seat and felt my face flushing even before I asked my next question, but it had to be asked. 'I hope you won't take this the wrong way, Dr Alvarez, but the circumstances surrounding Mr Mora's death make it necessary for me to ask my next question, awkward though it is.' I focused on Alvarez's eyes. 'Did Mr Mora ever mention, or even hint at, an offer of financial inducement in order to secure an early transplant?'

I waited, expecting an explosion of denial or indignation, but Alvarez offered only a wry smile.

'That's quite all right, Captain Fernandez. I got to know Mr Mora very well during the period after his initial diagnoses and whilst he was receiving dialysis. Knowing him, I can understand why you might ask the question. He was a man used to getting his own way, arrogant some might say. But being told you are suffering a life threatening condition and knowing that your salvation lies in the generosity and expertise of others, is a very humbling experience. You have to understand that within this hospital, patients waiting for transplants become part of a community. They would meet each other on a regular basis as in-patients or at dialysis sessions and they would quickly recognize the commitment and dedication of everyone on the unit. They would also realize that whatever their circumstances, there are others equally or more deserving of the operation that can change their lives. I doubt very much whether even a man like Mr Mora would ever get the impression that he could buy his way to the top of the list.'

A clever answer, I realized. Alvarez had not denied that Mora had offered, or attempted to offer, a bribe, nor had he implied that any such offer had been rejected. He had simply implied that such a circumstance would be unthinkable.

'Then Mr Mora was indeed a lucky man,' I said, implying I accepted Alvarez's version of events.

Before leaving the hospital, I called forensic pathologist Pilar Vidal, making polite conversation before getting to the point. I waited in trepidation for her response.

'That's a most unusual request, Captain Fernandez, but this is a most unusual case. I can't see any reason why not, but it will take a few days.'

'I'm very grateful, thank you and I haven't forgotten the lunch I promised you.'

'I look forward to it.'

CHAPTER ELEVEN

I checked my watch as I left the hospital. It was 4.30pm on Friday afternoon and I wondered whether to return to Jalon or call it a day; call it a weekend in fact. It only took a moment to convince myself. After all, I wasn't hunting a serial killer who might strike again at any moment. I called Mariela and left a message that I was heading home.

Home to Parcent. Home to a family I had only recently encountered and who were as unsure of me as I was of them. My first call was to my grandmother, Carmen Maria. The memory of our first meeting, just a few months ago was still fresh in my mind, as was the discomfort I felt at being suddenly thrust into confronting a part of my life I had steadfastly spurned.

Carmen Maria had shed tears of joy at meeting the grandson she had never known and I had squirmed with embarrassment when she cradled my face and peered into my eyes, declaring I was just like my father. My grandmother's joy turned to sorrow and self-recrimination when, later, I had forced her to reveal the truth about my father's virtual expulsion from the village when the leprosy was first diagnosed in 1951. Even the revelation that my father's exile had not been imposed by the villagers of Parcent but had been engineered by a bitter old priest, had failed to vanquish my long held bitterness and antagonism towards the village of Parcent.

Carmen Maria greeted me joyously as always, fussing and fretting as grandmothers do. It was so good to have me living nearby. Was everything all right in the recently refurbished house? Was I settling in at work? Had I made friends? Was I eating? Did I want a nice cup of tea? I fended her enquiries with patience and reassurance, turning the tables to ask how she was coping alone. Could she manage the house on her own? Did she need any shopping?

I felt comfortable and relaxed as I sipped the tepid tea from a gold rimmed china cup that I was sure had been reserved for special occasions. The small talk with my grandmother was a pleasant distraction from the complexities of my investigation and we both seemed to understand that reminiscence about my father was taboo. Instead, Carmen Maria gossiped about village life and though most of the people she mentioned were outside my acquaintance I was happy to let her ramble sensing that, starved of conversation, Carmen Maria found pleasure in talking to anyone. I was shaken from my reverie when she switched the conversation to Rosana. How sad it was to lose her mother. What a shame for Asunción to lose her daughter, and poor Rosana left to care for her grandmother. She shouldn't take on the burden alone, others could help, but Rosana had determined that it was her duty. She was a young intelligent woman, with so much to offer and it seemed such a waste to shut herself off from life in this way.

I sensed where the conversation was heading.

'Have you seen Rosana?' she asked.

'Not recently, no.' I made my excuses and left.

After a shower and change of clothes – I opted for jeans, polo shirt and boat shoes – I made my way to Bar Casino in need of a beer. As I plunged through the plastic fly screen the babble of conversation continued unabated, my arrival unnoticed. A group of a dozen or so men huddled together at the near end of the bar and as I passed by I picked out the familiar sound of British voices debating the week's football results. I could have been in my local pub in Nottingham with the regulars winding down at the end of the working week, except these men were all in their fifties or sixties and, far from winding down at the end of the working week, they were all tanned and relaxed in shorts, T-shirts and sandals. One of the group, a wiry man with short ginger hair, wore the green shirt of the Northern

Ireland football team. He was clearly the worse for drink as he yelled across the group in a slurred Belfast accent.

'So what have England won since 1966? And you only won then coz you was playing at Wembley and had that Russian linesman to help you out.'

As I passed behind the man, his shoe slipped from the metal footrest at the base of the bar causing him to stumble backwards into my path. Our shoulders brushed as he regained his balance, grabbing the edge of the bar and nudging a near-full tankard of beer, causing a few drops to spill over the rim. He turned and straightened so that our faces were inches apart.

'Watch what you're doing mate, you almost made me spill my beer,' he said, his face set in a menacing scowl.

I hate being called 'mate' especially by someone I have never met before and I hate being challenged by people who cannot take their drink without becoming boorish and bothersome. A knee in the groin was the least he deserved followed by a butt to the bridge of his nose, both of which should remind him in the morning that he needed to mind his manners.

'*Lo siento mi amigo borracho*,' I said, stepping to one side.

'Yeah, well just watch it mate,' he replied, oblivious to being called "my drunken friend."

I continued to the far end of the bar noticing the group of four old men squatting at a baize-covered table shuffling a set of dominoes. My great uncle Rafael was amongst them and for a moment I thought of approaching him, but Rafael's eyes flickered in my direction and, without the slightest hint of recognition, returned to the table.

Relief from my growing unease came when I found Pepito standing alone at the far end of the bar. A brown toothed smile greeted me when I tapped my uncle on the back.

'Michael,' he said, 'good to see you. What can I get you?'

I looked at the small glass of opaque white liquid on the bar. 'What's that you're drinking?' I asked.

'This is *candela*,' Pepito said, lifting the glass and taking a sip. 'It's the local version of anis, only stronger.' He waved the glass, wafting a powerful smell of aniseed that almost singed the inside of my nostrils. 'Care to try it?'

'Not for me.' I recoiled. 'A beer will do fine.'

'A *caña*, or something larger?'

'I suppose a pint is out of the question?'

'A *tanque*, you mean? That's for the English.' He nodded towards the row of pint-sized jugs at the other end of the bar. 'Paco, *un tubo*, for my nephew,' Pepito called to the barman and a tumbler of pale amber beer topped with two inches of froth duly appeared. 'No self-respecting Spaniard would be seen drinking beer by the bucket-full.'

I thought of protesting that I was not a self-respecting Spaniard, but changed the subject instead. 'Isn't that Rafael, playing dominoes over there?' I asked.

Pepito nodded.

'What is it with him? I'm sure he recognised me, but he just turned away when I glanced in his direction.'

'Ignore him; he's just a bitter old man.'

'But why?'

'He was on the wrong side in the war, or the right side, depending on your point of view.'

I was thinking of the Second World War and wondering how Rafael might have been involved given Spain's supposed neutrality. Pepito soon put me right.

'Most of this village sided with the Republicans, but Rafael was a staunch Nationalist. When Franco's Nationalists finally triumphed, they took their revenge on villages like this and ruled them with a rod of iron. Socialists and suspected communists were rounded up and interned; a few never returned. Even the village priest, father Ignacio, came under suspicion and was forced into hiding in the mountains where he was supported by a few dedicated followers and continued to conduct a regular clandestine mass from a cave. Rafael and a few other supporters of the regime were given privileged positions after the war and were always regarded as Franco's eyes and ears in the village. It caused huge resentment.'

'But the Civil War ended in 1939. How old is Rafael?'

Pepito thought for a moment. 'He was just eighteen or nineteen when he left to join the Nationalist forces, so I guess that would make him eighty-eight or eighty-nine.'

'He doesn't look it,' I said. 'But all that was nearly seventy years ago and you say he still bears a grudge?'

Pepito turned his shoulder to the bar and moved closer, lowering his voice and breathing more aniseed fumes into my face. 'People have long memories and it's not Rafael who holds a grudge, it's the others who hold a grudge against him – at least those who are old enough to remember.'

I frowned. 'It all seems so petty.'

'Petty.' Pepito exclaimed, raising his voice before returning to a whisper. 'Don't ever let anyone in this village hear you describe the divisions of the Civil War as petty. You have to remember that neighbour fought against neighbour, passions ran deep and some families were driven apart by the conflict, supporting opposing sides. Our own family is a perfect example. Your grandfather, Josep, fought with the Republicans. Can you imagine that, brother against brother? After the war there was a huge rift between Rafael and Josep, they hardly spoke to each other for the next fifty years.'

I puffed my cheeks.

'So you see, Michael, there's nothing petty about it. There was never any real reconciliation after the war. Despite his victory, Franco's hold on power was tenuous. He was paranoid that there would be an uprising against him, so he imposed rigid discipline and control on every town and village. People like Rafael were his enforcers. There was real suffering and hardship for years after the war – I'm talking about brutality, torture, incarceration even starvation.'

'Even so, it all seems such a long time ago. Franco died in 1975 and I'd have thought people would have learned to forgive and forget by now.'

Pepito signalled for another candela and second *tubo* for me. 'You'd have thought so yes, but the truth is that after the restoration of the Monarchy, Spain never went through the kind of reconciliation process that has occurred in other countries emerging from an era of harsh dictatorship. When King Juan Carlos shunned Franco's careful tutelage and worked to introduce democratic government, there was a kind of pact of silence; an agreement not to rake over the embers of the past. As a result, the average Spaniard knows little or nothing about the reality of Franco's regime; or if they do know, they don't talk about it. Crimes committed in the name of the state have largely been hidden, brushed under the carpet. And so the corruption and injustice of the Franco era have been overlooked and in many cases the beneficiaries of those crimes still hang on to their ill-gotten gains and the power base they established for themselves at the time. And that applies at local as well as national level.'

I cast a glance in the direction of the domino table. 'You're referring to Rafael?'

Pepito looked around again, checking that no one was within hearing distance of our conversation. 'Rafael returned from the war an angry man. He saw action at the end of the siege of Madrid in 1938. The Republican stronghold had been under siege for almost two years, blockaded and virtually starved into submission, until it finally fell in March 1939. It marked the end of the war. But it was not a victorious conclusion to Rafael's war. He was captured in October 1938 by one of the International Brigades formed from foreign volunteers committed to fighting fascism alongside the Republican forces. He claims to have suffered terribly at their hands, but the truth is he probably suffered no more privations than the average Madrileño, given the conditions they endured towards the end of the siege. Even so, when he returned to Parcent he made the most of his support for the winning side and gradually wheedled his way into a position of power and influence in the village. He and his cohort virtually ran the village for two decades or more, granting favours to themselves and their acolytes, rooting out opposition and denouncing them to the authorities. In the process they were able to acquire wealth and property either by forced acquisition or simple confiscation. And many of those wrongs have never been righted. Now, Michael, perhaps you understand why people have long memories and harbour hostility and resentment to this day.'

I raised my eyebrows. 'Do they still hold sway in the village, Rafael and his cohort, I mean?'

'That's an interesting point. When democracy was eventually restored and new political parties emerged, the likes of Rafael were tainted goods. No one, at least no political group hoping to gain legitimate power, would be associated with them, at least not openly. But the wealth and power base they established in the forties and fifties still exist. They exercise their influence covertly, never seeking election themselves or campaigning publicly for any party or candidate. But behind the scenes, that's a different matter. '

I looked over at the four seemingly innocuous old men and wondered what conspiracies, what subterfuge, they had practised, still practised, in their lives.

'But enough of that,' Pepito continued. 'How are you settling in to your new house?'

I snapped from my musings. 'Oh, fine thanks. I haven't really spent much time there, too busy at work.'

'And how's the job going?'

'Let's just say it's different.'

Pepito hesitated as if thinking how to frame his next question. 'Have you seen Rosana?'

I frowned. 'Not since the funeral. Why do you ask?'

'Well... I... your grandmother actually... thought you might have called on her. Only you seemed to get along so well when you first came to Parcent.'

I gave a weak smile. 'And Carmen Maria thought we made a lovely couple, is that it?'

'Something like that.' Pepito blushed.

'What have you in mind? An arranged marriage, an alliance between the clans Fernandez and Ferrando Moll? Perpetuate the local bloodstock, is that the idea?'

'No, no, of course not.'

'Then what?'

Pepito cleared his throat. 'Dinner.'

'Sorry?'

'Dinner. Tomorrow night actually.'

'I see,' I said trying hard to quell my irritation. 'So it's all been arranged?'

'Well, no, not exactly. It's just that Rosana has hidden herself away since her mother died. She hardly ever goes out. She says she must look after her grandmother, which

101

is fair enough, but there are plenty of others who could help. She doesn't have to be tied to the house. We just thought you might like to take her out, if only to give her a break from caring for her grandmother.'

'We?'

'Your grandmother and I. Carmen Maria is going to sit with Asunción and I'll be on hand if they need me.'

'And what does Rosana think about this?'

Pepito looked sheepish. 'She doesn't know.'

Not for the first time I felt the tentacles of small village life creeping around me, pushing and cajoling me in directions I would rather avoid. This was, I supposed, the way of things in these remote villages. In the era when people never went further than a donkey could travel in a day, young people had a small selection of the opposite sex to choose from. A limited gene pool, I mused. And when the spark of natural attraction failed to ignite, relatives had grown used to lending a helping hand through conspiracy or subterfuge and, if all else failed, outright interference. Well, I had news for them, the donkey had been replaced by the internal combustion engine, the gene pool was global and there was no way I was going to live my life in the goldfish bowl of some backward mountain village where the electric light bulb was regarded as a recent innovation and running water was still a novelty.

Rosana looked around edgily as she entered the walled terrace garden at the back of Restaurante La Tasca and gave no more than a faltering smile when she spotted me, already rising from my seat at a small table nestling in the far corner. Her natural olive skin appeared paler than I remembered. She was thinner too, her face drawn with faint dark crescents beneath subdued eyes. But her long auburn hair was sleek and shiny, and framed her face with natural elegance. She slid gracefully onto the chair I thoughtfully lifted away from the table, and removed a black pashmina from her shoulders, gently shaking her head to allow her hair to bounce back into shape, tumbling in waves beyond her shoulders.

For some reason I was nervous and nudged the corner of the table as I returned to my seat, causing one of two wine goblets to topple over. I grabbed at the goblet managing only to knock it against a porcelain cruet set cracking the glass.

I still wasn't sure why I had changed my mind and called at Rosana's house earlier that day to invite her for dinner. It was not, I realised, a good idea to have told her that the invitation had been prompted by Pepito and Carmen Maria. Some muttered reassurances that I really wanted her to accept, sounded less than convincing even to me, but Rosana had accepted all the same, even if she had not seemed ecstatic at the prospect. I had spent an anxious afternoon wondering what we might talk about and drifting in and out of a half sleep dominated by recollections of our previous times together.

Ever since our first meeting, when Rosana had coaxed me, against my better judgement, into meeting my Spanish family, she had used a mixture of charm and guile to take me on a journey of discovery, challenging my values and convictions about Spain and my Spanish ancestry. At times she had adopted an almost sisterly manner, confronting my opinions and opposing my ideas; at times she was more subtle, using all her feminine charms to virtually seduce me into acquiescence. Even now I wasn't sure whether she had accepted the invitation to dinner out of interest or curiosity; with enthusiasm or resignation.

'We need another wine glass, this one is cracked,' I said to the waitress as she finished scribbling our orders on a pad.

To this point our conversation had been perfunctory; the weather, the restaurant, the menu. It was as if we were both reluctant to touch upon anything more meaningful for fear of breaching an emotional barricade and releasing a tide of recrimination and regret.

I contrasted the mood with the last time we had dined at La Tasca four months ago. We had only just met and the conversation had flowed with the natural ease of two people captivated with each other; attentive, fascinated, probing without reticence and exploring feelings and emotions without inhibition or embarrassment. I had always believed that easy conversation was the hallmark of friendship; the cornerstone of any relationship. But now an awkward silence had descended and I found myself struggling for words, trying to find some uncontroversial topic to break the quietude that set us apart from the buzz of conversation all around.

'Carolina's not working tonight, then?' I said at last, remembering the waitress, a friend of Rosana's, who had served us on the last occasion and who had fussed around us exchanging cryptic glances and furtive smiles with Rosana as if they shared some enigmatic secret.

'She doesn't work here anymore,' Rosana said. 'She had a disagreement with the owner and left. Now she has a new boyfriend. They've moved in together and she's expecting a baby.'

'Someone from the village?' I enquired.

'Yes, why do you ask?'

'Just curious.'

'Curious as to who he is, or curious that she should find a lover so close to home?'

I was surprised Rosana had read the underlying import of my question and the sentiment it implied. I shuffled in my seat and glanced away.

'As I said, just curious.'

Rosana sighed and cast her eyes downwards, twirling the one remaining goblet between her finger and thumb. 'I'm curious, too,' she said. 'Curious about why you invited me to this dinner. Was it out of preference or pity? I mean, I know your grandmother and your uncle set things up, but you could always have told them to mind their own business. I'd have been none the wiser.'

'I'll be honest with you, the thought crossed my mind. Ever since I first came to Spain, I feel I've been pushed and tugged in all directions. Coerced into meeting my family in the first place, pressed into delving into my father's background and cross-examined about my feelings and beliefs. I'm used to being independent, doing and thinking what I want, and now I find myself surrounded by people who think they know what's best for me and who seem determined to control my life.'

'And you include me in that gloomy assessment of your fate?'

'No, no, of course not. Well, at first, perhaps. If it wasn't for you, I'd probably have left Spain three months ago without even coming to Parcent.'

'And that would have been preferable?'

'No, I'm not saying that, not preferable, just simpler.'

The waitress returned, placing a new glass in front of me and displaying a bottle of Comportillo Rioja Reserva. I nodded my approval and sat back as the waitress removed the cork and half-filled the two glasses, before turning towards the kitchen.

'I see,' Rosana mocked. 'You're saying life would have been so much simpler for you if you had continued in blissful ignorance of your grandmother and the rest of your father's family; simpler if you had been allowed to indulge your malevolence and the prejudice it has fostered. Is that it?'

Here we go again. I bristled and jutted my chin as my temper flared. I took a deep breath and sighed, holding back my first inclination to argue.

'I'm not looking for sympathy, if that's what you're getting at. I was simply trying to explain my feelings. I'm not even saying I regret what has happened, just that my life has changed, is still changing, and I need time to make adjustments. But I'm here in Spain aren't I? I could have scurried back to Nottingham when my last investigation ended, but I didn't and that should tell you something.'

Rosana lifted her eyes. 'And this has something to do with me?'

The conversation had reached a watershed. It would be easy, I thought, to retrench; brush aside Rosana's suggestion with a disdainful denial, as if... no, of course I'm not suggesting... but that would have eschewed my real feelings. My natural inclination was to stall, prevaricate and avoid the risk of disappointment or worse, rejection that I knew from experience, could be the outcome of revealing my feelings or exposing my emotions. Too often in the past I had taken the easy option of denial, preferring silence to any overt expression of my true thoughts.

I stopped fiddling with the napkin in front of me and looked into Rosana's eyes, trying to determine if her expression signified hope or ridicule. 'In a way, yes,' I said, immediately regretting my ambiguity and cursing my inability to say what I really meant.

Rosana's eyes narrowed and her lips parted as, inhaling, she prepared to speak...

'Who's having the goat's cheese salad?' the waitress said, before placing the plate in front of me in response to my nod. 'And Serrano and melon for the señora. *Buen aproveche.*'

'You were saying?' Rosana enquired as she set the cutlery on the side of her plate, empty except for a few pieces of stringy fat she had carefully separated from the thinly sliced jamon Serrano.

I pushed a pile of over-dressed salad leaves to the corner of my plate. For a brief moment I thought of pulling back – oh, nothing, what were we talking about? – but, glancing across at Rosana, I thought I read a look that seemed to be imploring me to express my true feelings.

'I was saying that you were one of the reasons I decided to remain in Spain.'

'Only one?' I imagined her saying in response, but she remained silent, her lips tightening to suppress a smile as she held my gaze.

'Well okay,' I said, 'the main reason.'

Still Rosana remained silent, further suppressing the smile and adopting a manufactured frown.

'Don't look so surprised,' I said. 'We had our differences the last time I was here, but I thought we both felt we had come through that. At least I felt we had come through it and... well, I thought we both felt there was something... tangible between us.'

Finally Rosana's tight lipped expression slackened as a hint of a smile crossed her face and her frown subsided. '*Tangible*?' Her smile broadened.

'I think you know what I mean. It was something we both felt, a spark... an affinity.'

'*An affinity!*' Rosana giggled, and then regained enough control to force her brow into a half frown. 'You mean you fancied me.'

I could feel my face reddening. 'No, I meant that you felt something too.'

Rosana reached across the table to touch my hand. 'I can't deny it, Michael, I felt it too... that affinity.' She giggled again.

I pulled my hand away in feigned indignation, but couldn't restrain myself from smiling. 'Oh... good,' I said. 'I was hoping you did.'

I returned my hand to gently grip Rosana's and we both burst into laughter, prompting a curious look from the waitress a she returned to clear our plates.

A hazy sky veiled the stars in the narrow gaps between the rows of houses as we strolled through the village streets which echoed to the tinny sound of televisions audible through open shutters. A few elderly residents sat on chairs set on pavements outside their front doors, grabbing a few last breaths of fresh air before retiring to the embedded heat of houses whose walls had absorbed hours of sunshine during the day. '*Bona nit*' some of them said in their native Valenciano to which Rosana replied without pausing to initiate further conversation.

The balmy night air muffled a single chime of the church bell as we reached my house. I paused for a moment, interrupting Rosana's stride and causing her to turn and take a reluctant step backwards.

'I'll walk you to your door if you like,' I said hesitantly.

Rosana cocked her head to one side.

'Or... you could come in...'

Surprised, she hesitated. 'Oh... my grandmother. I ought to...'

'Pepito said he would stay the night. I mean if...'

Rosana adopted a pained expression. 'Don't you just hate it when the people of this village try to interfere in other people's lives?'

I was still wiping the sleep from my eyes as I bounced on the hard bench-seat of the trailer hitched to Pepito's *mula mecánica* chugging its way along a dusty track through the orange groves on the outskirts of Parcent. It was just past nine, and the church bell was calling people to Mass. Already the sweat was oozing beneath the brim of my straw hat and trickling down my brow. The nape of my hair was soaked and I was wondering why I had agreed to help

Pepito with "a few jobs on the land" as he had put it. It was actually my land, or more accurately, mine and Pepito's.

Pepito was far too polite to ask directly about the events of the previous night and Rosana had said nothing when she returned to her grandmother's house, brusquely taking over the breakfast preparations Pepito had just begun. And I was giving nothing away either other than, 'It was a very nice evening, thank you.'

'We just need to check the irrigation to the oranges,' Pepito said as he cut the rattling motor and brought the ancient contraption to a halt. 'It's critical at this time of year. The fruit is swelling and if the trees are starved of water for just a day or two, the whole crop will fail.'

Pepito hopped from the *mula mecánica* and I followed him down a weed-choked path along the side of the orange grove. The trees were planted in neat rows each about three metres apart. There were twenty or so rows each with a dozen trees rising from rock-strewn red parched earth. The ground was criss-crossed with a network of black plastic tubing fanning out from a larger plastic pipe running through the centre of the grove. I studied the trees finding it almost impossible to see the young fruits, about the size of a plum, camouflaged in the dense foliage. But on closer inspection there were fruits in abundance, hard and green, soaking up the summer heat as if storing up the sunshine for the winter harvest.

Pepito pulled a bunch of keys from his pocket and inserted one in a rusty padlock set into a sheet of galvanised metal lying flat on the ground. He lifted this lid to reveal a buried chamber housing a collection of pipes connected to an ancient meter consisting of a single dial and a row of discoloured numerals. The main pipe was connected to a modern automatic timer.

'I'll just set the system to manual and open the valves for few minutes then we need to check the pipes for leaks.'

'What, all of them?'

'I'm afraid so, Michael, water is a precious commodity in these parts so we can't afford to waste it. You start at this end and I'll start at the far end. You need to walk between every row and pay particular attention to the connections. The pipes become brittle in this heat and can easily split or burst from the joints. Come on, it won't take long and then we can have *almuerzo*.'

'What do I do if I find a leak?'

'If it's a connection that's popped, just press it on again; if a tube has split, give me a shout and we'll patch in a new piece.'

Despite a freshening breeze that gave welcome respite from the escalating heat, my T-shirt already bore dark salty stains beneath my armpits. A sleeveless vest like Pepito's would have been much more practical, I thought, though I would never have been seen dead in such a thing. Pepito's footwear might also have been more practical than my socks and shoes, but, though I might be adjusting to my Spanish side, I was definitely not ready to be seen in a pair of peep-toed canvass espadrilles with laces twice wrapped around the ankles and tied in a bow.

Leaks repaired and joints reconnected, Pepito shut off the water and relocked the metal lid. He lifted a wicker basket from the trailer, raised his straw hat, and wiped his brow with a handkerchief. 'Come on, let's find some shade.'

A low dry-stone wall beneath an ancient fig tree provided seating and Pepito reached into the basket, placing the contents in the space between us and removing aluminium foil from a number of small parcels.

'Carmen Maria made this up. Let's see what we've got.'

A *barra*, the Spanish equivalent to the French baguette, was first to emerge, followed by two gnarled green tomatoes, a chunk of dry cheese, a small jar of purple olives and a cork stoppered bottle of cloudy olive oil. Last to be unwrapped was a small foil parcel of pale green pickled peppers. I wondered if they had been picked by Peter Piper.

Pepito split the bread with his hands and laid it on the opened-out foil before removing the cork from the tiny bottle and carefully drizzling the oil up and down the bread. He handed me a chunk then took a penknife from his pocket, opened the blade and laid it between the parcels.

'Help yourself, Michael. *Almuerzo*, best meal of the day.'

Despite its green skin, the tomato I bit into was sweet and red inside and the warm juices trickled down my chin. I confessed it was better than any perfectly red, perfectly round supermarket tomato I had ever tasted in England.

'Emelio grows them on a plot he cultivates on the other side of the village. They're called *mucho miel*, the king of tomatoes don't you think?'

Mucho miel – a lot of honey – was entirely apt, I thought as I cut a piece of cheese from the chunk and allowed its salty taste to mingle in my mouth with the tomato. The flesh of the plump olives was surprisingly hard and difficult to nibble from the pips, but the flavour was stunning.

'Here, try one of Carmen Maria's specialities,' Pepito said offering the peppers. 'She pickles them herself.'

They looked innocuous, smaller than a standard capsicum and paler in colour, more yellow than green. I tore away a piece of oil-soaked bread and then bit off a chunk of pepper, chewing the crunchy flesh. The familiar, slightly bitter taste of raw capsicum was first to hit my taste buds followed by the tang of vinegar, mingling with a slight saltiness and then came an explosion of heat, overpowering everything else, burning the back of my throat and numbing my tongue. I spat out the whole mouthful, then spat and spat again trying to remove every last morsel of the blisteringly hot pepper from my mouth.

'Sorry, Michael, I should have warned you,' Pepito said, slapping me on the back. 'You need something to wash it down,' he added, reaching into the basket to pull out a label-less bottle of red wine. He extracted the loose-fitting cork with his finger and thumb and handed me the bottle. I lifted it to my mouth and swallowed heartily. It wasn't the best wine I had ever tasted, in fact it was harsh and acidic, but as a neutralising agent it did the trick, temporarily at least, until the heat began to re-emerge and I took another gulp, followed by another.

Pepito stood and reached into the tree above our heads plucking two bulbous green figs, their skins swollen and beginning to split.

'Here, this should help,' he said, handing me one of the figs.

The delectable flesh was soft and warm, sweet and delicate; the perfect antidote to the harshness of the pickled pepper that still pervaded my mouth. I savoured the texture of the bright red flesh and massaged the juicy pulp with my tongue, allowing it to roll around my mouth. I was convinced there was no more exotic, more erotic, fruit than a luscious ripe fig plucked straight from the tree.

'How are things in the campo this year?' I asked.

Pepito shrugged. 'Same as always; some good some bad. We'll have a bumper crop of oranges by the end of the year, but the almonds are not so good. The blossom came early in January and was hit with a frost. The grapes are poor, too. We had too much rain and humidity in April and May and the mildew has taken hold. More than half the crop has been lost already and the rest will be hardly worth harvesting come the end of August. I sometimes wonder if it's worth carrying on.'

'Are things really that bad?' I asked, remembering that farmers the world over were never happy with their lot.

'Pretty much. You've seen those men in Jalon selling oranges to the tourists at two euros for five kilos; they're the lucky ones, if you can call it lucky to sit by the roadside for eight hours a day. The juice companies pay a fraction of that price when they gather the crop in autumn. This whole orange grove will yield less than three hundred euros, a pittance when you think of the work involved, and then we have to pay for the water. You can see why some people would rather sell out to the property developers.'

'But you can't build on every bit of agricultural land in the valley, that would destroy the very thing that makes it attractive.'

'You're right, of course, Michael, and that's why some people make their fortune and others are left to carry on scratching a living.'

'So who decides? I mean where you can build and where you can't?'

'That's an interesting point. Every village is supposed to approve a General Plan designating land for agriculture or for housing, land for commercial use or for public services and protected land. It's a good idea in principle, if everyone had their say and if there was some rationale behind the plans. But far too often it's the people with a vested interest, the big landowners, who dictate what's in the General Plan. They wheedle their way into power, directly or indirectly, and they use their influence to get their land designated as urbanisable. Hey presto, their land is worth a fortune and the rest get left behind. There's no proper environmental assessment, no consultation, no thought for the adequacy of water resources, in short, no proper planning, just the forces of greed and corruption dictating the future of whole communities.'

'And is this happening in Parcent?'

'It's been tried, but luckily, the new council is trying to halt the process and bring about more rational plans. At the moment there's stalemate, but who knows what will happen in the future. The opposition party only just scraped in last year by just forty votes, and that was because almost all the foreign residents voted for them. Who knows what will happen at the next municipal elections. If the other lot get back in, then all bets are off.'

Pepito stood and beckoned me to the side of the fig tree. 'You see the base of the mountains over there.' He waved his hand. 'From Col de Rates on the right to that hillock on the left in the distance.'

My eyes followed the sweep of Pepitos's hand taking in a vast swath of pine forest and rolling foothills covered with shrubs nestling in the lee of Carrascal, the mountain range that provided the backdrop to Parcent and gave rise to the village's claim to be Paradise in the Mountains.

'That, Michael, is what is known as Sector Repla. The previous council provisionally approved a plan to build 1,500 three-storey town houses up there covering more than a million square metres. Can you imagine the effect that would have on the countryside and the view from the village?'

I stared out over the picturesque vista and recalled the avalanche of concrete seeping over the hillside at Residencia Gata. Surely, I thought, this would be worse, much worse, if that were possible. Why, I thought, would anyone in their right mind contemplate such devastation?

'Who owns the land, Pepito?'

'You might well ask, Michael. Let's just say it doesn't belong to the poor people of Parcent. And it doesn't stop there. The last draft General Plan envisaged the construction of another 1,500 houses dotted around the village. Taken together they would increase the population of the village tenfold.'

'Let's just hope it never happens.'

'Hope may not be enough,' Pepito said with an air of resignation as he packed the leftovers into the basket.

As we returned to the *mula mecánica* Pepito spoke again without interrupting his stride or looking in my direction.

'There's something you should know, Michael.'

I sensed a certain hesitancy in his voice.

'About Rosana's grandmother's house.'

'Oh?'

'It's mortgaged up to the hilt. Rosanna took out the mortgage to pay for her mother's care when she became ill. The health service paid for her initial treatment after a stroke, but Rosanna wanted more. She was determined her mother could make a full recovery after she was left partially paralysed and with speech problems. She spent a fortune on intensive physiotherapy and speech therapy with little practical benefit. Rosana covered the mortgage while she was working, but when her mother died she gave up her job to care for her grandmother and now the debts are mounting. I've spoken to her about it, but she just refuses to see sense. She's determined to put her grandmother's care above everything else.'

The thought crossed my mind that in trying to push me towards Rosana, my grandmother and Pepito were attempting to engineer more than just a romantic connection. Perhaps they were also striving to forge a neat little economic alliance. Worse still, perhaps Rosana saw this as a solution to her problems as well.

'Why are you telling me all this, Pepito?' I asked.

'I just thought you ought to know.'

CHAPTER TWELVE

'Excellent, thank you,' was my response to Mariela's polite enquiry about my weekend.

'And how was your weekend?' I asked.

'Mundane,' Mariela replied. 'I spent most of Saturday in the office with Teresa Blazquez, trawling through files and searching the internet.'

'I'm impressed. Do I put you in for a medal or is there a chitty I have to sign for the overtime?' I smiled benevolently.

'Both, and you still owe me lunch.'

'I'll start saving now.'

'In that case, make it dinner.'

I wondered if there was something more than banter behind Mariela's suggestion. Don't be ridiculous, I thought, an attractive young woman like Mariela must have a string of boyfriends queuing up to take her to dinner.

'I know a cheap paella restaurant in Parcent.' I said. 'And over dinner I could bore you with details of the demise of the rural economy and the threat of over-development. You do eat paella, I take it?'

'I love paella, but there's something you should know.'

I lifted my eyebrows.

'A real Spaniard would never eat paella for dinner. It's strictly a lunchtime meal; a prequel to siesta.' A wry smile dimpled Mariela's cheeks and her eyes sparkled suggestively.

'I guess I still have some way to go before I qualify as a real Spaniard. For now I've still got my "L" plates.'

'Well, you know what they say, Michael, practice makes perfect.'

The conversation was becoming awkward. I cleared my throat. 'So, was your Saturday fruitful?' I asked.

Mariela straightened in her seat and pursed her lips peevishly before shuffling through the bundle of paper on her desk. 'We think we've found a source for the Torc posters from Tony Robinson's bedroom. It's a back-street shop in the Moroccan quarter of Alicante. They specialise in the occult – masks, books, posters, jewellery and religious paraphernalia. They even do tattoos. Officer Blazquez is paying them a visit this morning.'

I was hoping for more, especially as I still regarded the disappearance of young Robinson as secondary to Mora's murder. Still, if we managed to find the boy signed up to some obscure boar-worshipping cult, we could tick the case off the list and file it away under "mystery solved". Just so long as they didn't ask me to facilitate a reconciliation between the boy and his parents. I was not, and never would be, a social worker.

'Good, well done,' I said, trying not to sound disappointed. 'But it hardly justifies dinner.'

'Ah well,' Mariela sighed. 'It seems my Saturday was wasted.'

I shrugged as if to agree with her assessment.

'Sunday was much more productive,' Mariela said teasingly.

'Oh? Are you going to explain?'

'I spent the afternoon at Club Erotica on the N332. Most... interesting.' Mariela shuffled through the files in front of her.

'A Sunday afternoon?'

'It's a busy time at clubs like that. Some men like to enjoy a hearty lunch with the family and then slope off for a bit of private relaxation.'

Mariela glanced at me as I wondered what other norms of Spanish life I had yet to encounter.

'You look shocked.'

'Surprised,' I corrected. 'I'm just getting my head around the idea of Sunday Mass, followed by lunch with the family, then a siesta with seedy sex thrown in. So what did you turn up?'

'I met the "manageress" a Romanian, Sofia Filipescu, and a few of the "hostesses" – mostly eastern European girls in their late teens or early twenties. The place is not as seedy as you might imagine, by the way. It's quite respectable on the face of it.'

'You were saying?'

'I showed Sofia the photos we found in Mora's house and she was able to put names to some of them. Records are checking the names now, but on the face of it there's no one of any significance. However, when I showed her the photo of Salvador Guardiola, she recognised him immediately, but said she didn't know his name. She thought he had only been there on a couple of occasions in the last two months and she knew him because she had been told to "look after him" and that he must not pay for anything.'

'Interesting,' I said, still trying to assimilate the significance of this information.

'It gets better,' Mariela said, excitement growing in her voice. 'It was when I showed her the photo of Walter Wilkinson that things really changed. She tried to hide it, but I could see she recognised the photo so I pressed her. She still denied it, but eventually she told me she knew him. She seemed embarrassed though, and claimed he was not a "customer" just an acquaintance. She told me how she felt trapped in the club. She wants to get away, but she can't. It seems she came to Spain nearly twenty years ago on the promise of proper work, but she was forced into prostitution in order to pay off the cost of her travel and the exorbitant interest that accrued. But she was never able to pay enough after costs were deducted for food and accommodation. She threatened to walk out at one stage and return to Romania, but her passport had been confiscated and she was told that even if she went back to Romania, she would be followed and forced to return – after her family and neighbours had been told about the work that she did. So she has stayed, and worked, even though she doesn't want to. At least now she is the manager – I suppose "madam" would be a better description – and she doesn't go with the "clients" but she still feels trapped.'

My impatience got the better of me. 'Never mind the sob story, what has this to do with Walter Wilkinson?'

'I was getting to that. Filipescu says he is just a friend.'

'A friend?' Where had I heard that before?

'Yes, that's what she says. According to her, they met in a supermarket car park near her flat in Pedreguer. She was being harassed by a couple of suspicious youths who she thought were trying to snatch her bag. She shoved them with the supermarket trolley and screamed. The trolley toppled over, spilling all the contents in the car park and Wilkinson came to the rescue. She was very flustered and Wilkinson helped her load the bags into her car, then took her back inside for a coffee. They chatted for a while and struck up a friendship. They met a couple of times after that and at first she lied about where she worked, but eventually she told him the truth — the whole story about how she came to Spain and was forced into prostitution. She expected Wilkinson to end the friendship there and then, but according to her, he was sympathetic and said he wanted to help if he could. After that he visited her a couple of times at Club Erotica — she says he just bought a couple of drinks and chatted with her but never went with any of the girls. She seemed surprised, shocked, by the photograph and claimed she knew nothing about it.'

I puffed my cheeks. 'And do you believe this unlikely story?'

'I know it seems implausible, but I asked myself this: if Wilkinson was just a regular punter, like the others in the photos, why would she lie to protect him?'

'Mmm,' I thought for a moment. 'Why indeed? And when did all this take place, I mean our knight in shining armour riding to the rescue?'

'About four months ago, early in March. There's something else though. When I asked Sofia how Wilkinson intended to help her she became evasive. She says he just talked to her and that was help enough as she has no other real friends. They discussed the prospect of her returning to Romania to see her family, but she never thought it was a realistic possibility. I pressed her further about what they talked about but she just clammed up. I was sure she was hiding something. Then I asked her if there was anything sexual in their relationship – a bit blunt, I grant you, but an obvious question in the circumstances.'

'Her being a prostitute you mean? Seems reasonable to me.'

'Well, she didn't think so. She became very angry, indignant even, and flew into a rant about me being just the same as everyone else, wanting to believe the worst. Just because she used to be a prostitute everyone believed she was incapable of having a normal friendship with a man. At that point I thought I'd better back off and leave it at that.'

Very wise, I thought. 'I wonder what she meant by "everyone"? I also wonder if their relationship and that photograph have anything to do with the fact that Mrs Wilkinson is on indefinite leave of absence in Leeds.'

Mariela shrugged.

'Right,' I said. 'First we're going to pay Walter Wilkinson another visit, then I want you to contact as many of the other people in those photographs as you can to see if any of them were being blackmailed by Mora or anyone else.'

'Including Salvador Guardiola?' Mariela said, incredulously.

'No, not Guardiola. Not for now at least, we can leave him until later, I think.'

Walter Wilkinson looked tired and dishevelled when he finally trudged to the gate in response to Mariela's second, prolonged jangle of the bell. There were salty stains beneath the armpits of his plaid shirt, the sleeves of which were rolled up beyond the elbows exposing deeply tanned forearms. His knee-length shorts were a cut-off pair of beige cavalry twill trousers with frayed edges exposing equally tanned calves. The whole outfit, including a pair of sloppy brown loafers, convinced me that Wilkinson was either living on a tight budget or he was dedicated to recycling his English wardrobe.

'Sorry to disturb your siesta, Mr Wilkinson, but we just wanted another quick word with you, if it's convenient?' My tone left little doubt that we were not offering to come back later.

'Well, it's not really convenient. I've been working in the garden all morning and I was just about to shower. But if you don't mind the smell of body odour you're welcome to come in.' Wilkinson was already removing the padlock and unravelling the chain around the gates.

I ushered Mariela through the gates in front of me and watched with mild amusement as she wobbled on her high heeled sling-back shoes crunching across the loose gravel before recovering her poise as we reached the paved terrace on the shady side of the house. Taking one of the foldable hardwood chairs set around a matching table, Mariela inspected the delicate leather-covered heels looking for scuff marks, but seemed satisfied they had sustained no permanent damage.

Wilkinson removed the top from a small plastic water bottle and drained the contents in three gulps, swallowing hard as his Adam's apple bobbed in his throat. He was clearly in no mood to offer refreshment to his two visitors.

I tried to look cool and collected in a short sleeved white shirt open at the neck and tucked into lightweight chinos. As I crossed my legs, I noticed a couple of inches of white flesh between the bottom of the chinos and the top of my socks. I must find the time to get a tan, I thought, tugging at the hem of my trousers.

Mariela removed the over-sized sunglasses she habitually wore outdoors and placed them on the top of her head using the side arms to pin back her fringe. I couldn't determine whether, as the logo suggested, they were genuine Coco Chanel or cheap imitations and I couldn't help noticing tiny flecks of gold in Mariela's hazel eyes as she caught my glance.

'So what is it this time?' Wilkinson said. 'Have you found Mora's murderer yet? Please tell me if you have, I'd like to shake his hand.'

His bravado was short lived as Mariela pulled the photograph from a folder and slid it across the table.

'Have you seen this before, Mr Wilkinson?' Mariela asked in a matter-of-fact kind of voice so as not to give any hint that she knew the location in the background the photograph.

We both studied Wilkinson carefully, watching his reaction as he poured over the photograph, keeping his eyes on the image for longer than it took to recognise its content – long enough, I thought, for him to be considering his answer very carefully.

'Where did you get this?' Wilkinson said at last, his face set in a look of defiance as he flicked the photograph back towards Mariela.

'It doesn't matter where the photograph came from. The question was, have you seen it before, Mr Wilkinson?' Mariela pushed the photo back across the table.

Wilkinson's eyes flicked between the two of us before he settled his gaze on me. I could almost see the cogs whirring in Wilkinson's head as he tried to figure out how best to answer the question.

'Look, what's this all about? You can't just barge into my home and question me like this.'

I knew he was stalling for time. 'I don't recall barging in anywhere, Mr Wilkinson. You opened the gate and let us in. Now if you would just answer Sergeant Poquet's question.'

Finally the cogs stopped and Wilkinson made his gambit. 'Yes, I've seen it before.'

Expecting a denial, Mariela seemed momentarily startled, but regained her poise as quickly as she had recovered her high-heeled steps once she found level ground. 'Would you mind telling us where you have seen this photograph before?'

'A copy was sent to this address by post.'

'Do you still have that copy?'

'No, I destroyed it.'

'And the envelope it came in?'

'That as well.'

Mariela paused to recover the photo and replace it in the folder. 'Do you have any idea who sent it to you or why?'

'No.'

'Do you recognise the location in the photo?'

Wilkinson's shoulders slumped and he shuddered visibly as he realised Mariela already knew the place where the photo had been taken.

'All right,' he said with an air of resignation. 'The photograph was taken outside Club Erotica near Pedregeur. It was sent to this address by Mora. He tried to use it to force me to back off from opposing the development plans and withdraw the court case, but I refused. The photograph proves nothing, I told him that. I just happen to know someone who works at the club and I have been to visit her there. Not for "business" as you might be thinking, just to meet someone for a chat.'

'That would be Sofia Filipescu,' I said, turning the screw by demonstrating we knew a lot more than he expected. I was quite enjoying myself.

Wilkinson's surprise was short-lived. 'If you know Miss Filipescu, you'll know I'm telling you the truth.'

'You were trying to help her I understand,' I made no attempt to hide my sarcasm, hoping to provoke Wilkinson and move him away from his carefully constructed replies. It worked, but not as I had hoped.

'I suppose that years of wallowing amongst the dregs of society, fraternising with the filth of the earth has left you incapable of understanding the concept of genuine friendship or compassion. And since you have so obviously made up your mind about my relationship with Miss Filipescu, I see no point in further explanations.'

I felt suitably chastised, but was not about to apologise. 'Has your relationship anything to do with Mrs Wilkinson's current sojourn in Leeds?'

Wilkinson's patience snapped. 'How dare you? What has any of this got to do with Mora's death, or are you on a new investigation now? Snooping around the seedy sex clubs on the N332 is right up your street, I imagine. Much more interesting than finding the killer of a corrupt old villain like Mora. Is that it?'

Mariela felt the need to intervene, sensing that tempers were about to flare. 'You were not the only one to be photographed outside that club, Mr Wilkinson. And we'll be contacting all the others. We know that Mora has an involvement in that place and we are trying to discover if he was using the photos to blackmail people. If we can confirm that was the case then it would suggest there are other people who might have a motive for wanting Mora dead. You have helpfully confirmed that Mora sent you the photograph and that he was willing to make use of it, if not to extort money in your case, then at least to benefit his own ends.'

I was impressed. Mariela had expertly diffused the situation whilst still putting over the point that the photograph gave a further possible motive for Wilkinson to want Mora out of the way.

The point was not lost on Wilkinson who sat back in his chair looking smug. 'I'm glad I've been able to help. And since you should, by now, have been able to check the flight details I gave you last time, you will already know that I was not in Spain at the time Mora died. Now, if there's nothing more, I will go and take my shower.'

Wilkinson rose from his seat and strode towards the gate, replacing the padlock and chain with a flourish as soon as we departed. He turned and walked back to the house without acknowledging the polite thanks proffered by Mariela.

'I'm not sure where that got us, especially as you were so rude to him,' Mariela said as we returned to Jalon.

'I just don't like the man. He gets up my nose.'

'Is that your intuitive detective's nose or your everyday antagonistic nose?'

I grunted. 'Are you sure you checked those flight details?'

'You don't really want me to answer that do you?'

'Well at least we know Mora was prepared to use those photographs for his own ends. You'd better get on and check the rest of the people in the photos and see what else he was up to. But make sure you do it discreetly.'

'Discreetly,' Mariela snorted. 'You have a saying in English, I think, something about grandmothers sucking eggs.'

CHAPTER THIRTEEN

With Mariela discreetly chasing the mug shot victims, I was left alone in the office trying to shut out the noise of a rattling air conditioning unit that was about as much use as an ice cube in an oven. My shirt, fresh and clean that morning, was now catching the salty stickiness of my skin. I undid a couple more buttons and tugged the shirt laps from my trouser belt, wafting the fabric to allow the air to circulate around my body. If only I could have done the same with my trousers and boxer shorts.

Mariela's rebuke had left me chastened. It brought to mind something my old Chief Inspector said to me when I first joined Nottingham CID as a raw Detective Constable. "We sometimes want the facts to fit the preconceptions. When they don't, it is often easier to ignore the facts than to change the preconceptions." Perhaps Mariela had been right. I closed my eyes and tried to sift through the fog of information that was swirling around my brain, growing ever denser, obscuring my perception and clouding my judgement.

Juan-Jose Mora had been murdered, suffocated according to Pilar Vidal on the evidence of those petechial haemorrhages. There was no way of knowing for certain whether he fell or was pushed from the road above the ruins, but he had clearly been moved after the fall and then smothered. Therefore, in all probability, he had been pushed, otherwise how would anyone know he was lying there in pitch darkness? The presumption must be that the same person who pushed him intended to kill him and later went down to the ruins to finish the job.

Suspects? Walter Wilkinson had been the obvious choice. He had been heard to threaten Mora and what's more he made no secret of his hatred. Even his false bravado, expressing his pleasure at Mora's death, seemed to be a ploy on Wilkinson's part and this had further aroused my suspicions. But faced with a cast iron alibi, I had to set aside my enmity and mistrust and look elsewhere for a culprit.

Paco Santos, Mora's deputy Mayor? He knew about the money in Mora's house and he also knows where it came from even if he won't say so. After my circuitous conversation with Eduardo Moreno, there seemed little doubt the money was a bribe, a backhander, probably paid by the developers Guardiola Property SA to ease the smooth passage of their development plans for Beniforell. It could simply be that on hearing about Mora's death, Santos decided he'd better get hold of the money before anyone else did. But what if Santos and Mora had fallen out over the money and Mora wanted to keep more than his fair share? Might they have argued? Might Santos have wanted Mora out of the way so he could keep all the money for himself? As deputy Mayor, he would take over from Mora and it would be down to him to make sure the plans went ahead. A quarter of a million euros was a lot of money by anyone's reckoning and people have certainly killed for a lot less. And Santos had no alibi.

But what of Salvador Guardiola himself? What if Mora had become greedy, demanding even more black money? Guardiola was not a man to be messed with by all accounts. Someone with his power and influence would not take kindly to being held over a barrel and though it was unlikely Guardiola would dirty his own hands to deal with a petty politician like Mora, he would almost certainly know someone who would. And then there was that photograph of Guardiola outside Club Erotica. Could Mora possibly have had the temerity to invite Guardiola to the club and then try to blackmail him? It seemed implausible, but from everything I knew about Mora he was a man used to getting his own way, by whatever means necessary.

Then there was Mora's kidney transplant. Had it really been mere luck that put him in the right place at the right time when a donor kidney presented itself? Dr Ernesto Alvarez had carefully denied impropriety of any kind, but then he would, wouldn't he? If it were anyone else but Mora, I would have accepted Alvarez's denial, but I did not believe in coincidence, nor did I believe that Mora was the type of man who would trust his own fate to chance if there was a way of improving the odds in his favour. Perhaps that was why he needed the money – to buy his way to the top of the list. Perhaps he had already made a down payment for the operation and the quarter of a million was the balance to be paid when he was sure the transplant had been successful.

And what of those other photographs? Might Mora have been systematically blackmailing people who used the services on offer at Club Erotica? Spanish attitudes to the sleazy, seedy world of paid-for sex might be more liberal than in prudish Britain, but not every wife or girlfriend would be happy to overlook their partner's peccadilloes. That being the case, Mariela might well be working through a whole new list of suspects prepared to kill Mora in order to protect their reputations or their marriages.

And then there was...? Just about anyone Mora had crossed in his greedy, grasping, avaricious determination to get his own way.

So much for introspection, I thought, rousing myself from my reflections and rubbing my eyes to find Mariela standing in front of my desk, a sardonic smile illuminating her face. 'Taking a siesta I see. You're becoming more Spanish every day, Michael.'

I fastened a couple of buttons on my shirt and felt a trickle of sweat beneath my armpits. Luckily the shirt was white and there were no visible signs of the stickiness I felt. I had learned in hot weather not to do a Tony Blair and end up in two-tone blue or pink.

'I've been reviewing the case.' I said less than convincingly.

'And have you come up with any answers?'

'I was hoping you would do that. Any luck with those photographs?'

'I managed to track down all but three of them and have a word.'

125

'And?'

'Embarrassment, indignation, outrage in one case, but no one I have spoken to admits to being contacted by Mora, let alone blackmailed.'

'And you believed them?'

'Well, you wanted me to be discreet, didn't you? I could hardly threaten them with going public. So I made it clear that if they told the truth now about any possible demands, we would do our best to keep the information under wraps. Something we might not be able to do if anything were to come to light at a later stage.'

'Very discreet, I'm sure. What about the three you haven't been able to track down?'

'Two of them are complete mysteries. No one seems to know who they are. They could be out-of-town people, possibly even tourists looking for something to do on a rainy day.'

There was a flaw in that argument, I thought. From what I had seen it never rained in Spain. 'And the third?'

Mariela shuffled through the photographs and slid one across my desk. It was an enlargement of one I had seen before. The man in the picture was casually dressed in a tight fitting polo shirt that exaggerated the pot belly hanging over the belted waist of his jeans. He appeared to be in his mid-forties with a full head of wavy black hair thrust back from his face, though distinct patches of grey in his unkempt beard suggested he might be a little older.

'Do we know who this one is?' I asked.

'That, Michael, is Hilario Sanchez.' A smile ghosted on her lips. 'He's the _Tecnico_ – planning officer, you might call him – for the municipality of Beniforell.'

'Well, well, well,' I said understanding the reason for Mariela's satisfaction. 'And you haven't spoken to him yet?'

'Not yet, no. I thought you might like to join me on this one.'

I smiled at the thought. This could be very interesting. 'No time like the present,' I said, rising from my chair.

'Sorry, it will have to wait. The town hall is closed on Wednesdays. I've made an appointment to see him tomorrow morning at 10.30.'

I sat down in my chair again, imagining the public outcry if a notice appeared on the front door of Nottingham town hall, "Closed Wednesdays."

'Oh, by the way,' Mariela said. 'Teresa Blazquez was looking for you earlier. She has some news from the poster shop in Alicante.'

News from the poster shop in Alicante was the last thing I was interested in. Mora's murder was vexing me and there was something I was missing. Posters of wild pigs were not going to help me discover what it was. I had never been a team player, preferring to work things through on my own and in my own time. But that was in England. In Spain, as I was discovering, I needed all the help I could get, so I'd better not dismiss officer Blazquez's efforts.

With 'Z' pronounced 'TH' and 'QU' pronounced 'K', Teresa's surname was a real mouthful even for someone as fluent in Spanish as me. Izquierda (left) was bad enough, but Blazquez was almost impossible unless you had a natural lisp. I once heard a story that centuries ago one of the old Castillian kings had a lisp and found it difficult to pronounce the 'S' sound of a soft 'C' as in cerveza or gracias. To avoid embarrassment he had ordered everyone in the kingdom to speak as he did and hence a beer became 'thervetha' and thank you became 'grathias.' I had no idea if the story was true, but it sounded plausible to me.

'Come in Teresa,' I said. 'You don't mind if I call you Teresa do you? You can call me Michael if you like.'

In the days before political correctness Teresa might have been described as roly poly, now she was simply well built; a five foot powerhouse with roughly equal measurements to hips, waist and bust struggling to fit inside the unflattering standard Guardia Civil uniform of heavy green serge. For all that, her cheerful cherubic face might have been described as pretty, though I knew better than to make any such comment.

'You have some information for us, I believe.'

'Yes, Captain Fernandez, that's right. I went to "Brujería" this morning, a shop in the Moroccan quarter of Alicante run by a Rastafarian couple called Mocha and Murat – no last names so they said. They specialise in all the paraphernalia of witchcraft and wizardry – crosses, stakes, gaudy jewellery, incense – that kind of thing as well as masks and robes. They also sell pictures and posters and when I showed them the poster of Torc, they recognised it straightaway; they even had half a dozen identical posters in stock. It seems they buy them in from a specialist printer in Prague.'

I was becoming impatient and stifled a yawn.

Sensing my irritation, Mariela intervened. 'That's really interesting, Teresa, what else did you find out?'

'I showed them the photograph of Tony Robinson, but they didn't recognise him. Then I asked about recent sales of the posters, but not surprisingly, they didn't keep records. However, Murat recalled someone buying six of the posters. She remembered because it was unusual for them to sell more than one at a time. The same person, a woman of eastern European extraction, also bought a hooded robe, white with a red cross of St George embroidered on the front.'

My eyes drifted to the ceiling, tracing the lines of cracked plasterwork to a corner hosting a wispy cobweb. Mariela issued a deliberate cough, prompting me to refocus on Teresa as she continued.

'It was such a good sale – six posters and a robe – that Murat struck up a conversation with the woman who spoke reasonable Spanish. Murat remembered some of the conversation, in particular there was mention of a Centre somewhere in Lliber, but that's all Murat could remember.'

It took a moment for this to register with me. 'Lliber? As in the village of Lliber, just down the road from here where the Robinsons live?'

'Exactly,' Mariela exclaimed, obviously having discussed Teresa's information beforehand. 'And there's more. Carry on Teresa.'

Teresa's face flushed. 'I did some digging to see if I could find out more about this so called "Centre" and I came across something in Records. Three months ago the Guardia Civil received complaints from neighbours about activities in a chalet on the outskirts of Lliber just off the road to Benissa. It seems there were people coming and going at all hours during the night. There were also reports of loud screams. Six Guardia Civil officers raided the chalet in the early hours of the morning and arrested three people on suspicion of running some kind of religious sect. They removed various articles, including some ancient books, the robe I described, and one of the Torc posters. They also took away a crossbow, two scimitars and several knives with jewelled bone handles.'

Teresa paused and looked across at me as if to check that I was still listening. I was. 'And what happened next?' I asked.

Teresa cleared her throat. 'Well, there was a problem. The place was called the *Centro de Desarollo Espiritual* and the people arrested claimed they had been running spiritual and personal development courses for interested young people, mainly at the weekends. Unfortunately the police raid took place on a Wednesday night and there were none of the so-called "students" present. They made further inquiries but never found anyone who had visited the place and the people who were arrested were definitely not giving any names. They checked financial records, but there was nothing out of the ordinary – just a couple of personal bank accounts with small sums on deposit. All the information gathered was presented to a judge in Denia who dismissed the case for lack of evidence of any wrongdoing.'

'Sounds like no one took the case very seriously,' I mused. 'What happened to the people who were arrested?'

'Two men and a woman.' Teresa answered. 'The men were Spanish, and the woman was a Ukrainian. After they were released they returned to the chalet, but it was only a rental place. Shortly afterwards they left the chalet and it has been empty ever since. We have no record of where they are now.'

'Great.' I said. 'So all this takes us exactly nowhere.'

'I don't think we should be so dismissive, Michael,' said Mariela. 'At least there's a link with Lliber and possibly with the Robinson boy. It's more than a coincidence that he had the same wild boar poster as those people in the chalet. My guess is that he got his posters from them which suggests he might have spent time there before he disappeared. At the very least we should ask Officer Blazquez to dig around some more and see what else she can find out.'

'Very well,' I said, my thoughts already returning to Mora's murder and that nagging feeling that there was something I had overlooked.

'Should I contact Mr and Mrs Robinson about this?' Teresa asked.

'No, definitely not. It's all too vague at this stage and we don't want to raise false hopes, or fears for that matter, on the basis of some bungled raid on a bunch of odd-ball religious nutters who have disappeared into thin air. Just see what else you can find out about the people who were arrested and that chalet they rented.'

I had better things to do, though I was not sure what they were. I rose from my seat and headed for the door. Mariela barked another loud cough, attracting my attention as she cast her eyes deliberately towards Teresa.

'Oh, um... great work, Officer Blazquez, thank you. And just keep digging; you never know what else you might turn up.'

CHAPTER FOURTEEN

The town hall at Beniforell had a certain olde worlde charm. A broad oak panelled door glistening with a fresh coat of varnish led to an inner vestibule that doubled as a waiting area for those hoping to access the inner offices. The floor was in marble mosaic, worn with the passage of feet over what I imagined to be the past forty or fifty years. White glazed bricks set in a herringbone pattern lined the lower half of the walls topped with a heavily carved dado rail. At the end of the vestibule more polished doors were distinguished with ornate glass panels etched with the words *Alcalde, Secretario* and *Tecnico*. The service counter was a marble slab slotted into an arch of Gothic proportions. The apex of the arch was adorned by a crest bearing the town's coat of arms comprising a quartered shield inset with a castle, trefoils, rampant lions and dragons topped with a royal crown.

Behind the counter two young women tapped on keyboards in front of modern, slim-line VDUs. The office clerk, a middle aged man dressed in jeans and an open necked shirt, shuffled papers between a row of filing baskets. He had told us the *Tecnico* had just popped out for a coffee and would be back soon. It was now 10.45 and I was growing impatient and uncomfortable on a moulded plastic chair that that seemed out of place with the rest of the pseudo-splendid surroundings.

I looked at my watch again and exhaled audibly through my nose.

'Relax,' Mariela said, sensing my frustration. 'He'll be here soon.'

'He'd better be. We are already more than a quarter of an hour late.'

'Michael this is rural Spain. No one pays much attention to the time. He's probably bumped into a couple of locals in the bar and stopped for a chat.'

'The bar!'

'Where else would he go for coffee? I don't see a drinks machine, do you?'

I huffed again. 'Didn't you tell him who we were?'

'No. I thought it best not to. That way he would have no time to prepare.'

That much was true, I thought, though at least he might have made an effort to be punctual if he had known his visitor was a Captain in the Guardia Civil – or then again perhaps not.

Hilario Sanchez was instantly recognisable as his portly frame formed a silhouette against the sunlight streaming through the doorway. He sauntered over to the service desk and exchanged a few brief words with the clerk before turning to examine us through eyes narrowed by a suspicious frown.

'Please come through,' he said, moving towards his office and removing a heavy bundle of keys from the pocket of his black denim jeans.

There was no desk in the office, just a large mahogany table in the centre of the room surrounded by leather backed chairs embossed with the coat of arms I had seen in the foyer. The desk was clear except for a tall bundle of files and plans placed at one corner and on open diary sitting on a pristine blotter. Sanchez took a seat at the far side of the table in front of the diary and beckoned us to sit opposite. As I bent to sit, I was sure I detected a whiff of cigarette smoke tinged with a hint of brandy.

'How can I help you...' He glanced at the diary. '...Señor Fernandez and Señora Poquet, isn't it?'

As he raised his eyes from the diary he settled an undisguised leery look on Mariela who flicked her hair behind her shoulders and met his stare with a glower.

'I am Sergeant Poquet of the Guardia Civil and this is my boss, Captain Fernandez.'

I looked for signs of surprise, concern even, on Sanchez's face, but he remained impassive.

'Ah, Captain Fernandez,' he said, settling back in his chair. 'I heard you had been asking questions in the village. I guessed you would be calling on us before long.'

So much for the element of surprise.

'What can I do for you?'

'You'll be aware that we are investigating the death of Señor Mora, the Mayor?' I deliberately avoided the term murder at this stage.

'Of course. So tragic, especially after all he had been through in recent months. You'll be aware that he was recovering from a kidney transplant and doing very well from what I could see.'

'So I heard. We're following a number of lines of inquiry one of which suggests that his death might be related to the controversial development planned by Tierra Nueva S.A. and approved by the council in January this year.'

Sanchez remained nonchalant, gently stroking his beard. 'I'm not sure why you use the term "controversial." The plans are all above board, they met with all the legal and technical requirements and they were approved quite openly by the full council. Yes, a few people objected, but that's bound to happen in a development of this scale. That doesn't make them controversial though.'

I was tempted to argue that any plan using the Valencian land laws to confiscate property without compensation and charge people outrageous sums of money for infrastructure charges was, almost by definition, bound to be controversial. But now was not the time for arguing the merits of the *Ley Regulador de Actividades Urbanisticos*. I needed to concentrate on the specifics.

'Tell me, Mr Sanchez; is there a General Plan for the municipality of Beniforell?'

For the first time since we entered the office, Sanchez looked uncomfortable. I noticed him swallow hard and blink rapidly.

'There's a *concierto previo* – a draft – General Plan, but it's not yet been finalised. Why do you ask?'

133

'It's my understanding that the law requires that each municipality draws up a General Plan before approving specific development projects.'

I noticed Mariela's eyes widen in surprise but Sanchez appeared unmoved.

'That's a somewhat narrow interpretation of the law,' he said, as he launched into what appeared to be a well rehearsed response to my enquiry. 'The process of approving and adopting a full General Plan can take several years. It would be unreasonable to expect any municipality to freeze all development plans whilst a General Plan is in preparation. In the case of Beniforell there is already a zoning plan – the *Normas Subsidiarias* – in existence and that was used to assess the merits of the most recent plan. All the land in the Tierra Nueva project is classified as urbanisable in the *Normas Subsidiarias* so it was clear that everything was legal and above board.'

'And that was the official opinion you gave when you advised the council on this matter?'

'Correct.'

'But it's a view that has been challenged successfully in the courts. Am I right?'

Sanchez cleared his throat. 'It's been challenged yes, but there are no authoritative precedents.'

No authoritative precedents – another way of saying it doesn't matter what the courts have said, I thought.

'Did the council undertake an Environmental Impact Study, before considering the project? I understand that's a requirement of Spanish law as well as European law, especially in the case of a plan involving more than a million square metres of forest and woodland.

Sanchez gulped. 'That wasn't necessary in this case. The environmental impact was considered when the *Normas Subsidiarias* plan was adopted.'

'I see. When was that exactly?'

'Um… 1989.'

'So, almost twenty years ago.' I glanced at Sanchez for a reaction, but he met my stare with a hard-set jaw. I pressed on. 'And has there been an official report from the Hydrographic Confederation on the availability of water resources to meet the needs of all the planned new houses? I understand that's a legal requirement as well.'

'No. That wasn't necessary in this case either because the local *Regiantes* have stated publicly that there is more than enough water in this valley to support present and future demands.'

The *Regiantes*, I knew, were nothing more than a farmers' co-operative whose principal purpose was to allocate water for irrigation. Their opinion fell way short of a technical assessment of the availability of water resources to support development on the scale proposed in the Tierra Nueva plan.

'I understand the plan was approved by the council on 28th January this year.'

'That's correct.'

'Just a few days before the *Ley Regulador de Actividades Urbanisticos* was due to be repealed.'

Sanchez squirmed. 'A coincidence. The plans had been under scrutiny for many months up to that time.'

'That's very helpful,' I said, meaning the exact opposite. 'Just to complete the picture, can you confirm my understanding that before the Council could consider the Tierra Nueva plan they would require an official report certifying that all aspects of the process complied in full with the technical requirements of the law?'

'That's correct.'

'And you provided such a report?'

'Correct.'

'Thank you,' I said. I could easily have challenged his view of the law, but decided not to. 'I'm rather new to Spain,' I continued. 'So perhaps you can explain the political make-up of the council for me.'

I noticed Mariela's eyes roll upwards.

Sanchez seemed relieved to move on. 'There are seven councillors in total, four from Mr Mora's party and three from the opposition.'

'And how did they vote when the Tierra Nueva plan was considered?' I knew the answer already, but wanted to hear it from Sanchez.

'Mr Mora and his colleagues voted in favour and the three opposition councillors voted against.' Sanchez forced a week smile.

'And would you say your report was in any way influential in that vote?' I returned his smile with a cynical grin.

Suddenly, Sanchez exploded. 'What are you implying? How dare you come into my office and question my integrity like this?'

'I wasn't aware I had questioned anyone's integrity, Mr Sanchez.' I forced a look of surprise. 'I am simply trying to understand the background to this case.'

'This case! You mean the death of Mr Mora. What has any of this got to do with that?'

'Mr Mora was murdered, Mr Sanchez, and there is every possibility that his murder was linked to the approval of the controversial development plans.'

Sanchez's mouth gaped. 'Murdered?'

I had him on the run. Now was the time to press home an advantage. 'Sergeant Poquet has a few questions she'd like you to answer.'

I glanced at Mariela and nodded towards the file resting on her knee. Right on cue she pulled the photograph from the file and slid it across the table. 'Have you seen this before, Mr Sanchez?' she asked.

I studied Sanchez's face carefully, watching his reactions. His first glance at the photo brought only a squint and no obvious sign of recognition. He lifted a pair of gold rimmed half-moon spectacles from the breast pocket of his shirt and placed them on the end of his nose to study the photograph more carefully. I noticed his eyes first narrow as he found his focus and then suddenly widen as he took in the content then widen further as he appeared to realise the significance of what was before him. There was a pause as he considered the implications, inhaled deeply and made a deliberate effort to compose himself. From his reactions I was fairly sure he had never seen the photograph before and he was wondering whether we were aware of the background.

'No, I've never seen this before. Where did you get it?' He was fighting hard to maintain his composure though the faint beads of sweat on his brow gave away his obvious anxiety.

'It was one of several similar photographs we recovered from Mr Mora's house.' Mariela's tone was flat, and she allowed the silence to linger before asking her next question.

Sanchez ran a forefinger across his brow, trying hard to make it look like a casual movement.

'Do you recognise the place where the photograph was taken?' Mariela asked, giving nothing away.

Sanchez's face began to redden as he realised Mariela's question was entirely rhetorical. His shoulders slumped and his whole demeanour changed as he grasped the significance of the photograph. His next reaction would be critical.

'Why do you ask when you obviously know this was taken at the Club Erotica? Look, this could be very embarrassing for me – my wife, my family. What do you intend to do with this?'

It was interesting that his first thought was for the potential shame that would result if the photograph became public. Either he was a consummate liar, cleverly using his embarrassment to divert attention from any more sinister connotations, or, as I was inclined to believe, he was genuinely unaware of the possibility that the photograph might have been used to blackmail him. Even so, I wasn't prepared to let him off the hook that easily.

'We have a problem here, Mr Sanchez, don't we?' I watched his face twist into a frown. 'You see, knowing that this photograph was in Mr Mora's possession, a reasonable person might well presume it had been obtained for a purpose. And that purpose might well have been to blackmail you. And that blackmail could have taken several forms. It could have been in the form of a demand for money...' I paused. '...or it could have been used to pressurise you into writing a positive report in respect of the Tierra Nueva project.'

'It was neither of those things,' Sanchez protested. 'I've told you. I've never seen that photograph before. Mora never demanded money from me and I stand by my report to the council.'

Time to switch tack. 'We found something else in Mora's house,' I said, watching dark sweat stains spread beneath Sanchez's armpits, turning his pale blue shirt to a darker shade. 'A considerable sum of money – a quarter of a million euros in fact. The deputy Mayor, Mr Santos, was trying to recover it. No one seems to know anything about it; where it came from or who it belongs to, or at least no one is telling us. Such a large sum of money, it's a mystery. I just wondered if you can help us.'

Sanchez maintained his frown, but it changed from one of puzzlement to one of contemplation. He was, I realised, considering his options.

'Look,' he said at last. 'If I tell you about the money, can we forget about the photograph? I mean, it doesn't have to be made public does it? I've told you, I've never seen it before so it has no relevance here, does it?'

We couldn't forget about the photograph, of course, but it would do no harm to dangle a carrot. 'If what you have told us is true, then the photograph may prove to be irrelevant to our investigation in which case it may never be needed as evidence. You were saying... about the money?'

Sanchez was thinking about my last statement. I guessed he had hoped for more of an assurance, but he must have realised it was as good as he was going to get.

'The money came from Tierra Nueva. It was an advance payment to secure water resources for the new development.' His answer had the ring of a pre-rehearsed statement.

'Then why was it in Mora's house and not the town hall's bank account?'

Sanchez kneaded his temples as if trying to ease a growing headache. 'It was just a matter of accountancy.'

I almost laughed. 'A matter of accountancy,' I said with exaggerated disbelief.

'Yes, Mora insisted the money was paid in cash. I'm sure it would have been paid into the council's bank account at some stage.'

I doubted that very much, but didn't argue. What Sanchez had said at least told me one thing. 'So you knew about the money?' I tried to look and sound perplexed, though the practical implications of Eduardo Moreno's little speech about not allowing process to get in the way of progress were becoming clearer by the minute.

'Well, um yes... at least I was aware of it, but I had no idea of what was actually discussed behind the scenes.'

It was time for me to be dumbfounded. 'But surely as an officer of the council you have a fiduciary responsibility to the taxpayers. Didn't you even think about reporting this to someone?'

Sanchez sat upright in his chair and folded his arms across his chest. 'I am the technical officer to the council. I have no responsibility whatsoever for financial matters.'

What surprised me most of all was that Sanchez actually believed that what he was saying gave him absolute immunity from any kind of responsibility for the misuse of public money.

'Besides,' he continued unabashed, 'as Mayor, Mr Mora had the power to decide these things. If he wanted the money in cash for reasons best known to him, then it was within his power to accept payment in that way.'

Dumbfounded became incredulous. 'Are you seriously trying to tell me that as Mayor, Mr Mora considered it acceptable to receive money ostensibly on behalf of the council and keep it tucked away in the base of the wardrobe in his bedroom?'

'He's the Mayor,' Sanchez replied with a shrug as if that explained everything. And indeed in Sanchez's eyes it did.

'Who's responsible for financial matters in this town hall?' I asked, assuming there must be a senior accountant; an auditor even.

'That would be councillor Santos.'

'You mean Paco Santos, the deputy Mayor?' I forced as much astonishment as I could, which wasn't hard in the circumstances.

'Yes.'

'And did he know about the cash paid to Mora?' The answer was obvious given that we had found Santos lifting the base of the wardrobe in Mora's bedroom.

'I believe so, yes.'

'You believe so? Did he or didn't he know about the cash?'

'I heard it mentioned in his presence, so he must have known.'

'And who else was present when the money was "mentioned"?'

'Mora, Santos and me... but it was just a casual conversation I happened to overhear.'

I bet it was. Sanchez was simply trying to distance himself from events. His face was stern, deadpan. I sensed he had said all he was going to say on the subject. I glanced towards Mariela who had been watching proceedings with a certain enjoyment though her face barely betrayed it. I met her eyes then raised my eyebrows. We were beginning to develop a sixth sense, I felt, as she came in right on cue.

'Where were you on the evening of 20th June this year, Mr Sanchez?'

I was waiting for a jolt, a startled expression on Sanchez's face, but this was one question he had anticipated well before we had arrived in his office.

'I was with Mr Mora here in the town hall. We were discussing a number of minor planning issues due to be considered at the next council meeting. He left just after 9.30pm and I stayed on for an hour or so to finish a report and tidy my desk.'

'Was anyone else in the town hall at the time?' Mariela asked.

'No. There was just the two of us and I locked up after I left.'

'And what time did you return home?'

'Around 10.30pm.'

'And someone can verify that?'

'My wife... but is that really necessary?' He was obviously thinking again about the photograph.

Mariela glanced in my direction and I gave her a gentle nod. 'In the circumstances, yes it is,' she said.

'You're sure you went straight home? You didn't stop off anywhere else on the way?' I interjected, twisting the knife.

'No. Check with my wife if you really must.'

Sanchez had already told us more than he wanted to, but only because of the photograph. Yet everything he had told us was designed to distance himself from any involvement in the questionable dealings of Mora and Santos. His protestations of innocence and his blatant avoidance of any kind of responsibility for the misuse or misappropriation of money would never have stood up in a British court where public servants were bound by a strict code of ethics. But this was Spain and from what I was beginning to understand, I suspected his actions (or lack thereof) would be deemed entirely reasonable in the circumstances. However, one thing was certain. Sanchez was in this affair up to his thick flabby neck.

'Thank you, Mr Sanchez. You've been very helpful,' I lied, signalling to Mariela that it was time to leave.

'Glad to be of assistance,' he said, rising from his seat and taking a handkerchief from his pocket to wipe his face. 'Um, about the photograph?'

'Sergeant Poquet will be hanging on to that for a while. It's far too early to say whether or not it will be of relevance to our investigation.'

Sanchez hesitated as if he was about to protest. I decided to fill the void.

'I have just realised,' I said, looking at Mariela, 'from what Mr Sanchez has told us he must have been the last person to see Mr Mora alive. Am I right?'

'That's correct, Captain Fernandez, apart from the murderer of course,' Mariela said, the gold flecks in her hazel eyes twinkling.

'You really enjoyed that, didn't you?' Mariela said as we left the town hall.

'I don't know what you mean,' I protested.

Mariela snorted. 'And where did you get all that stuff about planning law, technical reports and General Plans?'

'It always pays to prepare, Mariela.' I adopted a professorial tone. 'That way you can ask the right questions and know the answers before they are given; a distinct advantage when dealing with slippery customers like Sanchez. I spent a couple of hours on the internet last night. There's an organisation here in Valencia called *Abusos Urbanisticos No* – AUN – they've been campaigning for years against corruption and injustice caused by Valencia's planning laws. They've even taken cases to the European Parliament. Their web site contains a detailed explanation of the most common forms of abuse and there are detailed case studies, including one about the situation here in Beniforell.'

'And there was me thinking you didn't even know how to turn on the computer.'

'There's a great deal you don't know about me, Mariela.'

'And vice versa,' she said tersely. 'So what do you think about Sanchez?'

'I think Sanchez is as bent as the rest of them and I have no doubt he was on a promise of some kind if he helped get the plans through. But corruption is not our focus is it? This is a murder investigation and we can certainly add Sanchez to the list of suspects. I want you to check with his wife. We still don't have an exact time of death, especially as Mora died sometime after he fell, or was pushed. We need to be precise about what time Sanchez arrived home that night. He knew about the money and kept quiet. As I've said before, a quarter of a million euros is a great deal of money and corrupt, greedy people have a tendency to fall out when it comes to dividing up the spoils.'

'I suppose that's possible,' Mariela said, thumbing her chin. 'Mora had the money and was holding on to it. If you're right then Santos and Sanchez were in on the deal and expected their fair shares. But once the plans were approved by the council, Mora had little use for the others and perhaps he was trying to freeze them out. They could hardly go running to the police could they?'

It sounded plausible to me, but we were a long way from finding out who actually killed Mora and why. I looked at my watch, just past noon.

'You say paella is always eaten at lunchtime, yes?'

'Yes, why?'

'Come on then, let's go to L'Era in Parcent. I promised you a lunch, remember?'

'Actually you promised me a dinner, but lunch will do fine.'

A paella for two is a pitiful sight. The whole point of the dish, it seemed to me, was for friends to gather in numbers and share a giant dustbin lid-sized pan of steaming fish, meat and rice and we were surrounded by people doing just that. Our own paella was served in a pan about the size of a large serving plate and though the content was the same as everyone else's we looked and felt out of place sitting at a cosy table for two tucked away in a quiet corner.

The small metal *paellera* was burned black on the underside and caked with a layer of soot from the wood burning stove over which it had been cooked. The saffron-tinted, sticky-soft rice was dotted with pieces of meat that looked as if they had been hacked from a carcass with an axe. I could just about distinguish chicken, rabbit and pork but there could easily have been other sources of flesh. As I had ordered a traditional Paella Valenciana, there was fish too, though I had so far identified only a few chunks of squid and four whole prawns precisely placed on the top of the rice as if to prove that they were really there. Sliced broad beans, butter beans and wedges of red pepper completed the assortment along with a garnish of quartered lemons.

A bottle of red wine appeared, un-ordered, on the table and I half filled two chunky glass tumblers. My first sip confirmed my initial suspicions; it was harsh, heavy with tannin and with a strong after taste of wood – the perfect accompaniment to rustic food – as the label might have said, had there been one on the bottle.

I allowed Mariela first use of the serving spoon and watched her lift a modest portion of food onto her plate before dowsing it with lemon juice. My turn. I scraped the bottom of the dish with the spoon to reveal that most prized part of the dish – a layer of crispy caramelised rice.

'*Socarrat*,' I declared, 'my favourite part of the paella.'

'I didn't realise you were an *aficionado*,' Mariela said as she lifted a chunk of meat with her fingers and nibbled the flesh from a splintered piece of bone, licking her glossy lips when she had finished. 'You must have eaten quite a few to know about *socarrat*. Did your mother cook paella in England?'

'My father. He taught my mother as well, but she never really mastered it. Either the rice went mushy or she managed to burn it to a cinder.'

'And your wife?'

'My ex-wife, you mean. She was Argentinean and she never cooked paella in her life. In fact she rarely cooked, full stop.'

'Is that why she's your ex-wife?' Mariela asked with a hint of a smile.

There were many reasons why my marriage ended after just two years and my wife's inability to cook was not among them. But I had no wish to share the details with Mariela, so I simply reciprocated her smile and returned to scraping the bottom of the *paellera*.

'Is your mother still alive?' Mariela asked, and then stuttered. 'Oh, I'm sorry, I'm prying. It's just that you told me your father died and left you the house in Parcent, but you have never mentioned your mother.'

The conversation was straying into areas I preferred to avoid. I needed to regain control. 'My mother died shortly after my father. And you, what about your parents? You've never mentioned them.'

Mariela lowered her eyes and spooned another portion of paella onto her plate. 'My parents died when I was fourteen – a car crash. I was brought up by a maiden aunt, my father's sister.'

A conspicuous silence fell between us and I sensed we had both said all we had to say on the subject of our respective parents.

'So why the Guardia Civil?' I asked, trying to fill the void.

'I was eighteen. My aunt and I never really got on. It wasn't that we hated each other; it was simply that bringing up a teenage niece had never figured in her plans. She took me in out of a sense of duty and did her best, but I'd be the first to admit that I didn't always make life easy for her.'

I raised my eyebrows in mock surprise hoping to elicit further details, but Mariela sidestepped my tacit enquiry and moved on. 'We lived in Murcia and I needed to get away. Joining the Guardia Civil gave me the opportunity, since the initial training was based in the barracks at Alicante. I signed up in 1997 and spent the first seven years in uniform, then moved to the detective branch in 2004.'

Looking over at Mariela, the blond haired beauty with a face and figure that would have been the envy of many a budding super model, I found it hard to imagine why she would have been attracted to the harsh, pseudo-military regime of the Guardia Civil.

'It can't have been easy leaving home at eighteen and adjusting to a soldierly way of life.'

'That depends on where you've come from. It wasn't easy, no, but it gave me my independence and taught me to be self-reliant.'

'And you like the job?'

'I'm still here aren't I?'

That didn't exactly answer my question, but I guessed it was as far as I was going to get, on the topic of work at least.

'And is there anyone else in your life?' I asked with a degree of ambiguity. Mariela met my question with a frown. 'A boyfriend... or something like that?' I clarified.

'Something like what?' Mariela's frown deepened and her eyes narrowed.

'You know what I mean... someone you're seeing?'

'Why do you ask?'

This was getting silly. 'Forget I asked. I didn't mean to pry.'

'The answer is no. There's no boyfriend... for the moment at least. What about you?'

The first thought that entered my head was Rosana, but for some reason, I'm not sure why, I denied her presence in my life. 'Like you, I'm unattached, at the moment.' I glanced across at Mariela, met her eyes for a second then glanced away.

'*Terminado*?' the waiter said before responding to our nods and lifting the *paellera* from between us.

I wasn't clear where the conversation was heading, if it was heading anywhere beyond small talk. The chirp of Mariela's mobile phone broke the silence and she reached into her clutch bag to retrieve the phone and answer the call. She listened intently, but said nothing. Her grim-faced expression left little doubt about the seriousness of the call.

'I'll tell him as soon as I see him,' she said as she flipped the phone shut. 'That was Teresa,' she said. 'It seems

145

Colonel Cardells is on the warpath. He's demanding to know where you are. He wants to speak to you straight away. Haven't you got your mobile with you?'

'I switched it off when we arrived at the restaurant. I hate the damn things, don't you?'

'You're not supposed to like them, just use them so people can contact you if need be.'

'That's my point – if need be. In my experience there's very little in life that can't wait until later. Besides, we're entitled to a lunch break, aren't we? Now, what about pudding, or a coffee perhaps?'

'I think you'd better call Cardells first. I don't think he'll appreciate being kept waiting by an almond tart.'

'Almond tart? Sounds perfect to me. Does it come with custard?'

'Where the hell have you been?' Cardells demanded at the end of the telephone as soon I was put through. I was back in the office at Jalon with a substantial portion of paella resting heavy in my belly and still miffed that a swirl of squirty synthetic cream was the best the cook in L'Era had been able to conjure up to moisten the dry almond sponge cake.

'Out and about,' I replied, swallowing a burp that brought the taste of rough red wine back into my mouth.

'Don't give me "out and about." You're supposed to be investigating a murder, but from what I hear you've taken it upon yourself to open up a one-man inquiry into corruption in town planning.'

It wasn't so much the nature of the comment as the timing that struck me as odd. No sooner had we left Sanchez squirming in the town hall in Beniforell, than Cardells was on the phone questioning my actions. In less time than it takes to munch a paella and almond tart, details of my enquiries had filtered through to Cardells. I doubted Sanchez had Cardells' phone number in his Filofax, but I guessed he knew someone who did.

'I have just been following up relevant lines of enquiry,' I said ambivalently, waiting for Cardells' next move.

'Well, it doesn't seem like that to me. Sniffing around town halls, questioning political decisions and casting aspersions. This is a murder investigation and you'd do better sticking to the facts instead of poking your nose into matters that don't concern you.'

My suspicions were confirmed, but by Cardells' standards this was a mild rebuke, well short of keep your nose out. I tempered my response accordingly.

'You can rest assured, Colonel, that I'm sticking to the facts – method, means and motive – they're my watch words in trying to get to the truth about Mora's murder. But to get to that truth I can't afford to leave any stone unturned and if I happen across a can of worms in the process, I can't really turn a blind eye.' The clichés were flowing beautifully, I thought, so I ended on one more for good measure. 'You'll just have to trust me to sort the wheat from the chaff.'

The trouble with idioms is that they rarely translate directly into a foreign language. A fish out of water, for example, means absolutely nothing to a Spaniard, but talk about an octopus in a garage and he'll understand precisely what you mean. Cardells was suitably baffled by my onslaught.

'Well just make sure you do stick to the facts. Finding Mora's murderer is what's important, anything else is peripheral. And remember, when you go fishing for a sardine you might just catch a shark.'

I wondered if this was another misconstrued Spanish idiom or if it was meant to be a warning of some kind. 'I'll certainly bear that in mind, Colonel,' I said, still wondering what it was I was bearing in mind.

'Just make sure you do.'

CHAPTER FIFTEEN

It didn't come as a complete surprise when Eduardo Moreno called me early the next morning. He just happened to be passing through Jalon and wondered if I could spare the time to bring him up to date on the investigation so far as it related to his client, Paco Santos. I doubted that was the real purpose of the call, but went along with the charade all the same, even accepting his invitation to lunch. I was beginning to realise that in Spain lunch was more than just a midday meal it was something of an institution; a prequel to siesta and the time when serious business was conducted. It also occurred to me that Moreno wanted to talk on neutral territory.

Restaurant Cara Mull on the outskirts of Jalon is just a few of minutes from the police station. It was another fine day of the kind that was monotonously predictable at this time of year – cloudless, clear blue sky, hardly a breath of wind and temperatures rising from hot in the morning to searing by mid afternoon. I decided to walk the half mile or so to the restaurant, but before I was half way there the term "mad dogs and Englishmen" was at the forefront of my mind. I removed my jacket and carried it draped over my shoulder, but even so my shirt was sticking to my skin and my face was dripping with sweat.

It would be easy to miss Cara Mull, set well back from the road to Benissa and almost hidden behind a frontage of waist-high weeds. The discreet name board was so subtle it was almost invisible and, unlike most restaurants hereabouts, there was no road-side sandwich-board promoting the *menú del dia*. I had driven by the place several times and wondered if it ever actually opened.

I was picking my way through the pot-holed car park when a large silver BMW swung in from the road and parked immediately in front of the entrance, leaving a cloud of dust in its wake. Moreno emerged from his air-conditioned cocoon looking cool and confident in an immaculate pale grey suit and sparkling white shirt.

'You walked?' he said with a deliberate air of surprise as if to reinforce my own thoughts about mad dogs and Englishmen as his cold hand clenched my sticky palm. 'We'll be cooler inside, I think,' he said leading the way past the sun-drenched front terrace and into the welcome chill of the restaurant, elegantly laid out with neat rows of linen-topped tables set with precisely folded napkins, silver cutlery and gleaming goblets.

To my surprise there was indeed a menú del dia or more accurately, a *plato del dia*, since there was only one meal on offer and it turned out to be a welcome change from the previous day's stodgy paella and almond cake. A light salad of sautéed chicken strips with toasted pine nuts was followed by a small brochette of prime beef fillet accompanied by (as the menu stated) a timbale (or should it have been thimble) of grilled vegetables surrounded by a swirl of sticky balsamic dressing. The chef had obviously discovered *cocina nueva*, but I wasn't complaining.

Our conversation was guarded and cautious. Moreno was fishing for information and I was giving nothing away beyond, "pursuing several lines of enquiry." Moreno insisted on topping up my glass with the excellent Valdepeñas Gran Reserva he had ordered without consulting me, but he was wasting his time if he thought it would loosen my tongue. As we tackled the wine-poached pear with ice cream, Moreno changed tack, telling me that his eldest daughter was excited at the prospect of being crowned fiesta queen in his local village just south of Valencia. He bemoaned the expense of the occasion which necessitated a complete new wardrobe, not to mention several parties for friends and family. I doubted the cost would make a serious dent in his budget and sensed our conversation was finally moving to its intended purpose.

'Do you have children?' he asked.

'No,' I replied, unwilling to explain more.

'You're divorced, I understand,' he added hesitantly, raising an eyebrow as if anticipating my obvious response – how do you know that?. But I was not going to play his game.

'Yes,' I replied, focussing on the last of the pear and scooping up the cinnamon flavoured juice.

There was brief pause during which I suspected he was considering his next move. I resisted the temptation to ask him what he was after and why he had really asked to meet me.

'Coffee?' he asked at length.

I thought of saying no and inventing an urgent appointment, but curiosity got the better of me. 'Yes, I'd like an *Americano*, thank you,' I said, wondering if I had fallen into some kind of trap.

'Two Americanos and two brandies,' he said to the waitress as she cleared the dessert glasses. 'Do you have Cardinal Mendoza?'

'I think so,' she replied.

I thought of protesting, but Cardinal Mendoza is one of my favourite Gran Solera de Jerez brandies; a rival to any French cognac. Two minutes later we were served with steaming black coffees and two large brandy snifters half-filled with the rich, dark aromatic liquor. Moreno pulled a packet of Villiger Export cigars from his jacket pocket, lifting the lid and waving them under my nose. For a brief moment I was tempted, remembering the intense pleasure I had gained from the nicotine hit and the waft of tobacco smoke until two years ago when I had forced myself through the long and painful withdrawal from my addiction.

'You don't mind if I smoke do you?' he said, unwrapping the paper from the square-shaped cigar and flicking a silver Dunhill lighter into life. The aroma of Havana tobacco drifted across the table and Moreno wafted his hand to disperse the smoke. It occurred to me that with a gallon of coffee and brandy and Moreno's five inch cigar, we might be here for some time.

'Have you ever heard of *enchufe*, Captain Fernandez?' Moreno drew hard on the cigar raising his head as he exhaled, sending another cloud of smoke drifting towards the ceiling.

My father never mastered English beyond a very rudimentary level and my English mother had extended her school Spanish in order to accommodate my father's unwillingness to learn the language of his adopted homeland. As a result, Spanish was the language that dominated my childhood at home. In everyday conversation I was near fluent, though I was aware that I had picked up a trace of a South American accent from my Argentinean ex-wife who also preferred to use Spanish at home. But domestic conversation is limited in scope and, as I was discovering, not having worked amongst Spaniards before, there were some glaring gaps in my understanding of the subtleties of Spanish usage.

Enchufe, I knew meant a plug or a socket or a connection of some kind, but I couldn't quite see the linkage of these definitions in the context of my conversation with Moreno.

'You'll have to enlighten me,' I replied, trying not to sound embarrassed.

'It's a term used a lot in business these days. You're new to Spain I know, so I'm not surprised you've never heard of it.' Moreno narrowed his eyes and glanced sideways. 'How can I explain?' He turned his head to meet my eyes. 'In business or in one's working environment one is naturally going to make connections either by accident or by design with people in other professions or with differing interests or callings. These contacts may be frequent or fleeting but one never knows when they might be useful. We all have need from time to time to pick someone else's brain in a field of knowledge that may be outside our own scope or perhaps we need a favour when... how can I put this? When normal channels might prove inconvenient or cumbersome.' Moreno seemed to be scrutinising my face for a reaction.

I had an inkling where the conversation was heading, but said nothing.

'In Spain we call this *enchufe*. I guess you could call it pulling strings or using one's connections to exercise a degree of influence. There's nothing sinister about it, nothing at all, it's just a way of getting things done that helps oil the wheels of business. It's quite commonplace

151

and a routine part of working life in Spain. In fact I sometimes think it would be almost impossible to get ahead without it, given Spain's propensity for burdensome red tape. Are you getting my drift?'

I was getting his drift all right and realised he was practicing a bit of *enchufe* as we spoke; or at least trying to.

'I think so,' I said. 'It's rather like Masonry, but without the funny handshakes.'

I didn't realise it at the time, but in using the Spanish term for stone masonry – *albañilería* – I had left Moreno dumbfounded. The correct term for Freemasonry is *masonería*. Small wonder Moreno's response reminded me of Fawlty Towers' maniacal Spanish waiter, Manuel.

'*Que*?' he said, prompting me to chuckle.

I didn't think it worth the effort of trying to explain. 'I'm sorry,' I said. 'Something got lost in translation. You were saying?'

'Enchufe,' he repeated.

'Ah yes. You scratch my back and I'll scratch yours. Is that what you are trying to explain?'

'Well, not exactly, but close enough.' He puffed on the cigar again and sipped the Cardinal Mendoza.

My patience was wearing thin. 'Look, Eduardo...' I deliberately used his first name in an effort to suggest we were getting along, '...is there a point to all this?'

He took my cue. 'Well, Michael, my point is that we may be in a position to help each other.'

'Oh?'

'In the matter of the quarter of a million euros you recovered from Mora's house.'

'Mr Santos would like it back, you mean?'

'No, no, Michael,' Moreno smiled benignly. 'Santos is just a bit player in all this. My approach is on behalf of the rightful owner of the money, or should I say the original source.'

'And that is..?'

Moreno leant forward and shifted his eyes from side to side as if to check no one was listening, which was unlikely since we were now the only customers left in the restaurant and gradually disappearing in a cloud of cigar smoke.

'You're teasing, I think,' he said. 'I suspect you have already worked out for yourself that the source of the money was Salvador Guardiola, or at least one of his companies.'

'I see,' I said, then added, 'The thought had crossed my mind. And Señor Guardiola would like his money back?'

'No, Michael, you misunderstand me. I've explained before, the money is not important, but Señor Guardiola's reputation is.' Moreno waived away another drift of smoke. 'I can assure you Michael that the money was a quite legitimate payment as part of the normal planning process. You see, technically, it was a down payment to the council to help secure water resources for the planned new development.'

Where had I heard that before?

'*Technically?*' I enquired, forcing my face to a frown.

'Yes. It's just unfortunate that the Mayor of Beniforell chose to hold on to it.'

'So what's the problem? Guardiola can simply explain what the money was for and he can claim it back or better still, it can be paid into the town hall's coffers.'

Moreno was quick to see through my false naivety. 'I think we both realise it is not quite as simple as that. You see Mora has held on to this money for quite some time and for Señor Guardiola to come forward now might give rise to questions.'

'Questions he would rather not answer?'

'Exactly. As I have said, the money is entirely legitimate, it's just that if its existence became public knowledge some people might seek to put an unfair slant on it. You'll understand I am sure, Michael, that development plans such as those for Beniforell always attract a degree of opposition. And those opponents would seize any opportunity to denigrate the promoters or the town hall, however unfairly, if they thought it would help their cause. Señor Guardiola simply wishes to avoid that possibility.'

Moreno studied me closely, trying to read my reaction, but this time I was genuinely perplexed. 'You'll have to excuse my naivety, but I really don't understand. If Guardiola doesn't want the money back and if it can't be paid to the town hall how can he solve his problem?'

153

Moreno smiled; a kindly sympathetic smile of the kind you might show to a bemused child. 'We were rather hoping you might be able to help there, Michael.'

'Oh?'

'We have a proposition to make to you. If Señor Guardiola could provide you with sufficient documentary proof as to the source of the money and its intended purpose, we hope you might be able to satisfy yourself that it could quite legitimately be returned so that its existence need never become public knowledge.'

I'm not normally slow on the uptake, but now I was completely baffled. 'But I thought you said he didn't want the money back?'

A sheepishness crept across Moreno's face and he lowered his voice to a whisper. '*Enchufe*,' he said. 'All Señor Guardiola wants is for the money to disappear so that its existence could never be called into question. If you could find a way to sign off the money so that it left police custody and could never be used in evidence then – how can I put this? – the final destiny of the cash itself would be a secondary consideration.'

Now at last the penny dropped. Moreno was offering me a bribe, a bribe of a quarter of a million euros. My initial reaction was one of indignation. How dare he? But somehow the thought of all those noughts flashed through my brain. And this was Spain after all. Perhaps this kind of transaction was common place; an accepted part of everyday life in a country where it seemed everyone was on the take. The money was just sitting there in a secure room at the police station. Guardiola didn't want it back and it couldn't be paid to the town hall without arousing suspicion about Guardiola's motives for paying it in the first place. So I thought, why look a gift horse in the mouth? But what would I do with a suitcase full of notes? I couldn't just pop along to a bank and pay it in – there are rules and questions to be answered. My curiosity was sufficiently aroused to find out more. 'I see,' I said. 'I'll have to think about it. There are risks involved in what you have proposed.'

Moreno's lips narrowed to a knowing smile; the kind of smile that suggested he knew the bait had been taken. 'Of course there are risks, but there are ways of reducing them to an absolute minimum.'

I gained the impression that this kind of transaction was routine for Moreno and systems were already in place to ensure the money could be deposited in such a way that it would be well hidden from prying eyes. I also guessed there were systems in place to ensure that if something went wrong Moreno, and more importantly Guardiola, had their backs covered.

'As I said, I'll have to think about it. And I think perhaps I need to meet with Señor Guardiola to discuss the details.'

Moreno's eyes narrowed. 'I'm not sure that will be possible. Señor Guardiola likes to keep his distance from these things, but you can be assured I have his full authority in such matters.'

'I'm sure you do,' I said. 'But I have a problem. Much as this kind of thing may be routine to you, it's a big deal for me. A deal that requires trust on both sides and since you are merely the monkey, I think it only reasonable that I should meet the organ-grinder himself.'

The scowl on Moreno's face told me that this particular English idiom translated into Spanish without ambiguity.

'I'll see what I can do,' he said, stubbing out his half-smoked cigar before emptying his brandy glass in one gulp.

I should really have insisted on sharing the bill for lunch, but that seemed rather pointless given the nature of our conversation, so I didn't offer even the slightest resistance when he handed his platinum card to the waitress. I also declined his offer of a lift as we parted. Much as I would have preferred to avoid the walk back to Jalon in the peaking heat of late afternoon, I'd had enough of Moreno's company.

CHAPTER SIXTEEN

I can't blame my half-Spanish ancestry for being a loner in my youth. True, my Spanish name, Fernandez, not to mention the Miguel-Ángel, caused a certain amount of teasing in my school days, but I learned to cope with that by toughening-up and confronting anyone who tried to poke fun. Kids get picked on for all kind of things, but an unusual name is not so hard to bear when you can give as good as you get. I guess that made me a bully, and like all bullies I was able to surround myself with admirers who thought it was cool to hang out with someone who stood no nonsense from anyone.

All that changed when details of my father's leprosy filtered out. Suddenly those fickle friends began to shun me. They didn't mock or harass me – they knew better than that – but their silent spurning was more painful than any bullying blows. Though I never realised at the time, my parents must have suffered equally from being ostracised by former friends and neighbours. They reacted by moving away to another district where they hoped their secret could be maintained. But it's a small world, as they say, and it was never long before the gossips caught up. My reaction, as soon as I was able, was to distance myself from the source of the problem – my parents – and to close the book on what I saw as an unwanted obstacle to a normal life. I'm not proud of myself for doing that, but experience taught me that denial was easier than explanation, for such is the stigma of leprosy that few people are able to confront it with an open mind. This I understood all too well, since I shunned my own father when, as a thirteen-year-old, I first learned of his affliction.

We were reconciled several years later, but if I am honest, the warmth and tenderness that characterised my early childhood had disappeared down a chasm so deep it could never be fully retrieved. My father, and later my mother, both said they understood, but I have always felt their forgiveness was wholly undeserved.

University provided me with the first opportunity to escape my parents. I rejected a place at Loughborough because it was too near home. In truth, I was not an academic and my 'A' level results meant that my choices were limited, but my Spanish gave me a head start in finding a place on the European Studies degree course at Durham University. I was an average student, conscientious, but not gifted. I made few friends, since I always fought shy of revealing anything personal about myself and this gave the impression I was aloof. It was at Durham that I first dropped the name Miguel-Ángel and opted for Michael, believing it would make life easier and avoid the obvious questions about my Spanish ancestry. This, I kept secret from my parents throughout my three years at university, during which I returned home as infrequently as possible.

It was in my final year that I first met Angelica, an overseas student from Argentina doing a post graduate course in International Politics. It wasn't exactly a whirlwind romance. Our shared language seemed to bring us together, but our contrasting cultures eventually drove us apart. This was not before we married in the rose-tinted aftermath of newly found uninhibited sexual fulfilment that proved, predictably, to be insufficient to bind us together when the cracks appeared in our relationship. We separated without acrimony after little more than two years.

By this time my father was becoming increasingly ill, suffering liver and kidney damage as a side effect of the drugs he was taking to suppress the leprosy. So I returned to Nottingham in a misguided effort at atonement, and though I re-established contact with my parents we never managed to put past resentments behind us. I settled in a rented flat not far from my parents home and enrolled on a graduate training course with Nottingham Constabulary. I was one of the first intake of graduate trainees and fast-tracked to Inspector in just three years, causing bitter resentment amongst many of the longer serving rank-and-file officers. And so it was that my persona was moulded and I learned to hide behind a self-created façade of detachment and aloofness at work and in my private life.

It always surprises me that people think detectives work seven days a week. It's as if they believe that in the hunt for criminals there is never a moment to be lost. I've known some detectives who feel that way too, and they usually end up on the scrap heap, burnt out in their mid forties, unable to function on a normal level and leaving behind wrecked marriages and broken homes. Well, I've got the divorce on my record, but that had absolutely nothing to do my being a workaholic, since I am not.

It was Saturday and I decided have a look around Jalon, since I knew little of the place beyond the Guardia Civil Headquarters. As the largest town in the valley, Jalon was apt to flex its muscles from time to time, though the surrounding villages, which together form the area commonly known as the Vall de Pop, maintain a fierce independence, resisting any attempt to centralise power or public services. The Guardia Civil headquarters, or *comisaría* to give it its proper name, was one exception. In Jalon itself the ayuntamiento had recently decided, officially, to revert to the former Valenciano name of Xaló and, with a fervour rarely evident in Spain, the powers-that-be had replaced every signpost and direction sign within a matter of weeks. That fanaticism explained what happened that Saturday morning when I decided to explore Xaló for the first time.

Parking spaces were at a premium as the local rastro market attracted visitors from far and wide. Coaches spewed out hundreds of day-trippers from Benidorm and enterprising local farmers eagerly relieved frustrated drivers of a few euros for the privilege of parking in olive and orange groves on the fringe of the town centre.

After ten minutes circling the streets of Xaló, I decided to abandon the car at the *comisaría* and walk the short distance to the rastro. As I approached the edge of the town, a blue BMW pulled up at my side and the German driver, glistening with sweat, started jabbering in his native language as he waved a tourist brochure featuring a small scale map. My baffled expression prompted the man to try again in faltering English and it took me a moment or two to realise he was searching for Jalon. 'You are here.' I said. 'Look there's the sign.' I pointed to the signpost just a few metres ahead which featured the insignia of the Comunidad Valenciana above the name XALÓ. It is one thing to change a few road signs, but far more difficult to eradicate years of tourist literature and millions of references on the World Wide Web. I somehow doubted that the ayuntamiento of Xaló had fully thought through the practical implications of their nationalistic zeal.

The bustling weekend rastro market occupied the mile-long frontage to the dry river bed which ran along the edge of the town. The stalls varied from rickety trestle tables to simple blankets laid on the ground and sold everything from household cast-offs and dubious antiques to cheap watches and DVDs. I quickly concluded that much of what was on offer was either stolen, pirated or faked and as I pushed through the hoards of browsing tourists, I realised it was one of those occasions when you would do well to heed advice to keep your hand on your wallet.

Coffee in a nearby bar, La Risa, brought welcome relief from the hustle and bustle of bargain hunters who, having come this far, were determined to spend some of their holiday cash.

I had just sipped the last dregs of a café solo and was waiting for the waitress to bring my change when a flustered English lady in shorts, T-shirt and flip-flops entered the bar towing a large black dog on a length of frayed rope. She moved between the tables jabbering frantically and gesturing to the customers, most of whom were Spanish and greeted her with a look of baffled incomprehension. It was only when she reached a British couple seated at the table adjacent to mine that her predicament became clear. She had paused in the market to admire the dog which had been held in close order by a man whom she presumed to be Spanish. She had struck up a conversation with the man whilst patting the dog on the head. She had a smattering of Spanish and thought the man had said: "You like my dog?" When she answered in the affirmative the man had thrust the makeshift lead into her hand and departed with some haste, disappearing into the throng of market-goers. It was only then she had realised the Spanish man had actually said: "You want my dog?" Now she was desperately seeking either the rightful owner or someone to take charge of the dog as she was due to return on the tour bus to her hotel in Benidorm in twenty minutes time. I heard the listening couple explain that, much as they sympathised with her predicament, they had cats.

'¿*Sabes este perro?*' she said to me as she approached my table. I should perhaps have pointed out that the verb *saber* means "to know" in the sense of knowledge and that the correct verb in the circumstances was *conocer* in the sense of recognising someone or something. Instead I said, '*danke schön*' to the puzzled waitress as she returned with my change and I made my way to the exit.

Just along from the bar I passed an English-run computer shop which reminded me of something I needed to buy. For such a small outlet in an out-of-the-way place like Jalon I was surprised at the range of computer accessories they had in stock. I could have paid less in one of the bigger chain stores, but I found what I was looking for and it was worth the extra to avoid the need for a trip to the coast.

Rosana arrived at my house just before midday with a picnic basket on her arm and a timid smile on her face. Our day out was pre-ordained, arranged by my grandmother and uncle Pepito. I could have protested at their latest interference, but since I had nothing better to do, I decided to go along with their plan – it didn't seem too much of a hardship.

Perhaps it was the reflected light from her simple pink T-shirt, but even without makeup Rosana's complexion seemed more radiant than in the aftermath of her mother's funeral. The dark shadows beneath her eyes had disappeared and her cheeks blushed a pale rose pink. Her short white culottes revealed slender tanned legs that contrasted markedly with my own pasty white legs exposed

160

beneath the shorts I felt obliged to wear in deference to the weather. They reminded me that since I now lived in a hot sunny climate, I needed to give my own flesh an airing from time to time.

The natural curls in Rosana's long dark hair glistened and bounced around her face as we walked together out of the village and down a track leading to the foothills of Carrascal. I had done the gentlemanly thing and taken control of the picnic basket and, despite our recent intimacy, I still felt curiously apprehensive when Rosana linked my arm.

'Where are we going?' I asked, feeling like a schoolboy out on a first date.

'Coll de Rates, to the Font de la Foia,' Rosana replied. 'It's just a short stroll.'

I was sure I detected a hint of sarcasm in her voice as her stride quickened and became more purposeful.

The cultivated groves of oranges, almonds and olives gradually petered out and gave way to bracken and gorse as the track narrowed and inclined more steeply. The air was filled with the scent of wild thyme and rosemary growing in clumps, forcing their way out of the rocky terrain. We passed a straggling prickly oak tree clinging to the edge of a rocky outcrop and then startled a herd of goats foraging on the parched scrub. The goatherd, a wiry old man with a battered straw hat, stood above us in the distance having made the arduous climb to a precarious ledge from where he could keep an eye on his goats. He gave us a cursory wave.

I was relieved when Rosana followed a more level track in the opposite direction. We approached a narrow plateau dotted with a collection of around twenty ramshackle boxes that seemed to be made of cast-off bits of wood and metal, each one bearing a crudely painted number. It was only when we drew closer and I noticed the mass of bees swarming around the boxes that I realised their purpose.

'Does no one steal the honey?' I enquired, baffled by the lack of fencing of any kind.

'The bees provide their own security,' Rosana replied. 'And they know their owners personally.'

'Ah, yes, of course I forgot, everyone knows everyone else in this village.'

Rosana responded with a half-smile, half-scowl from which I was unable to gauge if my attempt at a joke had provoked mirth or irritation.

At the far end of the plateau, a patch of green marked the Font de la Foia where a babbling brook of crystal clear water emerged from a craggy rock and followed a man-made course through a series of small troughs before disappearing again into the ground. We spread a small blanket at the side of the spring in the shade of a gnarled carob tree and removed the contents of the basket. The collection of foil-wrapped parcels revealed cheese, pâté and chorizo along with a *barra*, some tomatoes and a selection of *empanadillas* that resembled small Cornish pasties filled with tuna, meat and spinach. A bottle of white wine, chilled with an ice sleeve, emerged from the bottom of the basket together with a square slab of almond cake. I looked for the red-hot pickled peppers and was relieved not to find them.

We chatted and nibbled our way through the picnic, constantly flapping to discourage the flies that were homing in on the scent of food. Rosana laughed when I told her the story of the woman with the rastro dog.

'I thought you British were supposed to be animal lovers,' she said when I concluded with my German impersonation.

'We are. That's why the woman found herself with the dog in the first place.'

'But not you?'

'I'm allergic to dogs.'

'In the sense that they make you sneeze or something?'

'In the sense that they need to be fed and walked and groomed and leave their hairs on your clothes.'

'What do you think happened to the dog?'

'I've no idea. Perhaps it's enjoying a short holiday in Benidorm, but more likely it's tied to a table outside La Risa, waiting for another animal loving Brit to take pity on it.'

I emptied the last of the bottle of wine and set it to one side. Rosana lay back on the blanket with her hands beneath the back of her head leaving her breasts protruding and the impression of a lacy bra outlined beneath her tightly stretched T-shirt. I nudged closer, feeling my pulse quicken as I looked down on her face. It was a moment to say something profound; something to capture the intimacy of the moment, but words seemed superfluous.

A gossamer thread of saliva stretched momentarily between our lips as we parted. I leaned back, propping myself on one elbow, gazing across at Rosana's face wondering if she was experiencing the same rush of emotions as me as a mixture of pleasure and apprehension fuddled my brain. She turned her head and glanced in my direction smiling shyly. I returned her smile with equal timidity.

'What?' she asked, as the silence between us became protracted.

I wanted to tell her how I felt; how I longed to repeat our kiss and progress beyond that, but I was held back by a nagging doubt and a fear that was borne of uncertainty.

What I wanted to say was, 'I was just thinking how beautiful you are.' Instead I said, 'I was just thinking how beautiful it is here.'

Rosana's smile faded and she turned her head to look at the sky. A gentle breeze fluttered the leaves of the carob tree, causing the dappled sunlight to flicker across her face.

'Are you happy?' I asked.

'Happy?' She seemed surprised by the question. 'You mean now... here... with you?'

'Well, I was thinking in more general terms. Happy here in Parcent? Happy with your life?'

Rosana sat upright and her face creased with puzzlement. 'You sound disapproving.'

'I'm sorry, I didn't mean to.'

'So why did you ask?'

'No particular reason. I just...' I knew what I wanted to say, but couldn't find the words.

'Go on,' she urged.

It was now or never, I thought. 'Rosana, you know I am fond of you.' I realised how corny I sounded, but pressed on. 'I'd like to think we have a future together.' Corny became clichéd. 'But I just don't know if that can happen the way things are.'

'The way things are? What does that mean?' Her tone was tinged with irritation.

'My family, your family, the whole Parcent thing.'

Rosana's face darkened to a scowl. 'Why don't you just stop beating about the bush, Michael, and say what you really mean?'

I felt myself pouting as a childish sense of self-pity enveloped me. 'You know what I mean. You know how I feel about Parcent and what happened to my father. You know I hate being cajoled and manipulated by my family.'

'*Cajoled? Manipulated?* Is that how you feel? Is that why you are here? Because you were pushed into it? And you have the nerve to say you thought we might have a future together. Well I have news for you, Miguel-Ángel Fernandez, there is no future for us.'

The remnants of the meal were suddenly flying into the picnic basket. Rosana grabbed the empty wine bottle by the neck and I flinched momentarily prompting a snort of derision as Rosana dumped it in the basket breaking the glasses in the process. I grabbed her arm, trying to regain a degree of calmness, but she snatched it away.

'Don't touch me,' she yelled. 'Just leave me alone. In fact, why don't you just leave Parcent altogether since you appear to hate the place so much. You obviously hate your family as well, so why don't you just go. And to think it was me that helped your grandmother to find you and now you sneer at her and look down your nose at all of us just because we have a sense of responsibility and family duty; something you would never understand since you abandoned your own parents when the going got tough.'

I could feel the anger rising in my body, my pulse was racing and my muscles tensed. '*Responsibility?*' I bellowed. 'Is that what you call it? Why don't you face the truth Rosana. You left Parcent for the high life in Madrid and Barcelona and when your marriage failed you slunk back here. It was the easy option wasn't it? Hide away rather than face the world and start again. And you're still hiding away, justifying your lack of ambition by tying yourself to caring for your grandmother, sticking your head in the sand, playing the loving granddaughter while you gradually sink in a mountain of debt.'

Rosana's face distorted with anger and surprise. 'So that's what all this is about is it? Who's been blabbing? Pepito I suppose. Well you can tell him to mind his own damn business. I can manage my own affairs without any interference from him – or from you for that matter. Now I see what this is all about. What is it you are more afraid of, Michael? Being stuck with my ailing grandmother or being saddled with a debt-ridden divorcee?'

I realised I had taken it too far. Fuelled by pent up frustration, I had voiced the doubts I had been harbouring since returning to Parcent. Still, I thought, it's best to get these things off your chest; get things out in the open, then you can move on – or not.

The picnic basket hit me full in the chest and crashed to the ground spilling the contents across the blanket. Rosana was on her feet and heading down the track.

'Rosana,' I shouted. 'I'm sorry.'

Not the best Saturday outing I have ever had, I thought, as I gathered the wreckage of the picnic.

I spent the rest of the weekend at home in Parcent trying to avoid all contact with the outside world and wondering how far news of the ill-fated picnic had spread through the village grapevine. By now, I expected I had been cast as the demon interloper of Parcent who mistrusted all of my family and friends and viewed my new neighbours as busybodies with nothing better to do than interfere in other people's lives. Their verdict might not have been too far from the truth, though I was still wondering how I had managed to turn a pleasant summer picnic into a catastrophe of such epic proportions.

I didn't regret broaching the subject of Rosana's view of her life, but there's a fine line between making an enquiry and inferring disapproval and I realised I had crossed it. Well, who cares, I thought, Rosana meant nothing to me, and the last thing I wanted was to be thrust into a relationship with someone saddled with an ageing grandmother and burdened with spiralling debts. The trouble was that though I tried to convince myself I had engineered a lucky escape, I knew I was lying to myself, and I couldn't dispel the feelings of excitement and sensuality I experienced when we were together, or the despondency I felt at the thought that we might never experience that same intimacy again. I would have to find a way to make amends, though I realised it would not be easy to repair such a cavernous rift and a part of me wondered if I might be attempting the impossible.

CHAPTER SEVENTEEN

My melancholic weekend had given me time to mull over the investigation into Mora's death. The trouble was that nothing productive had come of my endless churning of the facts and all my attempts to rationalise the jumble of details had been constantly interrupted by thoughts of Rosana and an overwhelming sadness at the way I had so clumsily brought about a rift between us.

Back at my desk on Monday morning and sifting the dregs of my second cup of coffee, my brain seemed numb and I struggled to find the motivation to think about what to do next in the investigation. As the sun rose sending shafts of light between the slats of the Venetian blind, the thought of a grey drizzly dawn in Nottingham suddenly seemed appealing, as did the idea of familiar surroundings and working amongst people I understood.

The door to the office burst open and Mariela breezed in looking bright and business-like in a tailored pale green suit with a skirt that revealed almost all of her slender legs, exaggerated by sling-backed high heels culminating in sharp pointed toes. Her fine blond hair flowed behind her with the speed of her movement as she rushed excitedly across the room. For a moment my mood was lifted, then plunged as Teresa Blazquez followed Mariela through the door, filling the frame in her sage green uniform and casting a gloomy shadow that darkened my spirits as well as the room.

'Teresa has some interesting news about the Robinson boy,' Mariela said excitedly as she ushered Teresa to the chair opposite my desk.

I should have sat up, leaned forward and shown some interest, but the lost Robinson boy was the last thing on my mind, so I remained slouched in my chair resisting the temptation to allow my eyes to roll upwards to the ceiling.

'Are you listening, Michael? This is important.'

I made the effort to sit upright and focus on Officer Blazquez who met my eyes with a nervous timidity I felt obliged to assuage. 'I'm all ears, Teresa, tell us what you have,' I said with what I hoped was convincing sincerity.

Teresa shuffled the file of papers resting on her lap and began to speak. 'I conducted a search of the *Catastro* records in respect of the chalet in Lliber where the *Centro de Desarollo Espiritual* operated.'

Mariela must have seen the bemused look on my face. 'The *Catastro*,' she said, 'it's the land registry holding property records and details of ownerships.'

Teresa pressed on. 'You can search the records on-line. It's easy. All you need is…'

She heard me deliberately clear my throat.

'Well, the records show that the house was constructed in 2003 and belongs to a company called Propiedades JJM. It seems, however, that the construction was illegal because there is a note on the file that the town hall in Lliber has registered notice of an infraction of building rules. The house is one of several in that area approved by the previous Mayor of Lliber and built without proper authority on rustic land which should never have been developed. The Mayor was ousted in the last municipal elections and the new administration has issued notices against all the illegal buildings.'

So what? I thought. Why should I be interested in another tale of town hall corruption? From what I could gather this was standard practice hereabouts. I tried hard to stifle a yawn, but failed and Teresa sensed my impatience.

'Next I made a search of the *Registro Mercantil*. That's the…'

'I know what the *Registro Mercantil* is,' I snapped.

Teresa looked downcast and glanced over at Mariela.

'Michael, please be patient,' Mariela said. 'This is important.' She nodded to Teresa urging her to continue.

'The Registro shows that the principal shareholder in Propiedades JJM is Juan-Jose Mora.' There was a hint of triumph in Teresa's voice.

It took a few moments for the significance of the information to register. My first thought was that here was evidence of more shady deals by Mora, this time in cahoots with another local Mayor. Then it hit me like a hammer blow. There was a connection, albeit tenuous, between Mora and the disappearance of the Robinson boy. My mind was whirling, trying to pull the threads together. Mora's murder, the money found in his house, Anthony Robinson's disappearance, that poster of the Torc, the *Centro de Desarollo Espiritual*, the chalet built illegally by Propiedades JJM and back to Juan-Jose Mora.

'Of course, it could be just a coincidence,' Mariela said. 'I mean the link between Mora and the *Centro de Desarollo Espiritual* and those posters and Anthony Robinson.'

'I've told you before, Mariela, I don't believe in coincidence.'

We arrived at the Robinson's house an hour later. Graham Robinson opened the door and greeted us with something less than enthusiasm. The thought occurred to me again that he was less concerned than his wife about the progress of our investigation. It was Eileen Robinson who fussed as she greeted us on the small terrace, and ushered us to the plastic table still strewn with the remnants of breakfast.

'Have you got some news about Anthony, Mr Fernandez? Please tell me you've found him.'

I left it to Mariela to calm her. 'We're making progress, but no, we haven't found him yet.'

I wasn't sure whether "yet" was the right word to use in the circumstances since it seemed to offer false hope.

Mariela continued. 'Some new information has come to light and we need to ask you some more questions.'

I still had a feeling that the Robinsons were hiding something or at least holding back, so I had agreed with Mariela that she would lead the questions, leaving me to read their body language.

169

Mrs Robinson looked slightly nervous, or at least concerned, as she sat stiffly in the cushioned chair, fiddling with the hem of her floral print frock. In contrast Graham Robinson looked more relaxed as he sat by her side, leant back and crossed his bare legs exposing a patch of hard cracked skin at the base of his heels where his worn rubber flip-flops dangled loose from his feet.

'Have you ever heard of the Centro de Desarollo Espiritual - the Spiritual Development Centre?' Mariela asked.

A look of what I deemed to be genuine puzzlement crossed both their faces as they exchanged glances.

'No,' Mr Robinson said. 'Why do you ask?'

'Those posters you gave us from Tony's bedroom, the ones with the pictures of wild boars. They depict a mythical figure called Torc considered by some people to have powers to enhance male strength and personal resolve. We wondered where Tony got the posters since they don't seem to be generally available and the only place we found them was a specialist shop in Alicante who had sold several copies to the Spiritual Development Centre. The Centre was based not far from here on the other side of Lliber, so we wondered if Tony had any connection with it.'

Again, the Robinsons exchanged glances.

'I've never heard of this place,' Mrs Robinson answered. 'And Tony certainly never mentioned it. What sort of place is it anyway? It's not one of those cults that brainwash young people is it? Please tell me Tony's not been abducted by Satanists or anything like that.'

Mariela felt the need to offer reassurance. 'No, no, nothing like that. It's just the connection with the posters that's all, and we wondered if Tony had spent any time at the Centre or met any of the people there.'

Graham Robinson interrupted impatiently. 'Why are you asking us? Why don't you arrest the people behind this place and ask them?'

'It's not that easy, Mr Robinson. The Centre closed down some time ago and we've been unable to trace any of the people involved.'

I noted Mariela deliberately refrained from telling them the Centre had been raided and the people involved interrogated before being released. A wise move, I thought.

'Is this all you've got? Is this the only reason you've come back, to ask us about those stupid posters you found?' Graham Robinson's face was turning red with anger. 'You're wasting our time and upsetting my wife. Why don't you just get out there and find the people behind this so-called Spiritual Development Centre or better still find Tony?'

I thought of intervening, but Mariela seemed perfectly in control. 'We're trying to do just that, Mr Robinson. I realise this is upsetting and you were hoping for more positive news, but we felt this was a significant lead and that you might have some more information that could help us.'

'Well we haven't.'

I could understand Graham Robinson's frustration, but it seemed to me he was trying to bring the interview to a premature end when I would have expected him to be more curious about the background to the Spiritual Development Centre and the people behind it. I glanced across at Mariela who responded with an almost imperceptible shrug. I reacted with a faint nod.

'There is something else,' Mariela resumed. 'Do you know a man call Juan-Jose Mora?'

Graham Robinson stiffened and his eyes widened in surprise. His wife's mouth gaped in shock and almost involuntarily her left hand grasped her husband's arm. I knew we had hit a nerve and decided to reinforce our brief advantage with my own intervention.

'It's obvious from your reactions that you know this man, so if you're hiding something from us then you must come clean, otherwise there's little point in us wasting more of our time trying to find Tony.'

It was harsh, I know, but it was time to get things out in the open.

Eileen Robinson tightened her grip on her husband's arm, her eyes became watery and her bottom lip quivered. Graham snatched his arm away and rose to his feet.

'We've never heard of him,' he yelled. 'This is getting us nowhere. You'd better leave now, you're upsetting my wife.'

171

Eileen snatched at his arm and yanked it back, forcing her husband to stumble back into the chair. 'We have to tell them Graham. They need to know, otherwise we might never see Tony again.'

Her eyes were streaming as a flood of tears streaked her face. I rummaged in my pocket in an unsuccessful search for a handkerchief, but Mariela obliged with a paper tissue from her handbag. Eileen dabbed her face then blew her nose hard prompting Mariela to hand her another tissue.

'Perhaps your wife would like a glass of water,' Mariela said.

Graham Robinson stood again and stomped from the terrace into the house. A moment later I heard the front door slam. At last Eileen was ready to pour her heart out. She started slowly and hesitantly, but was encouraged when Mariela shifted her seat and took her by the hand. As she spoke I sensed her story had been pre-rehearsed as if she had imagined herself telling it before.

Tony and Eileen Robinson married in England in 1971. They had lived a normal and relatively happy life. They both had full time jobs – Graham a fireman and Eileen a housing officer with the local council. They were, by most standards, relatively affluent. In the early years they imagined they would like to start a family, but it was not a high priority as they ploughed their joint earnings into establishing a pleasant home on a select development of detached houses on the outskirts of Dartford.

As Eileen approached her mid thirties, they both decided the time was now right and Eileen stopped taking the contraceptive pill. Almost two years passed and nothing happened. Graham had been content to put it down to fate, but Eileen was becoming desperate for a child. Tests showed that, medically, Eileen was perfectly capable of conceiving so she pressured Graham into having tests himself. Eventually he acquiesced, albeit reluctantly, and the tests showed him to be sterile, incapable of fathering a child. It was a desperate time for them both. Graham took the news very badly and started drinking heavily, often staying out all night. Eileen became depressed and pleaded with Graham to consider adoption, but he was adamant in his refusal. The stalemate continued for almost five years as Graham's drinking became worse; so bad that he was arrested on three occasions and finally prosecuted and fined for resisting arrest and assaulting a police officer.

Eileen's depression deepened and eventually became so severe she attempted suicide with an overdose of sleeping pills. She was saved by the providential intervention of a neighbour who just happened to call by. On the afternoon in question Graham was virtually comatose when the police collected him from a local pub and took him to Eileen's hospital bed where he maintained a bedside vigil for almost two days until Eileen eventually came round. It was a seminal moment in their relationship. Graham vowed to quit drinking, a pledge which he had largely fulfilled over the years, and they agreed to pursue the possibility of adoption to achieve Eileen's now desperate desire for a child.

Despite their re-established relationship, the route to adoption brought only frustration. They were both now approaching their forties, a fact that prompted raised eyebrows amongst the social workers considering their suitability as prospective adoptive parents, especially as Graham had by then been medically retired from the fire service. And then there was that prosecution for assault, compounded by the suicide attempt documented in Eileen's medical records. The final answer, when it eventually came, was a devastating blow to both of them.

At about this time the newspapers and television reports were full of stories about the desperate plight of orphaned children in Romania, matched in equal proportion by warnings about the foolhardiness, not to mention the illegality, of well meaning couples who sought to snatch the impoverished youngsters and offer them a home in Britain.

To Graham and Eileen it seemed so unjust. These poor children needed a loving home and family, and they could offer just that. Their desperation for a child became an obsession. They made enquiries of several official and unofficial agencies but met only obstacles. They contemplated going to Romania and smuggling out a child, but this had been tried by others and it had proved impossible to avoid detection by the UK authorities. In one distressing case a child had been snatched by social workers from a family in Bristol and eventually returned to

Romania leaving a desperate couple facing charges of child abduction and rumours of sexual abuse.

Through their enquiries they came across a shady contact in Spain who suggested it was possible for people who were seriously committed to alleviating the plight of poor Romanian orphans to circumvent the red tape of official adoption agencies. They travelled to Spain to follow up the contact and though they were suspicious throughout, they convinced themselves this was their last chance to become parents. There were two major obstacles. The contact was adamant that if they went ahead they must move to Spain. It was explained that, as foreigners, their arrival as a new family in Spain with a young child would be less likely to raise suspicion than if they returned to the UK. The need for official paperwork was also likely to be less of a problem in Spain where the absence of a birth certificate could be easily explained away as documentation lost or left behind in England. The second major obstacle was money. The contact required a down payment of 500,000 pesetas (£2,000) with a final payment on delivery of the child of 3,000,000 pesetas (£12,000).

They were shown photographs of three children lying or sitting amidst filthy bed linen, their faces distorted with anguish and streaked with tears. Having come this far, their desperation outweighed their suspicion and they agreed to go ahead. By the time they made up their minds, they were told their first choice, a doe-eyed girl with wispy blond hair, was no longer available. They opted instead for the tiny boy with a chubby round face, a shock of dark hair and a crooked mouth.

They were given just two weeks to effect their move to Spain and receive the child. Eileen quit her job immediately and they moved into a rented house in Senija pending the sale of their Dartford home. The child, whom they decided to call Anthony after Eileen's father, arrived, cash-on-delivery, two days later. Their Spanish contact, whom they realised was the principal mover in the whole deal, was called Juan-Jose Mora.

Eileen Robinson seemed calm, even relieved, as she reached the end of her story. Mariela removed her hand and offered another tissue which Eileen used to dab away the last of her tears.

'I know what we did was illegal,' she said. 'But we were desperate and the child was desperate, too. We just couldn't bear the thought of leaving him in that orphanage when we could offer him a loving home. And that's exactly what we have done for the past seventeen years. He's wanted for nothing; we've loved and cared for him as if he were truly our son.'

My thoughts drifted between understanding of the Robinson's motives and anger at this latest revelation about Mora's seedy affairs. Was there no end to this man's depravity? Prostitution, corruption, blackmail and now child abduction and trafficking. The fact that he may have rescued this child, and possibly others, from impoverished lives in Romania was irrelevant since his motives were never altruistic. He had acted out of pure greed. Mora was evil and I couldn't help thinking he deserved to be dead. Murder was a fitting end for such a fiendish man and a part of me wanted to shake the hand of his killer and congratulate him for ridding the world of this Satan.

Mariela roused me from my thoughts. 'Thank you for being honest with us Mrs Robinson. I know it must have been difficult for you in the circumstances.'

'What's going to happen to us? Will we be prosecuted?'

'I don't think you need to be concerned about that for now,' I said. The fact was I did not know the answer. 'The main thing now is that we consider how all this affects Tony's disappearance. Tell me, Mrs Robinson, did Tony know he was adopted, legally or otherwise?'

'Absolutely not,' she snapped. 'We've always been very careful to keep it from him. It was difficult at times, like when he asked about getting a passport because we have no birth certificate or official adoption papers. We managed to discourage him, but we both knew that at some stage things would be difficult and we just tried to put things off.'

'Do you think Tony ever suspected he was adopted?'

'No, the subject was never raised. Why would he even think such a thing?'

175

'Well' it's just that...' I was trying to choose my words carefully. 'No matter how close the relationship with adoptive parents, sometimes children can have an intuitive sense of alienation – a feeling of detachment.'

I thought my comment might have provoked anger, but Eileen Robinson responded with curiosity. 'I don't think Tony ever suspected. At least he never mentioned it to us. Why do you ask?'

'I was just wondering if Tony had known or suspected he was adopted, whether he might have tried to trace his true family.'

'Not to my knowledge. Surely he would have said something to us, if that was the case.'

I had to admit she was probably right. 'Mrs Robinson, after the adoption...' I didn't want to be so harsh as to preface "adoption" with "illegal" ... 'did either you or Mr Robinson have any further contact with Juan-Jose Mora?'

'Absolutely not.' Her eyes narrowed and her mouth tightened. 'We knew him for what he was – an exploitative crook who preyed on people like us. But there was no other way for us to get a child. We were desperate and he knew it. If we had not adopted Tony, I doubt Graham and I would have stayed together. So we went ahead even though we hated Mora for what he was doing. After Tony arrived we made sure we never saw Mora again.'

'So Mora has never contacted you in any way?'

'I've told you, no.'

'You know that Mora is dead, murdered?'

'We read about it in the newspapers. I'm glad. He deserved it.' Her lips stretched to a faint smile.

'Thank you Mrs Robinson, I think that's all for now.' I thought of ending there, but that would be letting Graham Robinson off the hook. Much as I believed Eileen Robinson's account to be true, I still wanted to hear her husband's version. 'We need you to make an official statement, and your husband, too. Please tell him when he returns that we will be in touch and you will both need to come in to the police station in Jalon.'

'I'll speak to him, but he will be very angry when he knows I have told you.'

'You have done the right thing, Mrs Robinson. Just tell your husband I said that.'

'So what do you think?' Mariela asked as we returned to Jalon.

'I think our job just got a whole lot more complicated. I'm convinced there's a definite link between Mora's murder and the disappearance of Tony Robinson but I just can't fathom what it is. All I know is that Mora was never so philanthropic as to allow the *Centro de Desarolla Espiritual* to use his place in Lliber free of charge without a reason.'

'And what about Tony Robinson's link to the Centre?' Mariela asked. 'All we have is that poster to connect them. And there's no evidence of any direct contact between Tony Robinson and Mora.'

'I agree there's no evidence as such, but I'm willing to bet they met each other. The question is why?'

'Perhaps your suggestion to Mrs Robinson was right and Tony had been trying to trace his true family.'

'It's possible, but the more likely scenario is that Mora initiated the contact.'

'But why, after all this time?'

'Think about it, Mariela. You know the kind of man Mora was.'

'You mean blackmail? You think Mora might have been trying to blackmail the Robinsons?'

'It's a possibility, and you know what that means…'

'What?'

'It means we have another suspect for Mora's murder.'

'Graham Robinson, you mean.'

'Exactly. We need to get him in to the station as soon as possible. Contact him when we get back and bring him in. Arrest him if you have to.'

'By the way,' Mariela said, 'I spoke to Hilario Sanchez's wife and she confirmed he returned home at around 10.30 on the night Mora was murdered. She says she had supper prepared and then they watched television before going to bed around 11.30.'

'And you believed her?'

'I've no reason not to.'

'Did you ask if they sleep together?'

'What do you think?'

CHAPTER EIGHTEEN

Graham Robinson came willingly in the end and the next morning we interviewed him and his wife separately to see if we could find discrepancies in their stories. Their accounts coincided in all but minor details. Despite being pressed, both were adamant in their denial of any contact with Mora or any knowledge of contact between Mora and their son. Eileen Robinson was easy to believe and seemed more nervous at the suggestion of any contact than anything else. Her main concern was to know if they faced prosecution – a question I deliberately evaded on the basis that the uncertainty would keep them under pressure.

Mr Robinson was more belligerent. He made no attempt to disguise his contempt for Mora or his pleasure at Mora's demise. We pressed him to account for his movements on the night of Mora's murder, which he did by stating he spent the evening at home with his wife. The fact that she confirmed this still left room for doubt, but I could find nothing in his body language to contradict his assertion that he and his wife were guilty of nothing more than a desperate act to adopt a child when all other avenues were closed to them. Even so, I still had my doubts, especially given the way he had stormed out of the house the previous day. However, the fact remained that unless we could prove there had been contact with Mora and/or break Robinson's alibi we were at a dead end.

I was convinced there was more to link Tony Robinson to the *Centro de Desarollo* Espiritual than just that strange poster of the Torc, so I set Mariela the task of trying again to track down the people associated with the Centre. All I could think of to occupy my time was to sit in the office, doodling and turning the pages of the two case files. It was the first time I had viewed them together and I hoped that examining the cases concurrently would bring something new to light. It was a forlorn hope and I was left with just a jumble of facts and meaningless scribbles that rendered me more bemused than when I started.

I left the office just before seven-thirty and headed for Parcent. It was only Tuesday and I had no idea how the rest of the week would pan out. In fact I had no idea what to do the next day except drag myself back to the office and start going over old ground again.

It was a fine evening and the sun was still high in the sky leaving another hour or two before the heat of the day would begin to dissipate. As I trudged through the narrow streets of Parcent, the thought of spending the evening alone in the gloom of my townhouse seemed less than appealing.

I considered the possibility of calling on Rosana, if only to apologise for provoking our rift, but I quickly came to the conclusion that it would need more than an apology to effect a reconciliation. And then I thought, did I want a reconciliation anyway? I had been trying to convince myself that things had actually worked out for the best. I had only met Rosana through her insistence on bringing me together with my hitherto estranged family and beyond that the only thing we seemed to have in common was that our families were linked through generations of insularity in the same village. And I had no desire to perpetuate that insularity by tying myself to Parcent, since I was not sure I wished to remain in the village my father had forsaken all those years ago. Indeed I was not sure I wished to remain in Spain. Yet, even as I tried to convince myself, my subconscious alter ego negated those arguments and impelled me to acknowledge that there was something more palpable to my relationship with Rosana.

A beer and some company suddenly seemed like a good idea and I was relieved to find Pepito occupying his customary position in Bar Casino. My great uncle Rafael gave me no more than his now customary cursory glance as I strode by the dominoes table to join Pepito at the far end of the bar. I declined the *tubo* proffered by the barman

180

whose memory surprised me and opted instead for a *caña*, though I still questioned the point of serving beer by the thimbleful.

I exchanged pleasantries with Pepito – the weather, the shortage of water for crops and the high humidity causing mildew to beset the grapes. It wasn't long before the subject of Rosana cropped up as I knew it would. In truth I did little to avoid it. Whether it was Rosana's deliberate interpretation or the distortions of the gossip mongers, I did not know, but Pepito clearly had the impression that my differences with Rosana were born of concern about her debts. I could have refuted the implication, but Pepito wasn't seeking to condemn me and so I let it lie.

'Things could have been so different,' Pepito said, 'if Rosana's father hadn't been swindled out of his land.'

'What do you mean?'

'Manolo owned a substantial tract of land on the outskirts of Parcent, between here and Orba. His family had cultivated it for generations, but in the end it got too much for him. Rosana is an only child and so there was no one to help. Finally Manolo abandoned most of the land except for a small parcel where he grew a few vegetables and even that was neglected when the daily walk became too much for him. He was crippled with arthritis by then and had never learned to drive. Neighbours helped him out when they could, but he always felt he was imposing on them. This was in 1998 when the decline in agriculture was at its worst. The European Union had just ended agricultural subsidies and the price of crops plummeted because of overproduction. It was then that Juan-Dominic Giner offered to buy Manolo's land. It seemed like a good deal since no one really wanted agricultural land at that time.'

I sensed what was coming next. 'Don't tell me, a developer came along and built houses there.'

'You're catching on,' Pepito said. 'But you're not quite right. Three months after Manolo sold the land, the town hall issued a new plan for the village and the land was re-zoned as urbanisable. Giner sold the land almost immediately and made a huge profit.'

'And this Giner? Don't tell me, he's the Mayor's brother or nephew or cousin?'

'Not quite. Giner's father, Jaime, was part of the ruling political group at the time and Jaime's brother was the councillor for *urbanismo*. In fact Jaime Giner is sitting over there playing dominoes with your great uncle Rafael as we speak.'

I craned my neck to look at the quartet of old men huddled around the baize-topped table, furtively shielding their dominoes from each other's prying eyes.

'He's the one sitting opposite Rafael,' Pepito said, drawing my attention to a balding old man chewing on the stub of a large cigar.

'What surprises me, Pepito, is that corruption and dirty dealing is so rife in these parts, and so blatant, and yet no one seems to care much about it. The victims take it on the chin and the perpetrators seem to be able to carry on with impunity.'

'I know what you mean,' Pepito responded. 'Things are changing, but nepotism and corruption became so deep-rooted in Franco's years it will take a generation to wipe it out.'

I somehow doubted that even a generational shift would eradicate the kind of practices I had encountered and which seemed to have gathered pace with the boom in development in the Costa Blanca. As far as I was concerned *enchufe* was an embedded way of life in these parts and most people seemed to work on the basis that it was normal practice. The indifference with which Eduardo Moreno had offered me the money from Mora's house was proof of that. So who could blame those who took advantage? Why should anyone look a gift horse in the mouth, as they say?

The next day I was staring at the walls of my office wondering what to do next when Pilar Vidal came to my rescue.

'I'm sorry it has taken me a few days,' she said as I answered the phone, 'but I have some news for you.'

'I'm all ears.'

'When you phoned me last week I wasn't sure if it was possible, but it proved much easier than I thought. I checked with our DNA specialists and they confirmed that a transplanted organ retains the basic DNA make up of the donor despite the effects of immuno-suppressant drugs. So we took a sample of Mora's transplanted kidney and ran some tests. They didn't do a full DNA analysis, just the standard tests that would be used to determine compatibility of donor and recipient.' She paused.

'And?'

'And they confirmed what you were told by Ernesto Alvarez. There was a good match across the range of factors normally used to assess compatibility.'

'I see.'

'You sound disappointed,' Pilar said, picking up the despondency in my voice.

'I was hoping that wouldn't be the case. You see, the more I've discovered about the type of man Mora is, or was, the more I have become convinced that he was not the sort of man to put his trust in luck when it came to waiting for a suitable organ donor. A good match is one of the key criteria for selecting recipients when organs become available, but with the development in immuno-suppressants, it is less important. I suspected Mora might have bought or bribed his way to the top of the list to get a new kidney even if the match was not ideal, but what you have told me suggests that Alvarez had good reason to offer this particular kidney to Mora when it became available.'

'I see,' Pilar said. 'I'm sorry to disappoint you.'

'There's no need to apologise. In my job I get used to dead ends.'

'I have some other news, but I'm not sure this will be of any more help to you.'

'Oh?'

'We ran some more tests on those fibres we found in Mora's nasal passages. Do you recall?'

'Yes, of course, the ones that suggested he'd been suffocated.'

'The fibres are a type of cotton and there are traces of a green dye, but that's as far as it goes for now. This type of material is commonly used in all kinds of cloth from dusters and towels to clothing and bedding.'

'I see.'

183

'There's one other thing, but I'm not sure it offers any more help. The fibres were impregnated with some kind of chemical substance. It's impossible to say whether it was something used in the manufacturing process or perhaps something spilt on the cloth. So far we have been unable to identify the substance. We'll keep trying, but the traces are minute and I'm not sure we'll be able to pin it down precisely.'

'You're right, it doesn't take us any further forward, but thank you for trying anyway. By the way, I haven't forgotten I promised you lunch, but now is not a good time for me, this case is driving me crazy and I'm not sure I would be good company.'

'Don't worry, I won't forget. I'll get back to you if I have any news.'

More dead ends. Rarely in my fourteen years as a detective, had I been so stumped. I was used to unravelling complex cases and in my experience it was mainly a question of studying the detail looking for discrepancies and pursuing loose ends until something clicked and brought things together. In this case nothing seemed to make sense. There were plenty of links between random pieces of information, but the links created confusion rather than clarity. I was contemplating an early lunch when Mariela burst into the office bubbling with excitement.

'We've traced Helen Basilienko,' Mariela said. 'She's downstairs in the interview room.'

'Who's Helen Basilienko?'

'She's one of the people arrested then released when they raided that place on the Benissa road three months ago.'

At last, something to go on. Now we might find out what they were up to at the mysterious *Centro de Desarollo Espiritual.*

'How did you trace her?' I asked as we headed down the stairs.

'You remember Teresa said one of the people arrested was a Ukrainian woman?'

I didn't.

'Well, it struck me that she could not have been in Spain illegally, otherwise she would almost certainly have been deported at the time of her arrest. So if she was here legally, there should be a record of her at the Foreigners Office. You see, everyone coming to Spain to work or live has to register there and obtain a residency certificate.'

'So why has it taken until now to trace her?'

'The file from her arrest had her listed as Helen Basilienko, which was the name she gave and that's how we had been searching the records. I thought Basilienko looked odd for a Ukrainian name, so I looked it up on the internet and found a dictionary of Ukrainian names. The Ukrainian name Basil written in Ukrainian script begins with a letter that looks exactly like the letter B and that's how it would appear in her passport. But the name translates to the Latin alphabet as Vasili, so I thought that might give me a clue. You know that in Spanish the letters B and V sound very similar so that's probably why the officer wrote it up as Basilienko instead of Vasilienko. Once I discovered the error it was easy to trace Yelena Vasilienko with the Foreigners Office.'

'And where did you find her?'

'She lives in flat near Teulada and works at a club on the N332 near Pedreguer.'

'Not the Club Erotica?' I said expectantly.

'No, the Club Jupiter. Same sort of place, though.'

'And – don't tell me – it's owned by our old friend.'

'Give that man a cigar!'

Yelena Vasilienko was a slim young woman dressed in cheap clothes designed to catch the eye and suggest her availability for more than just conversation – skimpy see-through top, short denim skirt and white knee boots. Heavy make-up barely disguised her haggard features and hollow eyes seemed to portray a toil-worn life extending longer that her thirty-something years. Dark roots to her brittle blond hair betrayed her natural auburn colouring and her aura was completed with the waft of cheap perfume. She was noticeably nervous, biting her bottom lip and picking at fingernails already chewed to the quick. Despite her edginess she affected a show of defiance, rakishly exhaling cigarette smoke, avoiding eye contact and maintaining an arrogant gaze to the ceiling.

Mariela started the interview, plausibly reassuring Yelena that it was simply a matter of routine, following up on the earlier enquiries into the activities at the Spiritual Development Centre. Yelena spoke faltering Spanish and though her grammar was far from perfect, she had a surprisingly wide vocabulary. So long as Mariela spoke slowly and in simple terms, there was no difficulty in communication. Once reassured, Yelena seemed content to open up about the activities at the Centre, but her explanation might have come directly from a pamphlet.

According to Yelena, the Centre was dedicated to exploring the inner self to enable young men to grow spiritually and achieve mastery over their own future, by releasing hidden strengths and emotions that enabled them to live a life of respect for themselves and others. By releasing negative emotions such as fears, insecurities and hurt feelings as well as ill health, it was possible to live in peace, joy, health, love, happiness, abundance and appreciation.

Baloney, I thought, but Yelena was on a roll and I didn't want to stop her.

Mariela pressed on, mentioning the wild boar posters and enquiring about the mystical Torc. I watched for a reaction from Yelena to see if the topic aroused wariness in her demeanour, but she continued, seemingly unflustered, though with a large degree of cynicism.

The Torc, she said, was just a gimmick; something to give a mystical quality to the essential beliefs of spiritualism; a kind of focus around which to develop a form of worship. She dismissed the idea as harmless, but irrelevant to the central themes of spiritual development, though she acknowledged that some people took it more seriously.

We needed to move on and shift Yelena from her comfort zone. Talking about theory and philosophy was one thing, but I wanted to get to the core of what actually occurred at the place in Lliber and the role of a certain Juan-Jose Mora.

Mention of his name sparked the first sign of alarm, as Yelena's face tightened and she shifted uncomfortably in her chair. Her tone, too, became noticeably more guarded. I left for later the question of how Yelena had come to work at one of Mora's clubs and allowed her to explain Mora's role at the Centre. He was, she said, the Centre's founder and funder-in-chief. He led group sessions and a kind of worship when he expounded the virtues of the Torc. For these he wore a robe with a red cross which he adorned with a gold medallion centred with what he claimed to be a wild boar pearl. Most of these sessions encompassed the whole group of followers, young men in their late teens or early twenties, but he also ran separate sessions for a smaller group. In these sessions he deviated from the central message of spirituality, self respect and self reliance, and focussed more on a message of empowerment, claiming that true dedication to the Torc enhanced personal strength, determination and leadership ability. From this group he selected a handful of more committed followers for more intensive training, but this was all done behind closed doors and she claimed to know nothing of what occurred in these sessions.

I deliberately resisted the temptation to raise the name of Anthony Robinson at this stage and moved on to examine her precise role in the Centre's activities.

Her task, she explained, was to recruit young men and coax them into joining the Centre. To do this she and some of the others working at the Centre would distribute leaflets and try to engage youngsters in conversations about the direction of their lives. After that she would make them welcome on their first visits to the Centre by offering refreshments and talking about what the Centre could do for them.

It was time to end the pretence; time to get tough.

'Bullshit!' I declared. 'We both know that Juan-Jose Mora was not the kind of man to operate a Centre like this for benevolent motives.'

Yelena shuddered in her seat, her eyes flashing in Mariela's direction as if seeking pity or reassurance. Mariela met her gaze with a steely resolve that unnerved Yelena even more.

'I've told you the truth,' Yelena pleaded.

'I'm sure you have,' I said, 'but there is more, much more that you haven't told us. We're in for a long haul Yelena, so let's take a break now. Sergeant Poquet will get you something to drink and we can start again from scratch in half an hour. That should give you time to think about the advantages of co-operating and the consequences of lying. You know, of course, that Mora is dead so he can't harm you now. You can only harm yourself by continuing to be evasive. We will get to the bottom of this no matter how long it takes.'

We left Yelena squirming, her eyes wide and watery with confusion and panic.

'You were ruthless,' Mariela said as we killed time in the office waiting to resume the interview.

'Thank you,' I responded.

'It wasn't meant as a compliment. She's frightened out of her wits.'

'Good. Now get someone in uniform to take her a cup of tea; a male officer and make sure he's wearing his pistol.'

'Michael, have you no heart?'

'Oh, come on, Sergeant Poquet, don't go soft on me now. This is the best lead we've had in this case. I do believe we are finally getting somewhere. Now, that cup of tea and you can make me one while you're at it, no milk, and a slice of lemon if you can manage that. Then we'll start again, unless you haven't got the stomach for a dissection.'

'I can't wait to see the butcher at work,' Mariela said with thinly disguised exasperation. 'Jack the Ripper probably showed more pity for his victims.'

'Kind of you to say so.'

Mariela met my simulated smile with a put-on grimace of her own.

'You live in Teulada, I understand.' This was my opening gambit as we resumed.

She nodded.

'And you work at the Jupiter Club.'

Another nod.

'That's a brothel isn't it?'

Yelena looked suitably shocked, but didn't respond.

'You don't appear to have any legitimate form of employment, so my guess is you are a prostitute.'

Mariela's eyes rolled towards the ceiling.

'A dancer,' Yelena said with a degree of indignation.

'*A dancer*,' I replied. 'So that's the job description these days. You came all the way to Spain to be a dancer at a seedy club on the N332.'

Yelena pouted.

'Look, Yelena, I'm not really interested in what you get up to at the Jupiter Club, that's your business, just so long as we both understand that you are here to answer questions relating to murder and abduction; very serious questions.'

'I know nothing of such things,' she protested.

'Well, let's see. Did Mora pay you for the work you did at the Spiritual Development Centre?'

Yelena paused, considering her options so I decided to reinforce the seriousness of her situation.

'I want the truth, Yelena. If you've done nothing wrong then there's nothing for you to worry about. But if you lie to us we'll find out and you'll be in serious trouble. Obstructing the police is a very serious matter.'

'Yes, he paid me.'

'And what exactly did he pay you to do?'

'I told you before, I helped to recruit boys to the centre and welcome them when they arrived.'

'But you didn't really believe in all this spiritualist mumbo jumbo did you?'

'It had a certain fascination.'

'But you were really only there because Mora paid you. Am I right?'

Yelena's silence gave me the answer.

'And Mora wasn't running the centre for the furtherance of spiritualism, was he?'

'I don't know what you are talking about.'

'Oh come on, Yelena, we both know what kind of man Mora was, and he was not the kind of person to waste his money on a place like this without a good reason.'

'I only know what I saw. We recruited people and Mora preached his philosophy. It all seemed quite genuine to me.'

'These group sessions Mora ran, was there any suggestion of brainwashing or anything like that?'

Yelena met my eyes with a defiant look. 'You have a vivid imagination, Captain Fernandez. No, there was nothing like that.'

Her defiance disturbed me. Yelena should have been scared witless by now, but instead she was putting on a show of bravado. Either she was telling the truth or she was a confident, practised liar. I didn't know which. Time to disturb her equilibrium again.

'These young men you recruited. You didn't offer them favours of any kind, did you?'

'Absolutely not. They were young kids for Christ's sake. What sort of person do you think I am?'

'I think we've already established that. Did the recruits pay to go to the Centre?'

'No, the sessions were all free.'

'And in these sessions, did Mora ever talk about money or encourage any of the recruits to make donations to the cause.'

'Not while I was there.'

'Now tell me about these special sessions; the select group of boys Mora took under his wing.'

'I can't tell you anything about them. I wasn't allowed to go into those sessions, so I don't know what went on.'

'But you must have known the people involved; did any of them talk to you about what went on?'

'No, never. I think they were sworn to secrecy.'

This was getting us nowhere. Mora must have had a hidden motive for running the Centre and I had an inkling as to what it might be.

'It was only young men you recruited to the Centre?'

'Yes.'

'No women?'

'No.'

'Why was that, do you think?'

'I don't know. It was just that the philosophy he preached and all that stuff about the Torc was based on enhancing masculine virility.'

'Did Mora ever display any... how can I put this... any affection towards any of the young men?'

'I don't know what you mean.'

'Did Mora have any physical contact with the recruits?'

'He was friendly towards them, yes.'

'What do you mean by friendly?'

'Friendly, you know, he was nice to them.'

My patience snapped. 'Yelena, you're covering up for Mora. You're in enough trouble as it is. Now tell us what really went on with these boys.'

'I've told you all I know.'

Time to get to the point. My suspicion was that Mora was using the Centre to recruit and then groom young boys for his own perverse pleasure. If I was right, we could be adding grooming or even homosexual rape to the list of Mora's twisted web of illicit activities. The thought occurred to me that young Tony Robinson might have suffered that fate. My heart sunk at the possibility and my fears grew for his safety. Suddenly, the disappearance of this young lad, which I had always dismissed as a trifling teenage tantrum, was becoming central to Mora's murder and the whole web of intrigue that surrounded it.

I was still convinced Yelena was covering something up, but I couldn't work out what or why. Mora was dead; she had nothing to fear from him, so why was she being so obdurate?

'You must have known the names of the boys who came to the Centre, especially those you helped to recruit.'

'Some of them yes, but usually we only knew their first names. It was a kind of policy that we never used people's full names.'

'Do you recall a boy named Anthony Robinson – Tony?'

There was the slightest flicker of recognition in her eyes. She subdued it almost immediately, but it told me all I wanted to know.

'No,' she said falteringly.

'You're lying, Yelena, it's written all over your face.'

She sank in her seat then mumbled. 'There might have been a boy called Tony, I can't recall exactly.'

I nodded to Mariela who took the photograph of Tony Robinson from the file and placed it on the desk in front of Yelena. She lowered her eyes to focus on the photo but didn't pick it up.

'Do you recognise this boy?' I asked.

Her face flushed and she seemed to be thinking about how to answer.

'Well?' I prompted.

'I may have seen him, I can't be sure.'

'Look again, Yelena,' I said forcefully, thrusting the photograph forward. 'And think very carefully. Now do you recognise this boy?'

'Yes, I saw him at the Centre a few times.'

'And was he one of Mora's special group?'

'I don't know. He might have been.'

She was lying, I could tell.

'How often did you see this boy at the Centre?'

'Just a few times, I think. Yes, that's right. He came to only a few sessions before the place was raided by the police.'

'And after that?'

'After the raid, the place was shut down completely. I've never been back there again.'

'Have you seen this boy or any of the other boys since the centre was closed down?'

'No.'

'Just how exactly did Mora close the place down?'

'He wasn't there when the place was raided and we all had strict instructions never to mention his name. After the judge dropped the case he just told all of us to stay away.'

Time to ratchet things up again. 'Yelena, you need to know that Tony Robinson has been missing from his home for almost four months now. His parents are desperately worried about him and we suspect he may have been abducted, possibly even murdered. You may have been one of the last people to see him alive so it's vital you tell us everything you know about this boy.'

I glanced across at Mariela who frowned at the suggestion the boy had been murdered since we had never even discussed the possibility before.

Yelena protested. 'I've told you, I only saw him at the Centre a couple of times. I haven't seen him since then. I don't know any more than that, and I certainly don't know anything about murder or abduction.'

There was a false bluster in her reply and I was convinced she was lying or at least covering something up. At least we now had some clear evidence of direct contact between Mora and the Robinson boy. But where did this take us? Mora was dead and the boy still missing. I was still working through the implications when Mariela turned to Yelena.

'Yelena,' Mariela said, 'you've been very helpful, and if what you've told us is true, you have nothing to worry about. You've done nothing wrong.'

I wasn't best pleased by this intervention. In my opinion it was better to keep Yelena on edge rather than offer her reassurance, but I decided to let Mariela continue. I was still not convinced Yelena had told us all she knew, but perhaps a different approach would give us results.

'What puzzles us most is that Tony Robinson has been missing now for more than three months. There's been a massive publicity campaign with his picture in all the papers and on TV as well. And yet no one has come forward with any information. At least some of the other boys who attended the Centre must have recognised Tony Robinson, but none of them has contacted the police. Can you explain why that might be?'

'That's easy to answer. Everyone was sworn to secrecy and Mora made it clear there would be serious consequences for anyone who spoke out.'

'What kind of consequences, Yelena?' Mariela put on her most sympathetic tone.

Yelena's sudden outburst took us both by surprise as her body shuddered and tears began rolling from her eyes.

'He was wicked, you have no idea. One minute he could be charming, even kind, but if you did anything to annoy him he could be brutal. Not physically brutal, but he had a presence, a kind of evil. He would just bear down on you with his bulky body, put his huge face in front of yours and glare at you with those dark eyes of his. He would speak to you in a kind of fiendish whisper. No one who even so much as upset him was left in any doubt about the consequences.'

Mariela dispensed the tissues again and I wondered if she claimed them on expenses, since she always had a ready supply to hand. One thing puzzled me though. If Mora was really such a monster, why would someone like Yelena continue to work for him? I needed an answer.

'How long have you worked for Mora?' I asked.

'About two years.' Yelena dabbed her face with the tissue and appeared to relax a little.

'And you say you came to Spain to work as a dancer in one of Mora's clubs?'

'Yes.'

'How old are you, Yelena?'

'I'm thirty-four. Why do you want to know?'

'It's just that most of the people we come across who do this kind of thing are much younger, some are barely out of their teens and they find themselves coerced into this kind of work for a variety of reasons. But you don't fit that profile, do you? You are not a naïve teenager; you're a mature woman, so you must have known what you were getting into before you came to Spain.'

Again a thoughtful look crossed Yelena's face as she considered how best to answer. I was convinced she was not some frightened innocent, but a shrewd and intelligent woman who was considering her situation carefully; weighing up her options. When, eventually, she responded I wasn't sure whether she had decided to come clean or whether she was simply trying to protect herself.

'Okay, so I knew what I was getting into and I knew it was more than just dancing. But I needed the money. You have no idea what life is like in the Ukraine. My family is poor; they live in a dilapidated farmhouse near Chebinenko and scratch a living off a tiny bit of land. My parents are both in their sixties and my father suffers from emphysema. I have a younger brother with cerebral palsy. He can't work and needs constant attention and there's no help from the state, so every day is a struggle just to get by. Without the money I send home, there's no way they could survive.'

I was almost reaching for one of Mariela's tissues, yet Yelena explained her family's plight without emotion as if she neither wanted, nor expected, sympathy. I made a mental note to have her story checked out.

'I see,' I said, 'you say Mora was such a fearsome brute but even so you were prepared to work for him for the sake of your family.'

Yelena suddenly flipped, her eyes darkened and her nostrils flared.

'You really have no idea do you? I suppose you think I'm just some common slut who sells her body for money to pay for drugs; immune to the pain and degradation of sleeping with men who treat you like a piece of meat. Well you're wrong. I'd give anything to get out of this life, but how would that help my family? As for Mora, yes he's an evil brute, he uses and abuses the people around him without a second thought; he preys on their fears and exploits their weaknesses, but still I work for him because I have no other choice.'

There were no more tears from Yelena, just a cold hard stare. I was unmoved by her whimpering excuses, but Mariela seemed to sense her despair and reached out to touch her hand, glancing at me with a degree of admonition.

I decided to back off, but I was left thinking about Mora. Could anyone really be so evil, so demonic, that they could impose their will by sheer force of character? After everything I had learned about Mora in the past few days, I was willing to believe this was true. But we still had little more than Yelena's wafer thin evidence of a connection between Mora and Tony Robinson. And we were no nearer to finding out what had happened to Tony Robinson or solving the mystery of Mora's murder, except now it seemed that anyone who had ever come into contact with the man might well be happy to see him dead.

And then it occurred to me. If Mora had abducted Anthony Robinson, or any of the other boys, or used them for his own perverted pleasure he must have taken them somewhere. It wouldn't have been to his house in Beniforell – that was far too public. He might have kept them at the Centre, but that had been closed down. There must be somewhere else. I could have asked the question directly, but I doubted Yelena would give us a truthful answer.

'Have you ever been to Mr Mora's house in Beniforell?' I asked.

195

'I didn't even know he had a house in Beniforell.'

'Really,' I said with mock amazement. 'Then where do you think he lived?'

Yelena quivered. 'I don't know,' she said with false indignation as her eyes flashed from me to Mariela and back again.

'You're lying, Yelena. You must know where he stayed. We'll just have to keep you here until you tell us the truth.'

Her eyes drooped, her head bowed and her shoulders sagged into a posture of capitulation. 'There's a flat above the Club Jupiter,' she mumbled.

Bingo!

'Thank you Miss Vasilienko,' I said. 'You are free to leave now, but we'll be checking your story so don't plan any trips.'

'So where has all your blustering and bullying got us?' Mariela asked when we returned to the office.

I ignored her implied criticism. 'I think the *Centro de Desarollo Espiritual* was just a front for Mora's homosexual predilections.'

'That's a leap in logic. Where's the evidence?'

'Sometimes, Mariela, you don't need evidence; intuition is enough.'

Mariela snorted in a show of scepticism. 'And if you are right, what about Tony Robinson?' she asked.

'Well, we know he was there with Mora, and that alone is a cause for concern. As to where he is or what has happened to him, we are no further forward are we?'

'I guess not,' Mariela said with an air of resignation. 'What do you think about Yelena Vasilienko?'

'I think she knows a lot more than she told us. Get Teresa to check out Vasilienko's family in Ukraine and then we're going on a little trip.'

It was lunchtime and whilst everyone else in Spain was thinking of food followed by a siesta, I had other things on my mind. The heat was at its fiercest and I still questioned the wisdom of closing up for three hours in the middle of the day only to return for a further three hours until eight in the evening. I could understand how, in a rural community, farmers would want to avoid working in the midday sun, but in these days of air conditioned shops and offices, and when the rest of the Europe was open for business throughout the day, it seemed bizarre that Spain should hang on to such an outdated way of life. But then, as I had already discovered, this was not the only inherent idiosyncrasy built into the Spanish psyche.

I was driving the hire car I'd been using for the past three weeks. Colonel Cardells had sanctioned the hire car as a temporary measure "whilst you are still on probation" and his office had arranged the contract with a local hire company in Alicante. I wondered if the battered, bright yellow Opel Corsa was Cardells' idea of a joke. Everything in the car rattled and the interior reeked of stale tobacco, even after I had emptied the ashtray in the front console which was so full of fag ends I had to prise it out with a screwdriver. It was certainly conspicuous, and worse still it lacked oomph, especially when the air conditioning drained the engine of what little power it had. I only hoped I didn't become involved in any high-speed car chases, for I might just as well have abandoned the car and followed on foot.

'It's known as the *Carretera del Amor*,' Mariela said as we headed out of Jalon to join the N332 at Benissa.

'I expect there's more lust than love on offer at the Jupiter Club.' My stomach rumbled. 'Do you think they do food?'

'I'm sure one of the staff could rustle up a sandwich; they probably do room service as well.'

Clumps of weeds pock marked the rough gravelled car park occupied by an ancient rusting Volvo and a battered old Range Rover. The club itself comprised a roughly rendered two-storey block, painted in vermillion with blacked-out windows. It could easily have been mistaken for a semi-derelict warehouse except for the word "Jupiter" emblazoned in shiny silver discs that resembled giant sequins shimmering in the breeze.

The entrance door needed a hefty shove and we shambled into a narrow corridor illuminated by the dim light of a bare light bulb above a sign announcing, "ENTRADA". Inside, the subdued lighting theme continued, achieved by a motley collection of table lamps randomly distributed across an equally motley collection of low tables and chairs. There were plenty of dark recesses and secluded corners devoid of any light at all. Perhaps the proprietors were conscious of their carbon footprint, I thought, as I blinked to adjust my eyes to the gloom. There was a lingering smell of stale tobacco smoke and, as if to complete the impression, Procol Harum's "A Whiter Shade of Pale" pulsated in muffled tones through a set of crackly speakers.

Judging from the empty tables, the average red-blooded Spaniard was more interested in satiating his hunger than nourishing his sexual appetite – the place was deserted. The bulky silhouette of a man perched on a bar stool caught my eye as he lowered the newspaper he was reading and stood to greet us. Even in the murky light I recognised the signs of someone nursing a hangover – dark hollows beneath bloodshot eyes. The uneven, two-day stubble around his chin matched the greyness of his complexion but contrasted sharply with the greasy black hair swept back off his brow and cascading over his ears. His brief smile of welcome, exposing a set of crooked, plaque-encrusted teeth, quickly disappeared as he seemed to recognise us as police officers even before Mariela produced her identity card.

'How can I help you?' he smirked with a degree of cocky arrogance.

'You are?' I said.

'Felipe Cabrera.'

'Are you the boss here?'

'I'm looking after the place,' he replied.

'Since Mr Mora died, you mean?'

His face became animated and his left eye twitched. 'If that's why you're here, you're wasting your time. I know nothing about Mora's death except what I have read in the papers.'

He was probably telling the truth, I thought, but that was not why we were there. 'Mora has an apartment here I understand. We'd like to see it.'

Cabrera's face hardened. 'Don't you need a warrant for that?'

'You're quite right; strictly speaking I suppose we should have a warrant.' I turned to Mariela. 'Sergeant Poquet, get on to headquarters and arrange to obtain a warrant to search Mr Mora's flat. In fact while you're at it, ask for the warrant to cover the whole of this place, we might as well have a good look round while we're here.'

Cabrera gulped. 'It's on the top floor. I'll show you the way, but Mr Mora had the only key.'

'Thank you Mr Cabrera, it's good of you to give us permission to search Mr Mora's flat. Lead the way please.'

My shoes were sticking to the threadbare carpet as we climbed the narrow staircase at the back of the building turning left at the top and following a short corridor interrupted by a series of doors crudely painted with numbers running from one to six. I listened for signs of life as we passed, but heard nothing. At the end of the corridor we reached a solid wooden door painted black with matching black architraves.

'This is it,' Cabrera said, 'but I've told you, I don't have a key.'

'Thank you Mr Cabrera, you've been most helpful. You can leave us here now.'

'What next?' Mariela said as Cabrera shuffled back along the corridor. 'We really should obtain a warrant you know.'

'Come on, Mariela, you heard Mr Cabrera give us permission to have a look round. Now stand back.' I eased Mariela to one side and took a couple of steps backwards.

'Wait, Michael, I have a better idea.' With that, Mariela took a set of lock picks from her handbag and jangled them in front of my face.

'Is there no end to your talents?'

'I took lessons from a professional.'

Within a couple of minutes we were in the room. If I had expected to see a seedy pad with black satin sheets and mirrored ceilings I would have been disappointed. The place was neat if Spartan; interior designers might have called it minimalist, except that the paucity of furnishings had, I suspected, more to do with a desire to spend as little as possible rather than any design concept. The spacious lounge contained a brown leather sofa set before a glass-topped coffee table resting on a worn Afghan rug and centred with a ceramic ash tray. A flame-effect electric fire filled a mock marble fireplace topped by an uncluttered mantelpiece. The room was unusually devoid of ornamentation – no photos or paintings, just bare walls painted in uniform beige. One side of the lounge opened into a narrow open-plan kitchenette comprising a small worktop, electric hob, refrigerator, kettle, microwave oven and a short row of cupboards.

A modern slim-screen television occupied one corner, positioned on a black-lacquered cabinet that housed a satellite receiver and a DVD player/recorder. The bottom shelf of the cabinet contained a pile of DVDs, all sleeved and apparently containing regular movies. Next to the television, on the far wall, a VDU sat on a basic metal and wood desk with a computer console on the floor to one side.

At the end of a short corridor, I opened the door to the bedroom which was as functional as the lounge. A standard double bed occupied the centre of the floor covered with a neat floral duvet and flanked by a pair of pine bedside cabinets. The only other room was a small bathroom containing a WC, shower cubicle and wash basin. A glass shelf set into a circular mirror held a beaker containing several toothbrushes and a razor. The rest of the shelf was occupied by half empty tube of toothpaste and a nearly full bottle of mouthwash.

Opposite the bathroom was another door of solid wood that looked like an emergency exit with a heavy brass knob to one side. I twisted the knob, noting that there was no lock on the inside, and the door opened outwards onto the landing of a metal fire escape staircase leading to the rear of the building. The exterior of the door housed a Yale-type lock set into the wood. There was also a heavy sliding bolt which had been left in the open position. I closed the door again, hearing the latch click into place and realising the arrangement meant that anyone with a key could come and go without having to enter the club downstairs. The sliding bolt also meant the door could be secured from the outside.

I returned to the lounge and gazed around the scene. Here we were in Mora's secret hideaway, but what were we looking for? Such was the entangled web Mora had left behind I wasn't sure. Was there a clue here to the identity of Mora's killer? Might we uncover more evidence of corruption or extortion? And what about the Robinson boy? Might he have been brought here and held against his will? It was difficult to know where to start.

'What now?' Mariela asked, mirroring my confusion.

'Have a look round,' I said, 'but be careful. I think we are going to need a full forensic search after we have left.'

A cursory search of every drawer and cupboard in the lounge and kitchenette revealed nothing out of the ordinary just a collection of crockery and cutlery, pots and pans and a stock of canned and dried foods. The fridge was empty, devoid of even a mouldy piece of penicillin-encrusted cheese, suggesting that Mora, or someone else, had cleared the place not expecting to return, at least in the near future.

'Anything?' I asked Mariela as she returned from the bedroom.

'There's a small safe set in the floor of the built-in wardrobe.'

'Can you pick the lock?'

'It's a combination lock, beyond my capabilities I'm afraid, but we have a contact we can use who'll be in there in no time.'

'Don't tell me, a reformed burglar?'

'My tutor.'

'Anything else?'

'Nothing. Just a few items of men's clothing, socks, underwear and a pair of shoes.'

'What kind of shoes?' I asked for no particular reason.

Mariela, knowing my penchant for assessing people's personalities based on the shoes they wore, answered haughtily. 'Brown leather, chisel toes, rubber soles, flat laces, size forty-two, hardly worn. Anything else you need to know?'

'Maker's name?'

'Gonzalo,' Mariela replied with an air of smug satisfaction.

I was tempted to ask how many lace holes they had, but thought better of it, since she would probably have the answer.

'We're finished here for now,' I said. 'Get forensics to give the place a once over and you'd better contact your friendly safe-cracker. For now, just grab the computer and those DVDs and we'll have a look at them when we get back to Jalon.'

'Do you think we can take them without a warrant?'

'I don't think Mora is going to object, do you? We'll give Cabrera a receipt on the way out.'

Cabrera had resumed his perch at the bar when we descended the stairs and returned to the club. 'Find anything interesting?' he asked.

'We're taking the computer and a few other bits,' I said. 'Sergeant Poquet will give you a receipt. The forensic team will be back later for a more thorough look around. In the meantime, make sure no one else goes in there.'

'I've told you, Mora had the only key.'

'Then that shouldn't be difficult, should it?'

Mariela scribbled a note on a sheet torn from her note book, signed it and handed it to Cabrera.

With the air conditioning at full blast, the Corsa's engine rattled and juddered as we encountered a steep incline on the narrow winding road back to Jalon.

'Bloody motor,' I muttered, slamming into second gear, missing, and grinding the cogs in the process, losing all forward momentum. 'You may have to get out and push in a minute,' I said, glancing at Mariela who burst into a giggling fit.

'Perhaps I should drive,' she said. 'It takes a bit of getting used to, I guess – driving on the wrong side of the road, I mean.'

'It's not me; it's this tin-pot excuse for a car that Cardells arranged for me. I'll have you know I spent two years on traffic in England and completed the advanced driving course.'

'And I bet you have a certificate to prove it.'

'As a matter of fact...' I realised my macho male ego was being tweaked.

The car finally made it to the top of the hill and we rounded a sharp bend before starting a steep descent towards the bottom of a deep, tree-lined ravine. At last the car picked up speed as I moved up through the gears. In the distance I could see the road follow a gentle bend and then rise steeply again. This time I would use the car's momentum to get us up the hill without decelerating to a crawl. I kept my foot to the floor as we reached the dip in the road, realising a little too late that the bend was sharper than I had anticipated. I stabbed my right foot hard on the brake pedal, but with little effect; it felt spongy and the breaks barely gripped. I lifted my foot and stamped down again. This time the pedal plummeted all the way to the floor with no effect as the car continued to accelerate towards the bend. Instinctively I pumped the pedal again, but this time it fell to the floor and failed to rise.

Sensing our speed was too high for the bend, Mariela yelled. 'Slow down Michael...' There was panic in her voice.

By now we were entering the bend and I wrestled the steering wheel pulling it over to the left and feeling the rear of the car beginning to slide. Ahead of us loomed an unprotected drop to the bottom of the ravine and I realised that was where we were heading. Mariela realised this too, as she gripped the dashboard in front of her and braced her arms.

I dropped the clutch and rammed the gear lever from fourth into second. In an ideal situation I should have slowly raised the clutch allowing it to bite gradually and use the drag of the engine to slow us down. But this was not an ideal situation. I lifted my foot from the clutch and heard the engine revs rise to an alarming level. I didn't need to look at the rev counter to realise it was well into the red. The car jerked and the engine rattled and grated and juddered, but it had the effect of reducing our speed, though not enough to convince me we could safely negotiate the bend. As we reached the apex, the car began to slide sideways, drifting ever closer to the unguarded edge. I kept a firm grip on the steering wheel hoping I could maintain direction and steer us through the bend, but at this speed that seemed unlikely. I tightened my left hand grip and released my right hand to grab the handbrake and yank it up. Almost immediately the back wheels locked and though our speed reduced, the steering became light and unresponsive. We were still heading for the edge, but at least we were decelerating. I released the handbrake and felt the rear wheels grip once more as feeling returned to the steering wheel. The engine revs had dropped, but we were still travelling far too fast to negotiate the bend. Ahead of us a large rock protruded from the edge of the road. The choices seemed stark; either we hit the rock head-on or we miss it and tumble over the edge and into the ravine. I brace my arms on the steering wheel and eased gently out of the bend, heading straight for the rock. At the last moment I yanked the steering wheel to the right causing the car to slur sideways so that the rear end hit the rock with a glancing blow causing the car to spin across the road. Mariela screamed.

I saw the tree for just a split second before the car's bonnet concertinaed, accompanied by the nightmarish sound of metal twisting and crumpling. The car's windscreen shattered a millisecond before the airbags exploded and my head flew forward into a suffocating darkness.

My ears were ringing, my head was woozy and my vision blurred, but there was nothing wrong with my sense of smell as petrol fumes acted like smelling salts to bring me to my senses. I glanced across at Mariela who had bounced back in her seat, with her blond hair flung forward over her face. She was motionless, but emitting a low whimpering moan. I started to reach over to her, but was constrained by my seatbelt. I felt at the side of the seat and depressed the release button feeling a sharp pain in my right shoulder. Disentangled from the seat belt, I reached over to Mariela and gently lifted her hair from her face. My pulse raced at the sight of a trickle of blood oozing down her cheek and streaking the hair at the side of her face.

'Mariela. Are you all right, Mariela?' I yelled, trying to maintain a sense of calm in my voice. Another soft groan. 'Mariela, we need to get out of the car… quickly. Can you hear me?' Still she remained motionless.

I pressed the release button for Mariela's seat belt and felt it go down, but the clasp failed to eject. I pressed again with no result, so I yanked the belt upwards but it was fast. By now, the pain in my shoulder was acute, but I twisted further in my seat and yanked again with all the force I could muster. This time the clasp came free from its catch and I flung the seat belt to the far side of the car then grabbed Mariela's arm and shook her vigorously.

'Mariela, come on, we need to get out of the car. Can you move?'

Her eyes flickered and her head turned slightly in my direction until she winced in pain. At least she's conscious, I thought, though it was obvious she could not move. I would have to pull her out. I grabbed the driver's side door handle and felt the door catch release, but the door opened only fractionally. I leant into the door with my good shoulder and felt a sense of relief as it flew open. I lifted my legs and twisted my body grabbing the door frame to lift myself clear. It was then I realised my right shoulder was probably dislocated.

Free of the car, I moved as quickly as I could to the door on Mariela's side. My heart sank as I noticed the paint on the crumpled yellow bonnet begin to blister as smoke emerged from the engine compartment. I took a deep breath, fighting the panic that was rising in my head and causing my heart to pound. One look at the distorted passenger door told me it was unlikely to open, but that didn't stop me trying. My right arm was virtually useless so I tugged at the door handle with my left hand only for the handle to slip through my fingers leaving the door unmoved. Nursing my right arm with my left hand, I returned to the driver's side door noticing the yellow bonnet turning black as flames licked up the side.

One handed, I was never going to lift Mariela out, so I leant into the car, kneeling on the seat, gritted my teeth and fought the excruciating pain to reach with both hands beneath Mariela's armpits. I tugged as hard as I could, causing Mariela's body to slump over towards me, but a second tug failed to move her further. I noticed smoke emerging from beneath the dashboard.

'Mariela,' I yelled. 'Can you hear me? I need you to help. Can you move your legs?' I cradled her head and her eyes flickered once more then focussed.

'Michael,' she said falteringly.

'Mariela, if you can hear me, I need you to push with your legs so I can lift you over to this side of the car. Can you do that?'

Mariela blinked. 'I'll try,' she said.

I heaved again with both arms and this time Mariela braced her legs against the floor of the car and pushed. With this help I managed to drag her shoulders across the driver's seat and then I stepped out of the car and pulled again, finally succeeding in freeing her from the car and on to the road. I looked at her face and she appeared to be drifting back in semi-consciousness. I had to get her away from the car. With my good arm behind Mariela's back, I managed to raise her body from the ground and stagger backwards away from the car, dragging her feet across the tarmac as I went. The heels of her expensive designer shoes were ruined, but I guessed she would forgive me. Exhausted, I reached a grassy bank at the side of the road about thirty metres from the car and carefully lowered Mariela to the ground. I hoped we were far enough away if the car exploded as it seemed it might, though glancing back the flames beneath the bonnet seemed to have died down leaving only wisps of smoke drifting upwards and an acrid smell of burnt paint and plastic.

I knelt at Mariela's side and cradled her head with my left arm using my injured right arm to lift away a few strands of hair that had fallen over her face. I tucked the strands to the side of her ear and my fingers came away sticky with blood from a small cut on her temple. Her eyelids flickered then opened wide and she blinked deliberately two or three times as if forcing herself to focus. Her lips parted and she muttered something inaudible.

'Mariela,' I said, lowering my face closer to hers. 'Are you all right?'

She blinked again and then I felt her head rise from my supporting arm as her lips parted again as if to speak. I moved closer to listen and she lifted her head further until her lips met mine. I should have moved away, but the kiss shocked me and held me rigid until, after a few seconds that seemed much longer, her head flopped back to my arm.

'Thank you, Michael,' she murmured, as her eyes closed.

CHAPTER NINETEEN

The ambulance arrived twenty minutes after I made the call
– not bad, I thought, given that I had no idea as to our
exact location, except that we somewhere on the road
between Gata de Gorgos and Lliber. The paramedics
quickly classified me as "walking wounded" and strapped
my arm across my chest. Mariela's injuries were treated
more seriously with a precautionary neck brace strapped in
place and a surgical dressing bandaged over the cut to her
temple. I was able to sit at her side and hold her hand
during the fifteen minute journey to the Emergency
Department of Denia Hospital. She said nothing and
seemed to drift in and out of consciousness despite the din
from the ambulance's wailing siren. Her kiss was preying
on my mind. Was it a mere expression of gratitude? An
impulse in a moment of severe stress? Or was it something
more meaningful? An expression of genuine feeling
released in an unguarded moment? I dismissed the idea as
a piece of wishful thinking.

We were separated on arrival and all my enquiries over
the next couple of hours met with the same answer, 'She's
fine and you will be able to see her soon.' An X-ray of my
shoulder confirmed it was dislocated, but they said it was
not too serious; it just needed to be manipulated back into
place. For this I could have an intravenous anaesthetic or a
local injection of Novocaine. I was impatient to see Mariela,
so I opted for the latter, though there were moments when I
regretted the decision as a nurse pinned me to the bed and
a doctor manoeuvred my upper arm with what seemed like
some kind of wrestling hold. Despite the Novocaine I could
feel tendons straining and muscles twisting until a very

discernable click finally put the joint back in place and the pain began to subside. The nurse put my arm in a padded sling, gave me a packet of Ibuprofen and told me to rest for a couple of days.

'Where is Sergeant Poquet? Can I see her now?' I asked, as the nurse eased my jacket over my injured shoulder and tucked the loose sleeve into the side pocket.

'She's waiting for you outside,' said the nurse, much to my surprise.

'Michael,' Mariela said, rising from a seat in the corridor. 'Are you all right?'

She had a light-weight support strapped around her neck and a couple of steri-strips pasted across the cut to her temple. As we came closer she placed her arms around me and squeezed gently, pressing her cheek against mine and bringing the smell of disinfectant to my nostrils.

'Ouch!' I said, pulling away.

'Oh, sorry, I didn't think. How is your shoulder?'

'It's fine now, but never mind about me, how are you? From the way you looked in the ambulance I thought you'd have been admitted.'

'Luckily no. I was just dazed, that's all, and they say I have minor concussion. The cut turned out to be little more than a scratch.'

'I'm so pleased,' I said. 'For a moment I thought I had caused you some terrible injury.'

'Don't be silly. If it wasn't for you we might both have been customers of Pilar Vidal.'

The thought of the two of us occupying matching filing cabinets in the ice-house sent a shudder through my body. I wondered if we would be side by side or one on top of the other.

'Did I say thank you?' Mariela asked.

I gazed into her face, looking for any hint that she remembered our kiss, but all I saw was the beginning of a black eye.

'You did.'

I wouldn't have thought of it myself, but at Mariela's suggestion I summoned a police car to collect us from the hospital. The uniformed sergeant ushered us into the back of the green and white squad car and set off for Jalon.

'Can you stick to the main roads,' I said. 'I've had enough of mountain tracks for one day.'

'Yes sir,' he replied. 'Sorry, sir, but you need to put your seat belt on.'

'Of course.' I leant to my left, realising that with my arm in the sling I could not reach the belt.

'Here, let me help.' Mariela leant over and reached across my chest to pull the belt from its holder. I could feel her breath on my cheek.

'There we are, all tucked in,' she said as she planted the clip in its holder at the side of the seat.

I wanted to say something about our kiss, something to clear the air, but I wasn't sure she even remembered it. Then I noticed the driver glancing in the rear view mirror with what seemed to be a wry smile on his face.

'Do you know what they have done with my car, Sergeant?' I said, prompting his face to straighten.

'I think it's been taken to the compound at Benissa.'

'Good. After you have dropped us off, I want you to go to the compound and have a mechanic check it over. Tell him to pay particular attention to the brakes. And there are a couple of things in the boot – a computer and some DVD's – I want them back in my office first thing tomorrow morning.'

'You're not serious about being in work tomorrow, are you?' Mariela said as the squad car reached Parcent to drop me off at home.

'It's just a dislocated shoulder, my brain still works,' I said. 'But that doesn't mean you have to come in if you don't feel up to it. Take a couple of days off if you like.'

'What, and let you play the martyr on your own. I'll see you in the morning.'

I thought of giving her a parting peck on the cheek, but the leery-eyed look on the driver's face prevented me.

'I'll see you in the morning then.' After I had extricated myself from the seatbelt, I turned to the driver. 'Pick me up at eight o'clock sharp.'

A combination of pain in my shoulder and befuddlement in my head resulted in a restless night. My thoughts raced uncontrollably from one scenario to another and as I tried to blank each scene from my mind it was replaced by another, then another, then back to the starting point. One minute I was pumping the brake pedal, staring over the precipice as the car veered ever closer to the edge. Then I was staring into Mariela's eyes as she lifted her head and kissed me. After that I was stroking Rosana's hair on the pillow beside me then flinching as the picnic basket flew in my direction. Finally, as the pain killers numbed my brain as well as my aching shoulder, I drifted into a fitful sleep, wondering how I had got myself into such a mess and how it would all work out.

Mariela's black eye had progressed nicely though it was partially disguised with make-up. She had abandoned the neck support and, with her hair freshly washed and waved, she looked much better than I had expected. The pain in my shoulder had subsided but I kept my arm in the sling to remind me not to move it more than necessary. After exchanging enquiries as to each other's state of health, I was about to say something about the previous day's events. I didn't want to appear as a besotted schoolboy, beguiled by an innocent kiss, but neither did I want to pretend that nothing had happened.

'About yesterday,' I said.

'Yes?' Mariela said quizzically.

'I… I just wanted to say…'

The office door flew open and the sergeant burst in carrying the computer and DVDs we had recovered from Mora's apartment.

'Are these what you wanted, sir?'

'Yes, thank you. Put them on the desk will you.'

'The mechanic from the compound has just called,' the sergeant said. 'He's made a preliminary examination of your car. He says the brakes failed because of a small split in the hydraulic pipe between the fluid reservoir and the master cylinder which would have caused the brake fluid to leak out gradually.'

'And?' I prompted.

'There were signs of chafing on the pipe, but the fire in the engine compartment caused a lot of damage and left deposits of soot and molten plastic on the section of pipe in question. Because of this it is impossible to say if it had been tampered with. But given the age of the car and its mileage – almost 90,000 kilometres – the mechanic couldn't rule out the possibility that the split in the hydraulic pipe was caused by normal wear and tear.'

'But surely that should have been picked up in routine inspection and servicing.'

The sergeant cleared his throat. 'Well, the mechanic also said the car had not been maintained very well. Apparently the front shock absorbers were badly worn and the tread on the rear tyres was bordering on the legal limit.'

Great, I thought, Colonel Cardells had fixed me up with a death trap.

'You don't think someone deliberately tampered with the breaks, do you?' Mariela said once the sergeant had left the office.

'The thought crossed my mind.'

'But who would do such a thing? Why would anyone want to cause you to crash or worse still, kill you?'

'You tell me, Mariela. You're the expert on local customs in these parts.'

Mariela looked peeved. 'You were saying something before the sergeant came in, I think.'

'Oh… yes. It was nothing. Now, we have work to do.'

It was the middle of the morning before we finished examining the items removed from Mora's flat. The DVDs were exactly as described on the labels – American action and adventure movies dubbed in Spanish, some of poor quality suggesting they were pirate copies. The computer proved more interesting with an internet browsing history showing regular contact with a range of homosexual pornography sites, some quite graphic, though nothing approaching paedophilia. Even so, it confirmed my suspicions that Mora was using the house in Lliber to meet and possibly groom young men to satisfy his homosexual proclivities. Perhaps the safe would yield something more useful when our friendly safe-cracker had done his stuff, but Mariela explained he was out on another job and wouldn't be available until after midday. A picture of a masked robber with a striped shirt and "swag bag" crossed my mind and I wondered if he might be blasting his way into a bank vault, before coming to our assistance. Perhaps he had been given immunity from prosecution in return for his favours to the Guardia Civil. I should have dismissed the idea, but I had reached the stage where nothing in Spain would surprise me.

My mobile phone chirped its standard ring tone that surprised many people because it actually sounded like a telephone ringing. The number shown on the screen was not one I recognised though the call turned out to be one I had been expecting.

I grabbed my navy blue blazer from the back of my chair and fiddled with the red cotton handkerchief protruding from the breast pocket. It was a bit pretentious I know, but I figured it complemented the image I was trying to portray of a stuffy, straight-laced Englishman.

'I'm just popping out for a while,' I said to Mariela who was still stooped over Mora's computer. 'I'll need the keys to the Seat.'

Mariela screwed her face inquisitively. 'Are you fit to drive – your shoulder, I mean?'

'I'm fine. I'm not going very far. The keys?'

She pulled the keys from her handbag and dropped them in my outstretched hand. 'Where are you going?'

'Out,' I said tersely.

'Don't you need me to come with you?'

'No. I didn't realise we were joined at the hip. I think I'm old enough to be let out on my own, even in Spain.'

'How long will you be?'

Her concern might have been touching, but the thought crossed my mind that Colonel Cardells might not be too happy if I was let off the leash.

'I'm not sure, it all depends.' I pocketed the keys and left before Mariela could continue her inquisition.

The car had been left at the side of the station in full sun so I opened the door and waited a while, ostensibly to release the heat, but also giving me time to keep an eye on the front entrance to be sure I was not being followed. I removed my arm from the sling and started the engine, directing the chill blast from the air conditioning straight into my face, though it barely cooled my brow which was already stippled with beads of perspiration.

My destination was about fifteen minutes away, but I skirted Jalon and then doubled back into the narrow side streets constantly checking the mirror before heading out of town on the road to Benissa.

The car park at the Consum supermarket was virtually empty and it was easy to spot the stretched black "S Class" Mercedes parked in the far corner. I pulled into a space some distance away and killed the engine then removed my pistol and holster and locked them in the glove compartment. My shoulder was aching so I rested my arm in the sling then sat for a few moments watching the entrance to the car park.

Satisfied that I had not been followed, I left the car and walked towards the Mercedes. As I approached, the driver's door opened and a burly young man with a swarthy beard and dark glasses stood in front of me. I half expected he might be in uniform with a peaked cap, but it seemed that was just a touch too pretentious, even for Salvador Guardiola.

The driver gestured with an upward movement of his head. 'If you don't mind,' he said as he proceeded to frisk me.

It was clear he was looking for more than just a gun as he ran his hands over the sleeves of my jacket then unbuttoned it and patted my chest and sides through my shirt, running his hands over my back and then moving on to my thighs and calves. Finally he pulled apart the two sides of my sling and felt my arm. Satisfied, he opened the rear door and waved a hand inviting me to get in.

The cool interior had the distinctive smell of newness mingling with aftershave. I settled into the tan leather bench seat, nudging against a central armrest.

'Sorry about that,' Guardiola said. 'Can't be too careful, I'm sure you understand.'

I gestured with my sling that I could not reciprocate the handshake he proffered. He was younger than I had expected; early thirties I surmised. He met my eyes with a faint smile before settling back into his side of the seat. The jacket to his pale grey suit hung from a hook at the side of the rear window. The slight sheen on the fine material and the hand stitching around the lapel suggested a quality well above my off-the-peg blue blazer. He settled back in the sumptuous leather and crossed his long legs comfortably, revealing a pair of tasselled brogue-patterned loafers with slightly pointed toes. Like the suit, there was no doubting the quality of the shoes, but I was not so sure about the suavity of brown shoes with a grey suit and blue socks.

'Of course,' I said, trying to act as if being frisked was an everyday event, though my attempt at calmness was undermined by the fact that my face was flushed and my brow dripping with sweat. I pulled the handkerchief from my jacket pocket and dabbed my face, replacing the handkerchief and fussing to ensure it was neatly displayed.

'You've been in the wars, I see.' He gestured towards my arm.

'Oh, yes...' I said, taken off guard by his enquiry. 'A motoring accident. Luckily it's nothing serious, just a dislocated shoulder.'

His curiosity apparently assuaged, he got straight down to business. 'Eduardo Moreno tells me you might be interested in a certain proposition he put to you on my behalf, but that you insisted on discussing it with me personally.'

'I just like to know who I am dealing with, especially when our business is so... delicate. You understand, I'm sure.'

Guardiola turned his head to the driver who had resumed his place at the steering wheel. 'Drive, Vicente,' he said, pressing a button set in the door which caused a smoked glass screen to rise, cocooning us the rear compartment. He returned his gaze to me. 'We have complete privacy,' he said. 'We can talk frankly without fear of being overheard.'

I nodded my understanding.

'As I think Mr Moreno explained, the sum of money you recovered from Mora's house could prove to be the source of some minor embarrassment to my company if it were to become public knowledge.' He was trying to sound blasé, but there was an edginess in his voice. 'There was nothing illegal about the payment you understand, but unfortunately the way in which Mr Mora handled the money leaves room for misinterpretation, especially if one has an ulterior motive. There are those who oppose our plans to improve Beniforell and they would do anything to sully the good name and reputation of our company. I'd much rather that didn't happen.'

He was staring directly at me, trying to gauge my reaction. I maintained a look of vague disinterest, trying to give nothing away.

'What do you have in mind?' I asked.

He paused momentarily as if thinking, though I had no doubt he had pre-rehearsed his approach.

'If we could satisfy you as to the legitimacy of the payment perhaps you might be able to release the money so that, on paper at least, it could be returned to us.' He raised an eyebrow as if to reinforce the innuendo.

'*On paper at least?*' I asked, trying to adopt a puzzled expression.

'Well, we could provide you with a bona fide explanation for the payment so that you could authorise its return. We could then provide you with a receipt for the money so that all appeared correct and above board.'

He paused again, still trying to fathom my response. I returned his gaze with a raised eyebrow of my own.

He continued. 'Whether the money was actually returned to us would be a secondary consideration, so long as the paperwork was in order.'

I was intent on not giving him any encouragement or appearing to solicit an offer. 'And this bona fide explanation?' I asked, as if merely seeking clarification.

'The payment was always intended to be used to secure new water resources for the development we proposed. It's quite usual for promoters to do this since adequate supplies of drinking water are a normal prerequisite to approval of any development plan. The money handed over to Mora was a down payment in that regard to facilitate preliminary investigations – geological surveys, that kind of thing – in order to determine the best place to sink a new borehole. There's plenty of water in aquifers beneath Beniforell, it's just a matter of determining the best way of extracting it.'

He said this quite convincingly as if it were true. My curiosity was genuinely aroused, but only by his seeming plausibility and so I decided to play along.

'Forgive my naivety, but how would you secure those water supplies, or at least the investigations, if the money were to be... ostensibly... returned to you?'

His lips tightened to a faint smile as if satisfied that I had analysed the situation and understood the import of what he was suggesting. 'There's no need to worry about that for the foreseeable future. The Beniforell development will be put on hold, for the time being at least. We don't want to court controversy on such a sensitive plan and in any event the economic downturn means we will be reviewing a number of such plans and focussing our attention on those that are already more advanced. If and when the economic situation improves, we may revisit the plan for Beniforell, but as things stand at the moment that would be some years down the line and we would have to start again from scratch. So if we could tidy up the loose ends as I have suggested, we could effectively draw a line under the Beniforell scheme for the time being. Close the book so to speak, if you understand my meaning.' Again his lips pursed to a rueful half smile.

'I see,' I said. 'You seem to have thought of everything.'

His smile broadened to a grin of satisfaction. 'In my business, Captain Fernandez – or may I call you Miguel-Ángel? – it pays to do just that.'

The intimation was clear. He had offered the enticement and in querying the detail I had implicitly agreed to go along with his plan. I did nothing to disillusion him. His background checks had clearly not gone so far as to discover that I had dropped my Spanish first name in favour of its English equivalent.

'I prefer Michael, if you don't mind.'

'Then we have an understanding, Michael?'

I responded with a faint nod.

'There are just a couple of things I need to be clear about,' he continued. 'I need to be sure that the matter can be dealt with discreetly. How many people know about the money?'

Now we were getting to the nitty-gritty. 'Just myself, my sergeant and one officer. Oh, and my superior officer, Colonel Cardells.'

'Antonio Cardells?' There was a clear implication in the question. Guardiola was hinting he knew the Colonel.

'Yes,' I said, resisting the temptation to ask more.

Guardiola moved on. 'And you are satisfied that you can deal with the matter without repercussions?'

'If you can provide authentic paperwork then, yes, I can deal with the matter discreetly.'

He nodded his approval, then pressed a button on the door and spoke into an intercom. 'You can return to the supermarket now, Vicente.' He looked back in my direction. 'There's just one last thing.'

'Yes?' I asked innocently.

'The money. Cash can be dangerous. It's not easy to hide and there is always a risk of discovery or even theft. Neither of us would want that would we?'

'What do you suggest?'

'It could be banked, of course, but these days banks within the European Union are obliged to confirm the source of such a large sum and that might prove problematic. A Swiss bank would be better; they can still be relied upon to maintain a degree of secrecy. But I'm sure you wouldn't want the bother of travelling to Zurich with a suitcase full of cash, so if you were to return the actual cash to us we could save you the trouble by setting up an account on your behalf and arranging a direct transfer from one of our own Swiss accounts.'

Suddenly, the seriousness of the situation struck me. To this point we had been talking almost theoretically; Guardiola sends me authentic paperwork to justify the return of the money, except that it never gets returned. Now we were talking international cloak-and-dagger banking and numbered Swiss accounts. I tried to remain calm, but the lump in my throat betrayed the fact that I was getting out of my depth. Guardiola must have noticed my unease.

'Relax, Michael, it's all quite straight forward; routine almost, and very secure.'

217

It might have been routine to him, but this was a big deal for me and, besides, there was another problem. 'But if the actual cash is returned to you...' I hesitated, still thinking, '...that means I would have to trust you to transfer the money to the account. And there would be a record of the transaction somewhere, however well hidden.'

Guardiola's face twisted to a grin of satisfaction, though I was not clear whether he was relishing the fact that our deal was virtually secured or simply that I had recognised the import of what I was entering into.

'I think we will have to learn to trust each other, Michael. Half now and the other half when the cash is returned to us. How does that sound?'

It was clear now that Guardiola had thought through every last detail. I couldn't help feeling I had been expertly manipulated to this position by someone who understood the power of money and who, for that reason, had the upper hand throughout our conversation. The money was a mere trifle to him, but he knew it was a big deal for me and he had played me like a pawn in a bigger game of chess. But then what did I expect? There had to be a price to pay for succumbing to temptation.

'Fine,' I said, trying to sound glib.

The Mercedes glided to a halt in the same space it had previously occupied in the supermarket car park. Vicente left his seat and, without being prompted, moved to the rear of the car and opened my door.

'Someone will be in touch with you tomorrow with the paperwork and details of the account we mentioned,' Guardiola said. 'I'm sure we'd both like to see this matter concluded as soon as possible.' He offered his hand, signifying our discussion was at an end and I waived my sling in response. 'Drive carefully, if you want to avoid another accident.'

I walked towards my car and turned to watch the Mercedes sweep out of the car park, offering a half-hearted wave. I couldn't see beyond the tinted glass of the Mercedes, but I somehow doubted my gesture was returned. A sickening feeling of anguish overwhelmed me as I sat in the car thinking through what had just occurred. I hadn't expected that selling out would be so easy, and knowing it was just a run-of-the-mill transaction to Guardiola, made me feel used and belittled. It was as if he had got the better of me, and using my first name without inviting me to call him Salvador seemed to signify our relative status in the relationship.

Then I recalled the way the driver, Vicente, had leapt from the car the moment we came to a halt back at the supermarket. It was as if he knew my discussion with Guardiola was at an end and it was time for me to leave. Yet how could he know if, as Guardiola had stated, we had complete privacy behind the screen that separated us from the driver's compartment? I had the uneasy feeling that Vicente had heard every word of our conversation and probably recorded it as well. Was it a mistake when Vicente left the car so promptly to open my door? I doubted it. Guardiola was much too meticulous to allow his driver to commit such an elementary error. I was meant to notice and it was intended as a message.

Most disconcerting of all was Guardiola's statement, "we will have to learn to trust each other." He could have said, "we have to trust each other," but I suspected his words were carefully chosen and the implication was clear. This affair was not the end of our relationship and he would be expecting more for his money in future. But why should I care? He probably had half the police force on his payroll. This was Spain, after all, and from what I could see I had just embraced the admirable Spanish ethos in its entire mercurial magnificence. What was it called? *Enchufe?* That was it, *enchufe*. It sounded so much less sinister than corruption, I thought.

I placed the keys in the ignition about to start the car when Guardiola's final words came back to me: "Drive carefully if you want to avoid another accident." I thought it was just a throw-away remark at the end of our conversation, but then I realised that what he had actually said was: "*Conduce con cuidado, si queréis evitar otro accidente.*" Unlike English, where the second person singular of any verb (the 'you' form) is conjugated the same as the second person plural, in Spanish they are different. By using the term *queréis* as opposed to *quiere*, Guardiola was referring to 'you' in the plural. Perhaps paranoia was setting in; perhaps it was just a slip of the tongue, but if not, the implication was clear – Guardiola knew I was not alone when the car had crashed. And that meant one thing – it was no accident; the brakes had been sabotaged. Was it a serious attempt to bump me off? I doubted it. More likely it was Guardiola's way of demonstrating the extent of his power and influence and, if need be, his ruthlessness and determination to get his own way. His use of the second person plural was no slip of the tongue; he wanted me to know, or at least suspect, that he was behind the accident.

I started the motor and, relieved that the car didn't explode, drove very carefully back to Jalon. Selling out had been easy, but the quid pro quo might prove more onerous than I first imagined. I consoled myself with the thought of the two hundred and fifty thousand euros soon to be sitting in a numbered Swiss bank account.

CHAPTER TWENTY

'Where have you been, Michael?' Mariela demanded as soon as I entered the office. 'We've been trying to contact you all afternoon. Your mobile has been unobtainable.'

I lifted the phone from my jacket pocket and flipped open the cover, giving it a puzzled look. 'Sorry, I must have switched it off by accident.' I was not going to account for my movements. 'What's so important anyway?'

Mariela gave me a quizzical look, but decided not to pursue it. 'We eventually got into Mora's safe and guess what we found?'

I was in no mood for guessing games. 'Just tell me.'

Mariela grabbed a large manila envelope and tipped the contents onto my desk. A collection of assorted passports fanned in front of me in various colours and sizes. I recognised the gold embossed maroon of a couple of European passports, but there were others I could not recognise in blue, black and green. I bundled them together.

'So what do we have?' I asked.

'There are fourteen in total, mostly young women. There are a couple of Spanish women and one British, but the remainder are Eastern European. I suspect they are all people Mora had pressed into prostitution at some stage and he held their passports as a form of security or perhaps simply to prevent them returning to their home countries.'

'So?' I asked disdainfully. 'We already knew that Mora was into prostitution amongst many other rackets.'

'Yes, but there are a couple of interesting names here.' Mariela flicked through the bundle and pulled out a green

Ukrainian passport. 'This one, for example belongs to Yelena Vasilienko.'

I opened the passport and studied the photograph. It was a typical stern pose; devoid of facial expression with eyes that stared blankly back at the camera. The woman's bleached blond hair had been drawn away from her face and tucked over her shoulders. She had prominent cheek bones, a squat nose and a square, slightly jutting jaw line. There was something severe about her hollow eyes that seemed to sum up the national characteristics of a race of people who had suffered years of Soviet repression.

'And this one belongs to Sofia Filipescu.' Mariela passed me a dark blue Romanian passport with tattered edges.

I opened the booklet and studied another expressionless photograph of another blond with stark features and intense eyes that seemed to glower back at me.

'So what do these prove, Mariela? We know that both these women worked for Mora, so why should we be surprised to find their passports amongst his collection?'

'Try this one.' Mariela passed me another Romanian passport, this one brand new.

I flicked the empty pages to find the printed details at the back. The name was Dumitru Filipescu, male, seventeen years old, born 12th October 1992. I was beginning to tire of Mariela's cryptic charade when suddenly my eyes were drawn to the photograph embedded in the page and embossed across one corner with an official stamp.

'Jesus! Is this who I think it is?'

'Anthony Robinson, yes. Either that or he has a twin.' Mariela folded her arms and sat back in a gesture of satisfaction. 'Take a look at the next of kin named at the bottom of the page.'

I adjusted my focus and read the print: Sofia Filipescu - *Mamă*. I put the two passports side by side. Sofia Filipescu's was issued in Bucharest in 1990. It was a twenty year passport with only a year or so to run. Dumitru's passport was more recent, issued four months ago from the Romanian embassy in Madrid.

'Could Anthony Robinson really be Sofia's son?' I asked.

'Take look at this.' Mariela passed me a folded sheet of paper. I opened it and read the details. It was a Spanish birth certificate for Dumitru Filipescu issued in Alicante in October 1992. Mother: Sofia Filipescu. Father: Unknown.

'So you think that Dumitru Filipescu is really Anthony Robinson?'

'It seems likely,' Mariela replied. 'Dumitru's stated date of birth in the passport and birth certificate is not the same as Mr and Mrs Robinson gave us, but it's only a couple of days out. And it would put Sofia at nineteen years old when Dumitru was born. But there's a problem.'

'Oh?'

'I think Dumitru's passport may be a forgery; a very good one, but a forgery nonetheless. Take a look at the embossed stamp on Dumitru's photograph.'

I screwed my eyes to concentrate on the page in front of me and Mariela continued.

'The embossing is very shallow and vague, not crisp as it should be. And there should be a detailed coat of arms in the centre of the stamp, but this one is just an outline. Take a look at the stamp on Sofia's passport and you'll see the difference.'

It was indeed easy to register the difference between the two. 'Can we check with the embassy?' I asked.

'It's already in hand, but it may take a while. Although the Embassy in Madrid can issue passports, all the records are sent back to Bucharest, so they have to check back and it seems the passport office in Bucharest is not very well staffed.'

'Great!' I said with exasperation. 'We need to know for sure and quickly.'

'I've done everything I can,' Mariela said with a measure of annoyance. 'They understand the urgency and we'll just have to wait.'

'There's a quicker way,' I said. 'Let's get Sofia Filipescu in here and ask her.'

Mariela cleared her throat. 'I've already tried that. Teresa Blazquez went to the Club Erotica again this afternoon, but she's not been seen there for several days. Teresa tried her flat in Pedreguer as well, but drew a blank. None of the neighbours remember seeing her for the last few days.'

I lifted my head and allowed my eyes to roll towards the ceiling, biting my lip at the same time to avoid a temperamental outburst that might have provoked Mariela into enquiring further about my whereabouts whilst she had been holding the fort.

'There's some other news though,' Mariela said, sensing my frustration. 'Teresa asked who was running Club Erotica whilst Sofia was away.' She paused as if seeking a prompt and I responded with raised eyebrows. 'Yelena Vasilienko. She wasn't there at the time, but Teresa asked around, because she was puzzled that Yelena had given us the impression she was just another one of Mora's put-upon pawns. The barman at the club almost laughed at the suggestion. He say's Yelena Vasilienko is one of Mora's key personnel. She helps to recruit new talent. She has frequent contact with someone in the Ukraine and regularly arranges for new girls to come over to Spain with offers of work. She also helps these girls and others from eastern Europe to "settle in" when they arrive.'

Somehow I wasn't surprised. With hindsight, Vasilienko's whole story about the so-called Spiritual Development Centre didn't ring true. She had convinced us that she was just a minion doing as she was told, but now it appeared she was an integral part of Mora's whole operation. It was almost three weeks since Mora's murder, but his sleazy sex operation continued as if nothing had happened. And yet Vasilienko's passport was there amongst the others kept in Mora's safe. Why had he kept her passport with the others if, as it now appeared, she was a key part of his business? The best I could conclude was that Mora had locked it away for safety along with the boy's passport and the others and perhaps it was simply that no one else knew where they had been hidden.

'We need another word with Yelena Vasileinko,' I said. 'Get her back here and let's see what she has to say.'

Mariela looked at her watch. 'What, now?'

The office clock showed a quarter to seven. Mariela was right, it was getting late, and besides, I was hungry.

'Okay, leave it until tomorrow morning – first thing.'

'You want me to arrest her?' Mariela asked.

'If she won't come voluntarily then, yes, arrest her.'

Mariela gave me her best frown. 'Are you sure you want her back here, Michael? We're investigating the murder of

Juan-Jose Mora and the disappearance of Anthony Robinson. I'm not clear how much more you think she can tell us.'

'I only know that she lied to us, Mariela, and in my experience people usually lie because they are trying to cover something up. I'm convinced she knows more, much more, than she has already told us and the best way to get to the truth is to put her in the frame. Despite our previous chat, she's been confident enough to carry on running the sex operation as if nothing had happened. So arrest her and bring her back in. Let's see what a few more hours in a cell do for her confidence. Who's checking out Vasilienko's story of family woes back in the Ukraine?'

'Teresa's on to it. She's waiting for a reply from the Ukrainian Embassy, but they have to contact the authorities in Kiev. It will be a while.'

'Tell her to keep chasing. And keep looking for Sofia Filipescu. And chase the Romanian Embassy for that information about the boy's passport.'

'Yes sir,' Mariela said mockingly, 'I'll get on to it first thing in the morning. And what will you be doing whilst I'm dragging in Yelena Vasilienko?'

'I'll be here bright and early waiting for you.'

Mariela grabbed her bag off the arm of her chair and placed the strap on her shoulder, tossing back her blond locks haughtily in a show of annoyance.

'You'd better take someone with you,' I added. 'You never know, she might not come willingly. You have a set of handcuffs in your bag don't you?'

'And my pistol,' she said sarcastically, 'though I'll try not to use it if that's all right with you?'

The officer door rattled in the frame as she left.

CHAPTER TWENTY-ONE

I spent a restless night thinking through the day's events. I could understand why Mora would retain the passports of the girls who worked for him. What better way of ensuring they remained at his disposal? The birth certificate for Dumitru Filipescu seemed genuine which meant Sofia Filipescu had given birth to a son a year or so after arriving in Spain. The photograph of Anthony Robinson in the passport was no coincidence. The only conclusion I could reach was that Anthony Robinson was Sofia's son and that Mora had taken the boy shortly after birth and sold him for adoption by the Robinsons. It made sense. Sofia Filipescu would be no use to him as a prostitute with an unwanted baby in tow. And it was in Mora's nature to exploit the opportunity to match up an unwanted baby with a couple desperate for a child.

But why the need to obtain a passport after all these years? We still needed confirmation that the boy's passport was a forgery, but I was already convinced. Had Mora smuggled the boy out of the country? And if so, why? Could it be that the boy's father had appeared on the scene and Mora had sensed an opportunity to seize the boy and return him to his father, no doubt for a hefty fee? But why forge a Romanian passport? If Mora had the means to obtain a forged passport, why not a Spanish passport, or British, or anywhere else for that matter?

Sleep eventually overcame me and I awoke the next morning with the same questions buzzing around my head.

I arrived at the police station in Jalon just before eight and gave the officer on the desk a cursory greeting. I couldn't remember his name.

'Captain Fernandez,' he said, 'this arrived for you about half an hour ago.' He was brandishing a large buff envelope. 'It came by courier and I signed for it. I hope that's okay.'

'That's fine, er…'

'Officer Gonzalez, sir.'

'Thank you Officer Gonzalez.'

I entered the office and dropped the Venetian blinds before sitting at my desk. The envelope was well sealed with adhesive tape reinforcing the gummed flap. I prised it open and removed two sheets of paper. Salvador Guardiola didn't hang about. The first sheet was a letter on official paper from Tierra Nueva SL, the subsidiary company of Guardiola Property SA in whose name the development plan for Beniforell had been lodged. It contained a detailed explanation of the payment of a quarter of a million Euros to the Mayor of Beniforell along the lines I had discussed with Guardiola the previous day. The letter wasn't signed by Guardiola himself but by someone called Carlos Garcia, Chief Executive of Tierra Nueva SL.

The second sheet was a copy of a fax from the Gesteitling Bank, Zurich confirming the transfer of one hundred and twenty-five thousand Euros to a numbered account running to fifteen digits. A hand written note at the foot of the fax gave a web address for the bank followed by a password and PIN number. Below this was a hand-written note stating: "It would be advisable to change the password and PIN on first accessing this account."

Reading the documents set my heart racing and when the office phone rang I almost jumped from my chair. I stuffed the papers back in the envelope and placed it in the bottom drawer of my desk, taking a bunch of keys from my pocket and locking the drawer, tugging on the handle to be satisfied it was secure. The phone was still ringing.

'Hello,' I said in English as I lifted the receiver.

'Don't you mean *Hola*?' the woman's voice said. 'Or have I caught you reminiscing. You're not homesick already are you?' It was Pilar Vidal.

'Homesick? How could I be homesick when Spain has so many fascinating traits to beguile and confuse me? To what do I owe the pleasure?'

'Well, you remember those fibres we found in Mora's nasal passage and mouth?'

'Yes...' I said hesitantly, trying to recall their significance.

'I told you they were impregnated with a chemical substance of some kind.'

'Yes, I recall. You were going to get the lab technicians to run some more tests.'

'Exactly. We have this young graduate, Maximo; he's only been with us for six months or so. He's very keen and enthusiastic, so I gave him the task. He's done a brilliant job. It's not easy you know. First he had to analyze the substance to identify the principal chemical characteristics. That's difficult enough, but then he had to trawl through literally millions of different samples recorded in a data base in order to find a match.'

This was becoming tedious. So much had happened since Pilar Vidal first mentioned the fibres that they now seemed irrelevant. The solution to Mora's murder was more likely to be found by following the trail of corruption and sleaze than from a chemical analysis of a substance found up his nose.

'And the answer is?' I prompted, trying to sound interested rather than impatient.

'The answer is that the fibres were cotton, coated with a kind of wax. Not a natural wax such as bees' wax or vegetable wax, but a petroleum derivative. And there were traces of an oxygenated solvent – glycol ether.'

'Interesting,' I said, not meaning it. 'Where does this take us?'

'Maximo says there are two possibilities. One is that the solvent was mixed with the wax as a thinning agent before being applied to the material in a production process. The other is that the solvent and wax were mixed in an aerosol – possibly furniture polish or perhaps a car polish of some kind.'

'I see,' I said. My thoughts were already returning to the impending arrival of Yelena Vasilienko, with or without handcuffs, and the questions I would put to her. I visualized her passport photograph; those sharp features and bleached blond hair.

'I hope it helps you in some way, Michael.'

It didn't. 'I'm sure it will, but I need to give it some further thought. Please pass on my thanks to Maximo.' I was about to bring the conversation to an end and my thoughts had drifted to the photograph of Sofia Filipescu and the forged passport for her son Dumitru. Just why had Mora needed that forged passport? Then another question occurred to me, not about fibres or dyes or chemicals, but about Juan-Jose Mora. I put the question to Pilar Vidal and waited for her answer.

'It's possible, yes,' she said in a bemused tone. 'I wasn't looking for it at the time, but I certainly wouldn't rule it out. I could run some more tests if you like.'

'That would be very helpful. I haven't forgotten, I owe you lunch.'

'That's the third time you've said that, Michael.'

'If my suspicions are right, you can make it dinner. You can pick the restaurant and take the most expensive bottle of wine on the list, but for now I have to dash. I'll call you later.'

I called Denia hospital immediately to find Dr Ernesto Alvarez, Consultant Renal Surgeon was in the operating theatre, but should be finished within the next half hour. I told his secretary I was on my way and would be there in thirty-five minutes to talk to him urgently. I didn't ask if it was convenient, I just said I would be there and put the phone down. I grabbed the file from Mariela's desk and the envelope containing the passports then headed for the car.

Alvarez's secretary gave me a stern look as she showed me to a public waiting area that was simply a corridor lined with chairs. 'He's still in theatre. I'll tell him you're waiting when he returns, but he's a busy man and I don't know if he will be able to see you.' She was obviously still smarting from my terse phone call, but I was not in the mood for a brush-off.

'Just tell him it's extremely urgent and won't wait.'

She turned and flounced back down the corridor, her high heels clicking on the tiled floor.

'I suppose a cup of coffee or a glass of water is out of the question,' I said to her back. It was indeed out of the question as she continued down the corridor without breaking her stride.

Twenty minutes later she returned wearing the same well practised sour expression she presumably adopted the minute anyone challenged her zealous protection of Dr Ernesto Alvarez. 'He'll see you now,' she said, turning once more and resuming her catwalk strut along the corridor.

Alvarez was still in his greens and had obviously been watching British hospital dramas, since his head was tightly wrapped in a scarf in the colours of the FC Barcelona. Clearly he was not from these parts and didn't mind offending his Valencian patients. I guessed that when you are in need of life-saving surgery, you don't much care what team the surgeon supports.

'Thank you for seeing me at such short notice, Dr Alvarez,' I said, getting the formalities out of the way.

'My secretary said it was urgent,' he replied with a scowl.

'It's about Juan-Jose Mora.'

'Of course it is,' he snapped. 'Now can you please get on with it, I have patients waiting.'

Obviously this was not going to be easy, but there was no point in pussy-footing around. 'I appreciate all you said last time about maintaining the privacy of organ donors and recipients, but in this case that information is critical to our inquiries into Mr Mora's murder, so I'm afraid I'm going to have to insist on knowing the identity of the kidney donor.'

His face reddened as he swiped the scarf from his head and tossed it onto the desk between us. 'You can insist all you like, Captain Fernandez, but I am not going to divulge that information to you or anyone else; and certainly not without a court order.'

I had anticipated this would be his response. Time to try another tack. 'I will seek the authority of the courts if I need to and believe me, such is the heinous nature of the crime in which you are implicated, there is no doubt I will obtain the courts' approval.'

His expression suddenly changed from controlled anger to outright rage. I was convinced he was on the verge of a furious outburst, but he managed to draw back.

'Are you threatening me, Captain Fernandez?' he said quite calmly.

'Not at all, Dr Alvarez. I merely wanted to emphasise the seriousness of the situation and to point out that the information I need is so vital that I will take all possible steps to obtain it. And of course it could be handled much more discreetly if it were divulged here in your office than in the full glare of a public hearing.'

He drew back to a more defensive posture. I had at least made him think. Time to press on. 'Perhaps it would be easier if I outlined what I believe may have happened and then you can simply confirm or deny my suspicions.'

'Go on,' he said hesitantly.

At least he had not thrown me out of his office. I just hoped my suspicions were right; otherwise I would be out of the door in the next thirty seconds.

'The donor of the kidney Mr Mora received was a young man named Dumitru Filipescu.' I studied Alvarez's face for a reaction but he remained impassive so I pressed on. 'Consent for the boy's organs to be used for transplantation was given by his mother, Sofia Filipescu.'

Alvarez blinked softly in what I took to be acknowledgment. 'It seems, Captain Fernandez, that you may not need my help. Are we finished? As I told you, I have patients waiting.'

So far so good, but I was a long way from finished. 'Not quite finished, no. You obviously needed to confirm the identity of both the boy and the mother and you did so on the basis of their respective passports.' I met his eyes, seeking further acknowledgement.

'Go on,' he said, without commitment.

I reached inside the envelope and withdrew the two passports, placing them on the desk. 'Are these the documents you saw?'

Alvarez picked up the two passports and opened them in turn. His viewed them cursorily and pushed them back in my direction.

'What if I were to tell you that the young man's passport is a forgery?'

Finally I had provoked a reaction. 'What are you suggesting?' There was a touch of anxiety to his voice as he began to realise the import of what I was suggesting.

'Please bear with me, Dr Alvarez. I'm not suggesting anything, merely trying to establish the facts.' I opened Dumitru Filipescu's passport at the page containing his photograph and pushed it back towards him. 'Are you sure this is the young man whose kidney was transplanted to Mr Mora?'

He gave it no more than a casual glance. 'Positive.'

I repeated the process with Sofia Filipescu's passport. 'And this is the mother?'

He lifted the passport and this time gave the small photograph a more careful examination. 'I'd say so.'

There was a trace of doubt in his voice. I opened the file and withdrew a larger photograph, placing it on the desk and pushing it towards Alvarez. My heart was racing and I could feel my pulse throbbing in my neck.

'Passport photographs are so small and often so old that it can be difficult. Perhaps this will help.'

'Yes,' he said, returning the photograph. 'That's Sofia Filipescu.'

'And this is the woman who signed the consent forms for the boy's organs to be transplanted?'

'Yes.'

'Thank you Dr Alvarez,' I said, concealing a sense of elation.

'Is that all? You seem to be remarkably well informed, or perhaps this is all guess work.'

'I prefer to call it intuition.'

'Whatever. It seems you didn't need my help after all.' He pushed his chair away from the desk and began to rise, gesturing that he was drawing our discussion to a close.

'Oh, but I most certainly did.'

He sat again.

'You see, Dr Alvarez, the woman you have just identified is not Sofia Filipescu. Her name is Yelena Vasilienko. She's quite similar in appearance to Sofia Filipescu, but in fact she is a Ukrainian citizen employed by Juan-Jose Mora.

'What?' There was a trace of panic in his voice.

'And the young man was not Dumitru Filipescu. His real name was Anthony Robinson. He's the adopted son of a British couple. He disappeared some four months ago and his parents have been frantic with worry.'

Beads of perspiration were beginning to appear on his face. It was time for reassurance, but there was one further bombshell before I did that.

'Dr Alvarez, I believe that Dumitru Filipescu – Anthony Robinson – was Juan-Jose Mora's son.'

His eyes widened in stunned amazement. 'This is incredible!'

All thoughts of the patients he had waiting were dispelled as he picked up the phone and told his secretary to bring through Mora's file and the file relating to Dumitru Filipescu. The officious secretary entered moments later, casting a scornful glance in my direction.

'Thank you, Dorina, that's all for now. Please cancel all my appointments for the rest of the morning. You can reschedule them for later in the week,' he said dismissively.

There were many important details still to be filled in and with Alvarez realising he was embroiled in an elaborate deceit, he was only too willing to co-operate. He started by showing me a copy of a police report taken from his file. Dumitru Filipescu (Anthony Robinson) had arrived at hospital by ambulance having sustained serious head injuries in a car accident. The car, driven by his "mother" had apparently skidded from a narrow country road near Gata de Gorgos having been forced to swerve by a lorry travelling in the opposite direction. The lorry had failed to stop at the scene, but the car had plunged down a ravine, rolling over several times before coming to a halt at the bottom of a dry river bed. The boy suffered serious head injuries, but the mother escaped with only minor cuts and abrasions and possible concussion. She had raised the alarm by calling the police on her mobile phone.

The young man was pronounced dead soon after arrival in the hospital's emergency department and the attending doctor had immediately notified the hospital's Transplant Co-ordinator. The co-ordinator had undertaken the delicate task of approaching the mother and had done so soon after the boy's death, realising the need for prompt action.

Dr Alvarez explained that a donor kidney remains viable for transplantation for just an hour or so after the heart stops beating and for a further 24 to 36 hours after removal, if placed in a cold preservative solution on ice. When he became aware of the possible availability of the boy's kidney he immediately started the process of cross matching the tissue and blood samples with those of patients on his waiting list. When the match with Mora came through, he decided to intervene and speak to the mother himself. He would not do this normally, but this was an exceptional case as the recipient, Mora, had just arrived at the hospital for a routine dialysis session and the tissue match appeared near perfect.

Alvarez related this information with a growing sense of unease as the extent of Mora's scheming hit home. As I listened to his explanations I, too, was shocked. Even by Mora's standards this was a truly despicable act. My suspicion was that he and Yelena Vasilienko had drugged the boy and then staged the car crash together. Mora had then headed straight to the hospital in order be on hand to take advantage of the fortuitous arrival of a suitable kidney donor. He had killed his own son to save his own life.

'This is dreadful,' he said, a shroud of despair enveloping his face. 'How could he do such a thing?'

'You shouldn't blame yourself, Dr Alvarez. I doubt anyone could even imagine someone so evil.'

Alvarez seemed to recover from his despondency. 'But how did you fathom out it was Mora's son?'

I was in a gracious mood and felt Alvarez deserved an explanation.

'It was a question of bringing together a series of seemingly unrelated facts and events. You see, I knew from Mr and Mrs Robinson that Mora had been instrumental in setting up the boy's adoption. Mora charged them a fat fee and they thought the child had been rescued as a baby from an orphanage in Romania. They kept quiet all these years because they knew the adoption was illegal. I thought nothing more of it until we began to uncover links between the boy and Mora after the boy's disappearance. It always struck me as too much of a coincidence that Mora should have contact with the boy so many years after the adoption. At first I wondered if he was planning to extort money from the Robinsons, but there was no evidence to suggest this was the case.'

'I see,' Alvarez said, following my words carefully.

'When we found the passports, we also found a birth certificate in the name of Dumitru Filipescu. It's genuine and the date of birth led me to conclude that Mora had arranged for the Robinsons to adopt Sofia Filipescu's child. We found the birth certificate with a collection of passports in a safe at a flat Mora used above one of his clubs. They included passports belonging to Sofia Filipescu and Yelena Vasilienko. The boy's passport was with the others, and it appears likely to be a forgery.'

'*Likely to be a forgery?*. You told me it was forged.'

'Just a detail, Dr Alvarez, I am convinced it is forged and that will be confirmed in the near future.'

'But you still haven't explained how you worked out that Mora was the father.'

'I couldn't understand why Mora would go to the trouble of making contact with the boy and then forging a passport in the name of Dumitru Filipescu. At first I thought Mora had abducted the boy and obtained the passport in order to get him out of the country. But I couldn't figure out why he needed a Romanian passport. Then it came to me. The forged passport was created four months ago – if the date of issue is to be believed. And four months ago Mora was desperately ill with kidney failure. You told me yourself that dialysis would not prolong his life indefinitely.'

'That's right,' Alvarez said.

'You recall the last time we spoke we discussed – how can I put this? – the possibility that Mora might have bought his way to the top of the transplant list. You assured me this was not the case and he had simply been in the right place at the time when a kidney with a good tissue match became available.'

'Yes,' Alvarez said cautiously.

'Forgive me, but I'm a detective and I like to check things out – force of habit I guess. After we spoke, I asked Pilar Vidal, the Chief Forensic Pathologist, if it was possible to perform a tissue test on the transplanted kidney and compare it with Mora's tissue. I wasn't even sure if it could be done, but Dr Vidal said it could and went ahead.'

'And?'

'And the result confirmed what you had told me. There was an excellent tissue match between Mora and the donor kidney. So I had to accept that Mora had indeed been fortunate to be in the right place at the right time when a suitable kidney just happened to become available. I thought no more of it.'

Alvarez snorted indignantly.

'It was just as I was trying to work things out earlier this morning that Pilar Vidal called me again. Her call was about something entirely unrelated, but it reminded me of what she had said about the match between Mora and the donor kidney. I put two and two together and realized the match was so good because Mora was Dumitru Filipescu's father. Of course, we'll need to do a full DNA match, but there is very little doubt in my mind.'

Alvarez was gawping back at me, speechless.

I had a question to put to Alvarez, but chose my words carefully so as not to sound accusatorial.

'There's just one point I need to clear up, Dr Alvarez.'

He gave me an enquiring look.

'I'm no expert, of course, but was it not possible to establish that Mora was related to boy when you did the tissue matches before the transplant?'

Alvarez twitched his shoulders. 'I can understand why you ask, Captain Fernandez, but the answer is no. In order to determine the compatibility of donor and recipient we only need to test a limited number of characteristics. A full paternity test would require a much more comprehensive comparison against a much wider range of DNA parameters. Such an analysis would take days not hours and in any event such detail is unnecessary for our purposes once basic compatibility is established.'

'I see.'

'I have a question for you, Captain Fernandez.'

'Yes?'

'How did you know it was Yelena Vasilienko and not Sofia Filipescu who presented herself at the hospital and authorised the donation of the boy's organs?'

'I couldn't believe Sofia Filipescu would be complicit in a scheme to sacrifice her own son to save Mora's life, especially after the way he had treated her. So it had to be someone else. Then, only yesterday, I discovered that far from being just another pawn, Yelena Vasilienko was one of Mora's most trusted servants. I had just been looking at Vasilienko's passport alongside Sofia Filipescu's and it struck me that there was a similarity between the two women, so I guessed it might be Vasilienko who helped Mora in his plan.'

'You guessed?' Alvarez said with a degree of surprise.

'It was an educated guess, but fortunately it turned out to be right, as you have been able to confirm.'

At that moment my mobile phone chirped and vibrated at the same time. 'Excuse me,' I said to Alvarez, flipping the cover to see it was Mariela calling. I knew exactly what she was going to say.

'Where the hell are you, Michael? We have Yelena Vasilienko waiting in a cell.'

As I made my excuses, promising to be back in Jalon within half an hour, but not hinting at my revelations, I noticed Alvarez turning the pages of the Filipescu file with increasing agitation.

'Something wrong?' I said, closing the phone.

'I hope not. Do you have an address for Sofia Filipescu?'

'I think so.' I rummaged through my own file. 'Yes here it is – Edificio San Carlos 27, Calle Ortiz, Pedreguer. Why do you ask?'

Alvarez's face flushed and bridled. 'Oh my God! You need to see this.' He passed me a sheet from his file. 'It's a letter to the Transplant Co-ordinator from the wife of a man who recently underwent a liver transplant. The man has made a full recovery. Of course they do not know the identity of the donor so they ask for their sincere gratitude to be passed on to the donor's family in the hope that it will give them some comfort to know that their loss gave someone else a fresh chance of life.'

I felt my pulse quicken as I realised what Alvarez was about to say.

'Dumitru Filipescu was the donor and the letter was sent on to his mother, Sofia Filipescu, at the address you have just stated. You'd better see this as well.'

He handed me another letter, this one from the Transplant Co-ordinator to Sofia Filipescu. I started to read.

Dear Mrs Filipescu,

I thought you would like to see the enclosed letter from the wife of a patient who benefited from a liver transplant following your son's unfortunate death and your compassionate decision to permit his organs to be used for transplantation. As I am sure you will understand the name of the author of the letter has been deleted in the interests of privacy.

I thought you might also like to know that the patient who received one of your son's kidneys has made a good recovery and the transplant has greatly enhanced the patient's life and future prospects....

I skipped the rest of the letter and my eyes went straight to the date at the top — 17th June. Three days before Mora was murdered.

CHAPTER TWENTY-TWO

Understandably, Mariela was hopping mad by the time I returned to Jalon, but despite her ruddy cheeks and flared nostrils, she looked as beautiful as ever.

'Yelena Vasilienko has been in the cells for almost two hours now. She came quite willingly and I didn't need my handcuffs after all. Where have you been all morning?'

I closed the office door. 'Yelena Vasilienko will have to get used to being in a cell,' I said. 'Sit down and I'll explain.'

It took half an hour to put Mariela in the picture and I ended with an apology for acting so impulsively and keeping her in the dark. She accepted the apology graciously and bombarded me with questions, testing the conclusions I had reached.

'Well,' she said when we finished, 'you seem to have it all neatly wrapped up.'

'Not quite.' I said. 'We have certainly got to the bottom of Mora's web of deceit and duplicity, and we now know what happened to the Robinson boy. But there is still one big question; the question we started with.'

'Who killed Juan-Jose Mora?'

To this point I had not mentioned the letter which the Transplant Co-ordinator had sent to the real Sofia Filipescu. When I told Mariela, her first reaction was one of astonishment, but she quickly became pensive as she appeared to be thinking through the implications.

'Of course you realise, what this means,' I said, trying to short-circuit her thought processes. 'We now have a new prime suspect. What better motive could Sofia Filipescu have for murder than knowing that Mora killed their son to save his own skin?'

239

'Oh my God,' she yelled. 'Michael, there is something I have to tell you.' Suddenly she appeared flustered. 'The Romanian embassy came through an hour ago. They confirmed that no passport has ever been issued in the name of Dumitru Filipescu.'

'I expected as much,' I said, puzzled by her continuing agitation.

Mariela took a deep breath. 'They also told me that a new passport was issued only last week as a replacement for one reported as lost. The new passport was for Sofia Filipescu. The application was dated 22nd June, two days after Mora was murdered and it was collected from the Romanian Embassy in Madrid only last week. Our new prime suspect may have already left the country.'

My initial anger quickly turned to frustration. No one was to blame. Police work is often like this; one step forward and another step back. If need be we would have to trace Filipescu in Romania, if that was where she had gone, and have her extradited. The thought of endless hours of bureaucratic paperwork filled me with dismay. There was one last hope.

'Last week you say. When?'

'Friday.'

'Today is Thursday. You know what you have to do Mariela, and quickly.'

'Check the airports. I'm on it.'

The first news seemed promising – there were no direct flights from Spain to Romania, but this only meant we had to widen the search to other international airports. Mariela had a plan.

'It's a long shot, I know, but my guess would be London. There are several airlines operating regular flights from London to Bucharest, but she would have to get to London first. There are loads of cheap flights to London from Alicante and they will be much easier to check than all the individual airlines operating out of the London airports. Teresa is checking with Alicante now.'

I filled the time thinking about why and how Sofia Filipescu might have killed Mora. She must have been aware that Mora was ill with kidney failure and she must also have known about his transplant operation. When the

240

unfortunate letter arrived from the Transplant Co-ordinator it wouldn't have been hard for her to work out what had happened, even if she didn't know the detail of how Mora had brought about the boy's death. Assuming the letter took a couple of days to arrive, she must have acted straight away since he died within a day of the letter being received. She would have had little time to plan, so my guess was that she acted on impulse and rushed to Beniforell to confront him. Perhaps she didn't mean to kill him. Perhaps an argument ensued and she pushed him off the precipice in the heat of the moment. I would have liked to believe this because I could understand how she would have felt and Mora deserved to die. The only problem was, according to Pilar Vidal, the killer returned to the scene to finish Mora off by suffocating him with something made of green cotton and impregnated with wax and solvent. If I was right, and Sofia Filipescu had killed Mora in an unpremeditated rage, then the material used to suffocate him must have been something readily to hand – an article of clothing, a scarf, a handkerchief, a rag. Unless we could identify the material and link it to Sofia Filipescu all we had was motive with nothing to back it up. If she denied the crime we would be hard pressed to disprove her denial.

Mariela burst into the office with a triumphant look on her face. 'We have it,' she declared. 'We drew a blank at Alicante airport, but then Teresa had the idea of checking with Valencia airport; it's not much further from here than Alicante and there are plenty of flights to the UK. Sofia Filipescu is booked on a flight due to depart from Valencia at 13.21 hours on Saturday bound for London Stansted.'

'Brilliant,' I said. 'Tell Teresa well done.'

'Why not tell her yourself. She would appreciate that. All we have to do now is wait until Saturday and pick her up at the airport.'

We were so close to solving the murder that the thought of kicking my heels for a couple of days was unbearable. Sofia Filipescu was out there somewhere and we needed to find her in case she changed her mind and disappeared.

'Get someone to watch her flat in case she returns' I said. 'And we should keep an eye on Club Erotica in case she turns up there.'

241

'We can do that, but it seems a bit of a long shot.'

'Long shots are all we have.'

Mariela's eyes narrowed in concentration. 'It's more likely she'll be hiding out somewhere else, perhaps with a friend.'

'You could be right, but who?'

Mariela's face suddenly brightened. 'Who do we know has befriended her?'

'Of course,' I said. 'Walter Wilkinson! Come let's get going.'

'I need a couple of minutes,' Mariela said, leaving the office.

I wondered if she was off to powder her nose, but I didn't complain. Mariela was not just a pretty face as she had proved more than once during the last few days. I mused at the irony of Walter Wilkinson in his plaid shirt, Hunter Wellington boots and corduroy trousers trudging to greet us at the gates of *Casa Buena Suerte*. I felt my lips tighten to a smile at the shock we would see in his face, especially if Mariela was right and he had Sofia Filipescu tucked away in his villa pending her imminent departure. At the very least we could charge him with hindering our inquiries, possibly harbouring a fugitive or perverting the course of justice. Pity it couldn't be more, I thought, for I had never liked the man, especially the smug way he had responded to our questions knowing he had a cast iron alibi for the time of Mora's murder.

And then it occurred to me…

Mariela returned to the office, hair combed and a fresh coat of lipstick applied. 'Ready?' she asked, unlocking the top drawer of her desk to remove her pistol and place it in the holster beneath her navy blue jacket.

'Not quite,' I said. 'There's something I want you to do first.'

Walter Wilkinson crunched his way across the gravel after Mariela rang the gate bell for the second time. His appearance did not disappoint. The county-set outfit comprised a pair of beige, almost yellow, corduroy trousers and another checked shirt with sleeves rolled up above the elbows as usual. He had dispensed with the Wellington boots in favour of a pair of battered, brown lace-up brogues. The age of the brogues was evident as the leather soles had curled and distorted to mould themselves over years of wear to the shape of his feet. Even the high gloss sheen to which the uppers had been buffed could not disguise the creases that had developed across the base of the toes through constant bending.

To my surprise, his demeanour was welcoming rather than hostile as I had expected. Perhaps my suspicions were unfounded. He opened the gate and gestured for us to enter, leading us round to the back of the house and a jasmine-covered pergola that offered welcome shade.

'What can I do for you this time?' he said with cheerful bravado as we sat at the hardwood table with matching chairs and padded cushions.

I was looking for clues that Sofia Filipescu might be there. Two cushions might have given a hint, but there were four. There was a single coffee mug in front of the chair he occupied – no clue there and I was having serious doubts.

Mariela occupied the seat opposite Wilkinson and crossed her long legs gracefully, leaning back and flicking her hair behind her shoulders, interrupting my train of thought.

'There are just a few details we want to clear up,' I said, not knowing what else to say.

I could have asked the direct question – is Sofia Filipescu here? – but a denial would have led us nowhere. I wanted to be sure before I confronted him.

'About Mora's murder?' he said with a swagger, cocking his head to one side and wiping a finger across his right eyebrow. 'Anything I can do to help, just ask.'

Either he was genuinely uninvolved or this was the consummate bluff. I couldn't tell which. To confront him would be a risky strategy; at best it would put him on his guard; at worst I would make a fool of myself. I was on the verge of abandoning all caution when Mariela attracted my attention by clearing her throat in an all-too-deliberate way. My eyes met hers and she steered my gaze towards the finger she was tracing around the circular stain on the table in front of her. She lifted her finger from the stain then rubbed her finger and thumb together before separating them in a gesture suggesting a certain tackiness. She raised her eyes again to meet mine and then half winked in my direction. I switched my focus to Wilkinson who had not missed Mariela's gesture.

I took my cue. 'Why don't you ask Miss Filipescu to join us?' I said with undisguised bluster.

Wilkinson buckled. 'Wait there,' he said, entering the villa.

Mariela looked in my direction. 'Should I go with him?' she asked.

'I don't think that will be necessary.'

Moments later Sofia Filipescu emerged from the villa and took a seat at the side of Walter Wilkinson. She looked tired with dark rings beneath her eyes and a puffiness to her face. There was no make-up and her skin was pallid. She wore a simple red and white gingham frock that amply covered her knees as she sat.

'What do you want?' she asked in a faltering voice.

This was not the time for subtlety. 'You pushed Mora off the road in Beniforell and left him lying in the rubble,' I said, as if making a statement of fact.

'Don't say anything, Sofia.' Wilkinson said, grabbing her hand. 'He's only guessing.'

I pressed on. 'On 20th June you received a letter from the Transplant Co-ordinator at Denia hospital that was never intended for you, but you realised immediately what had occurred. Mora had killed your son in order to get a kidney transplant and save his own life.'

I looked into her eyes, but they gave nothing away. 'Outraged, you hurtled straight up to Beniforell to confront him.'

Still she maintained a blank expression, but glanced fleetingly towards Wilkinson. 'And when you found Mora, you argued in the street and you pushed him over the edge of the road and into the ruins below.'

Her body slumped in the chair and her chin sank into her chest. I was sure she was close to breaking down, but Wilkinson interjected. 'Say nothing, Sofia. He can't prove any of this.'

I pressed on. 'But you didn't kill, Mora did you, Sofia?'

Sofia lifted her head and gazed at me with wide-eyed surprise. Her expression gave me the one piece detail I hadn't been able to figure out for myself. I turned towards Wilkinson. 'You killed Juan-Jose Mora didn't you, Mr Wilkinson?'

There was a momentary panic in his eyes which was quickly replaced with indignation. 'Don't be ridiculous,' he said. 'I wasn't even in the country at the time Mora died. I was in England.'

'You had *been* in England, we know because we checked the flight details you gave us. You left Alicante on Monday 18th June and returned from Stansted on Saturday 23rd.'

'So?' he blustered.

I looked at Mariela, who removed a sheet of paper and slid it across the table to Wilkinson. He glanced at the paper without reading it and it was obvious from the look of resignation on his face that he knew precisely what it contained.

Mariela filled in the details. 'What you didn't tell us was that you returned to Spain on a flight from Stansted to Valencia on 20th June arriving at 20.30 hours and you returned from Valencia to Stansted at 13.50 hours the following day. Both flights were booked at the last minute and paid for on your credit card.'

'Quite a busy week,' I said. 'You must have been exhausted.'

'So what?' Wilkinson said. 'This proves nothing.'

'My guess is that when Miss Filipescu received the letter from the hospital, she phoned you in England and told you she planned to confront Mora. She might even have told you she was going to kill him. You probably tried to dissuade her, but when it became clear she was determined to go after him, you jumped on the first available flight to try and stop her. But you were too late weren't you, Mr Wilkinson? And when you found her she had already pushed him off the road and left him lying there. That's when you decided to go up to Beniforell and see for yourself. You found him at the bottom of the precipice and he was still alive so you decided to finish him off by suffocating him.' I looked Wilkinson straight in the eyes and noticed his bottom lip quivering. I switched my gaze to Sofia to find her mouth gaping and her eyes wide open in bewilderment.

'This is nonsense,' he raged, looking towards Sofia. 'Don't believe a word he says, Sofia, this is pure speculation. He can't prove any of it.'

Sofia's look of confusion turned to unease as she reflected on what she had heard. Wilkinson noticed her anxiety and felt the need to reinforce his own posture. 'He's lying, Sofia. He's just trying to set us against each other.'

I paused, hoping Sofia might break, but she remained silent and motionless. Time for the *coup de grace*.

'Do you own a Barbour jacket, Mr Wilkinson?' I asked. 'A green, waxed Barbour jacket?'

Sofia Filipescu and Mariela both looked baffled at the question, unlike Wilkinson whose face froze in disbelief.

It is perhaps perverse to take pleasure from someone else's distress, but there are few more satisfying feelings than unravelling a mystery and unpicking the carefully constructed fabrications of someone as arrogant and conceited as Walter Wilkinson. And my elation was enhanced by the knowledge that Wilkinson had hidden his duplicity even from Sofia.

We recovered the Barbour jacket from a wardrobe in Wilkinson's bedroom. He continued to protest his innocence even when I told him of the forensic analysis of the fibres found in Mora's nasal passage and the post mortem evidence that proved Mora died, not as a result of injuries sustained when he fell, but of suffocation some time after the fall. True, we might have had difficulty proving that the fibres came from his Barbour jacket rather than someone else's, though I was sure there were not too many examples of that quintessentially English piece of country-wear to be found in this part of Spain. Wilkinson finally capitulated when I showed him the slight trace of blood we fortuitously found on the sleeve of the jacket.

I couldn't resist twisting the knife one last time as he resignedly scribbled his signature at the foot of his confession.

'The irony is that you didn't need to finish him off; he would have died anyway.'

Wilkinson sneered. 'I don't care, he deserved to die.'

He was right. If there was ever a case of justifiable homicide this was it. Juan-Jose Mora was an evil man; corruption, abduction, extortion, execution – there weren't enough damning epithets to describe the man. I even felt a brief pang of sadness as we charged Wilkinson with murder and a deeper sorrow as Sofia Filipescu was charged with attempted murder. However, I was sure the court would show her the sympathy she deserved, especially after she explained how Mora had raped her in January 1992 and then taken the child immediately after it was born to be sold for adoption. She told us she had later pleaded with Mora to tell her what had happened to the boy, but he steadfastly refused. She had even considered calling in the police, but she realised that would result in the whole shameful story becoming public and feeding back to her family in Romania.

Poor Mariela looked perplexed when I explained how I had made the link between the analysis of the fibres found by Pilar Vidal and a Barbour waxed jacket, and how such a jacket would be de rigueur for anyone seeking to conform to the mode of English country gentleman and complete the full attire of green Wellington boots, plaid cotton shirt and corduroy trousers in order to harmonise with the rest of the hunting, shooting, fishing brigade.

'I have a Barbour jacket myself,' I said in order to support my reasoning. 'Very practical and hardwearing.'

'Don't tell me you have a pair of green Wellington boots as well?' she said with mock amazement.

'Don't be ridiculous,' I replied with false irritation, failing to mention I had left them behind in Nottingham, never imagining for one moment I would have use for them in Spain.

The detailed DNA tests confirmed what we already knew – Mora was Anthony Robinson's father.

The forensic examination of Mora's flat above the Jupiter Club uncovered plenty of evidence that Tony Robinson had been there. We also discovered Yelena Vasilienko's fingerprints all over the flat and, when pressed, she confirmed that she and Mora had held the boy there for several days. Initially, Mora had tried to persuade Anthony to agree to donate one of his kidneys, even telling him he was his father. Tony had even acquiesced under pressure, but Mora didn't trust him, especially since he knew the transplant team would want to counsel the boy carefully before agreeing to any voluntary donation. So, in the end, Mora hatched his plan to stage the accident.

To my surprise, Yelena Vasilienko's family history checked out. Her father did indeed suffer from emphysema and there was a younger brother with cerebral palsy. Yelena maintained throughout that she had been forced into helping Mora through threats and intimidation, though her story was undermined by the discovery she had transferred ten thousand Euros to a bank account in Kiev two weeks after Mora's transplant operation.

CHAPTER TWENTY-THREE

'Good morning, Officer Gonzalez,' I said as I entered the police station at 7.30 the next morning.

He seemed surprised to see me at such an early hour and even more surprised I remembered his name. 'I need you to open the secure property office.'

He hesitated.

'There's something I have to recover. It's important,' I said sternly.

He took a set of keys from a filing cabinet on the back wall of the reception area then lifted a hatch and walked the short distance along the corridor to unlock the solid steel door.

'That's all, thank you,' I said.

He hovered for a moment. 'I'll have to ask you to sign a receipt for anything you take away, sir,' he said in a faltering voice.

'Of course,' I replied. 'You can return to the desk now. I'll be along in a minute. Leave the keys in the door.'

I found what I was looking for and quickly checked the contents, before leaving the room and locking the door.

'What shall I write on the form?' Gonzalez asked when I placed the keys on the counter.

I raised my left arm. 'Brown leather briefcase, one metal clasp.'

He scribbled on a pad and I signed at the bottom of the page. Gonzalez tore away the sheet. 'This copy is for you,' he said. 'The other one goes on the file.'

'Thank you, Officer Gonzalez,' I said, trying to maintain a confident tone and disguise the nerves that were jangling in the pit of my stomach.

I made the phone call then tapped out a brief note on the computer, pressing "Print" when I had finished before clicking the "Don't Save" option and closing the screen. I waited ten minutes before leaving and arrived at the supermarket car park to find the Mercedes already parked in the far corner. I hadn't expected Salvador Guardiola to be there in person, so I wasn't disappointed to see Vicente alone in the car.

'You have it?' he said through the open window.

'I need you to sign this,' I said.

'The money?'

I lifted the clasp on the briefcase and showed him the contents. 'It's all there. Do you want to count it?'

He took the sheet and reached for a pen on the dashboard then scribbled a signature and handed the sheet back to me. I passed the briefcase through the window and he tossed it on to the passenger seat then pressed a button on the door panel so that the window glided to a close. Moments later the Mercedes disappeared from the car park. Before I reached Jalon my mobile phone chirped. The text message read: "Transfer complete." That was it. It was so easy.

I always feel a sense of anti-climax at the end of an investigation. Perhaps that's because I know a problem solved is only a prelude to the next one coming along, which is probably just as well, otherwise I would be out of a job.

Someone had to speak to Graham and Eileen Robinson and though I offered to take responsibility, Mariela said she would do it first thing that morning. I didn't argue and told her to take the rest of the day off and have an early start to the weekend. Back in the office, I shuffled a few papers and resisted the temptation to log on to the Gesteitling Bank. I'm no expert, but I didn't want to use the office computer for fear I would leave a record in the memory. I would have to wait until I returned home, which I did at 4.30 that afternoon.

Telefonica had installed the land line to my house just a couple of days ago, but I had been told that ADSL was not yet available in Parcent. The dial-up facility on my laptop meant it took an age to navigate the entry pages, inputting my new username, password and PIN. The final screen had just opened, confirming what I expected to see when someone banged hard on the door knocker making me jump. I slammed down the cover of the laptop and yanked out the telephone connection, feeling my heart pounding in my chest.

I opened the door cautiously and my pulse quickened at the sight of a blue police uniform.

'I'm sorry to disturb you, Michael, but I've been trying to speak to you for a few days. I saw your car outside the Cooperativa so I thought I'd come round. I hope it's not inconvenient.'

It may seem strange, but despite years as a serving police officer the sight of a uniform still caused a slight flicker of nervousness, but my exaggerated response was, I realised, caused primarily by a guilty conscience. The realisation that it was Vicenta Sendra, did little to ameliorate my palpitations.

'No, it's fine,' I blustered. 'Come in.'

I still felt uneasy as Vicenta strode down the hall in heavy boots, cargo pants and a blue combat sweater topped with a yellow day-glow vest. Most disconcerting of all was the baton clipped to her belt and the jangling of a set of handcuffs.

'How can I help?' I asked, still struggling to recover my poise.

'We had another broken wing mirror on Tuesday night. That's thirteen in all and yesterday one of the British residents stopped the Mayor in the street to demand that something is done. The Mayor spoke to me this morning and she was not very happy.'

'This latest broken mirror was on a British registered car then?'

'Yes.' Vicenta removed the check-banded baseball cap that was shielding her eyes. 'I've marked it on the plan with all the others. Perhaps you could take a look.' She removed a rolled up plan from under her arm and moved towards the dining table.

'Just a moment,' I said, grabbing the laptop and moving it to a sideboard in the corner of the room.

'This is the latest case here.' She pointed to a red dot on the plan which was within the cluster we had previously identified. 'And I've added the date to the list.' She handed me a piece of paper with a list of dates.

The dates seemed random with three or four incidents occurring within a couple of weeks, then a break of a week or so followed by more incidents, another break and then two more a week before the latest attack.

'Did you check on other British cars parked elsewhere in the village as I asked?'

'Yes, I've done that. There are several British registered cars that regularly park on the outskirts and none of them has been attacked.'

My eyes switched between the dots on the plan and the list of dates. 'It seems to me, Vicenta, that whoever is responsible is not prowling around the whole of Parcent looking for British registered cars to attack, otherwise the incidents would be more widespread. That means they probably live close to this cluster of dots. I'd also guess that they travel along these particular streets on a regular basis, late in the evening.'

'Do you think they have a particular grudge against the English?' Vicenta asked.

'The British,' I corrected. 'There's a difference. Presumably all the vandalised cars have standard British number plates with the letters GB at one side and you can't tell whether they come from England, Scotland or Wales. Except...'

It just occurred to me that British car registration numbers included letters denoting the place where they were first registered. Of course, cars could be sold on to someone from a different part of Britain, but perhaps our attacker didn't realise that, or perhaps they didn't care.

'Vicenta, do you have a list of the registration numbers?'

'Yes, here.' She handed me another sheet of paper. 'The ones at the top of the list are the cars that have been vandalised. The rest of the list includes all the British cars that we found to be regularly parked around the village.'

I studied the numbers to find at least half the cars were more than five years old and the chances were that they had been sold on more than once. One number in the list of cars that had not been attacked stood out because it contained the letters CAZ. The letter Z, I knew, was used exclusively for cars registered in Northern Ireland and, if I remembered correctly, the letters AZ denoted the city of Belfast.

'Does that tell you anything?' Vicenta asked.

'This one here,' I said, pointing to the Northern Irish number. 'Do you know who it belongs to?'

'No, but I could soon find out.'

I was growing impatient. After days spent unravelling the evil deeds of Juan-Jose Mora, I was not in the mood for taxing my brain over a few acts of petty vandalism. I was wondering how I could get rid of Vicenta without appearing disinterested. Perhaps I could suggest some spurious new line of inquiry then send her on her way. With this in mind, I looked again at the plan and the two lists on the table. And then it came to me.

'Do you have a diary or a calendar?' I asked.

'I have a small calendar in the front of my notebook.'

'Let me have a look please.'

Vicenta pulled the Velcro fastener on the flap of one of the many pockets in her trousers and passed me the notebook. I studied the dates on the list against the calendar and handed the notebook back to her.

'Thank you, Vicenta,' I said, disguising my elation. 'Give me twenty-four hours to think about this and I'll get back to you.' I rolled up the plan and gave it back to Vicenta along with the two lists before ushering her towards the door.

'Do you want me to check the owner of that Northern Irish car?' Vicenta asked.

'That may not be necessary.'

It was like entering a familiar film set as I pushed aside the fly screen and walked into Bar Casino just after 7.30 that evening. The British contingent occupied a group of stools just inside the door taking up over half the length of the bar. One of the group, a burly man with more stubble on his face than on the top of his head, wore a white football shirt emblazoned with the three lions of England. As I passed behind the group it was easy to pick out a Geordie accent arguing vociferously with the ginger-haired Northern Ireland supporter I had bumped into before.

'England didn't even qualify for the last European Nations Cup.' I heard the green-shirted man jibe in his familiar Belfast brogue.

The domino quartet was ensconced around the same baize-covered table by the side wall, their hands clasped furtively around their dominoes to protect them from each other's view.

Pepito occupied his customary position at the far end of the bar, just beyond the glass cabinet that housed the day's tapas selection. The small glass of milky white *candela* was almost empty and he readily accepted the refill I ordered along with a *caña* for me.

'Had a good week, Michael?' Pepito said, raising the candela to his lips and wafting the now familiar scent of aniseed in my direction.

'Excellent, thank you. Almost perfect in fact.' I sipped the *caña* virtually emptying the tiny glass.

'Have you spoken to Rosana recently?' he asked.

'I've been meaning to, but I've been rather busy.'

'Michael, if you'll accept a piece of well-meaning advice…' Pepito glanced in my direction as if seeking permission to continue.

'Yes…' I said, giving him the encouragement he sought.

'Don't leave it too long. It's my experience that a wound left untended will fester.'

His cryptic message was clear.

'Actually, Pepito, I did want your advice on something.'

'Yes…' he said, gesturing to the barman to refill my glass.

'Well, it's just that… I may be in a position to help Rosana – financially I mean.'

'I see,' he said hesitantly.

'You told me she has significant debts on her house and I'd like to find a way to help her out if it were possible. I just wondered what you thought.'

Pepito twitched his shoulders. 'In my experience, Michael, it is better to mend a bridge before you attempt to cross it.' He cleared his throat. 'By the way, Vicenta was looking for you earlier.'

254

'I know. I saw her this afternoon.' I slid my barstool closer to Pepito and leant towards him. 'Pepito, remember you told me that at the end of the Civil War great uncle Rafael was captured by a contingent of the International Brigades during the siege of Madrid?'

'Yes, in 1938.'

'People from lots of countries joined the International Brigades to fight Franco's fascists. Do you know what nationality formed the contingent that captured Rafael?'

'British I think. Why do you ask?'

'No particular reason. Where does Rafael live?'

'At the end of Carrer San Lorenzo.'

'What days do the old men over there play dominoes?'

'Every Tuesday and Friday. What's this all about, Michael?'

'I'll be back in a moment.'

I left the bar and strode across the room to the domino table and tapped the shoulder of the old man wearing a greasy black beret. His head turned and his gnarled face met me with a scowl.

'Remember me, Rafael – Miguel-Ángel, Antonio's son, your great nephew.'

He screwed his eyes, squinting through the small round lenses of his spectacles. 'What do you want?' he said with a hiss of annoyance.

'I need a word with you.'

'*Vete a la mierda!*' he snarled.

I was not in the mood to fuck off just yet. 'We can talk quietly, or in front of your friends, or if you really insist we can talk at the *comisaría* in Jalon. The choice is yours.'

His face flushed with anger as he stood. 'I'll just be a moment,' he said to his friends.

I led him to an empty table in the corner of the bar and we sat facing each other.

'Just who do you think you are, barging in and threatening me like this? You may be the son of that leper nephew of mine, but you are no relation to me.'

I swallowed hard to suppress my anger. 'I have a small problem and I think you may be able to help.'

Rafael snorted.

'Vicenta Sendra tells me there has been a nasty outbreak of vandalism in the village in recent weeks.'

'You're wasting my time,' Rafael said, rising to his feet.

'Sit down, Rafael,' I demanded as sternly as I could. 'I haven't finished yet.'

He hovered for a moment then slumped back in the chair.

'Thirteen cars have had their wing mirrors smashed. All the cars were British registered and they were parked in the main square, Carrer Gabriel Miro or Carrer San Lorenzo. All the incidents took place late in the evening on Tuesdays and Fridays.'

Rafael's face grew pallid.

'Now, here's how you can help. Using my expert detective skills I have surmised that the culprit is someone who lives on one of the streets I have mentioned and that they have a reason to walk along the route of the incidents on Tuesday and Friday evenings. Oh, and they have a grudge against the British. I just wondered if you knew anyone who might fit those criteria.'

'I don't have to listen to this,' Rafael snarled.

I leant forward, pushing my face towards his. 'Understand this, Rafael, as far as I am concerned you are no relation of mine. I know you are used to getting your own way in this village and you are probably thinking that a chat with your political cronies will see this matter brushed under the carpet. Well, I just happen to be between cases at the moment, so I have time on my hands and I'll be taking over this case from the *policia local*. And remember this, Rafael – *El Caudillo* died in 1975.'

Rafael shuddered. His defiance subsided and he suddenly looked like the old man he was. I could almost have felt sorry for him except that he had just called my father a leper. If I were a vengeful person I could have enjoyed seeing him dragged through the courts and exposed as a bitter old man still living in the past. But this was Spain and I knew it wasn't the convention to rake over a part of history most Spaniards had conveniently erased from their collective memory.

'There is another way to deal with the matter,' I said, prompting a flicker of an eyebrow from Rafael.

'I noticed a small charity shop in one of the side streets near the town hall. I gather it is run by some British ladies who raise money for good causes locally. It would be nice to read in the Costa Blanca News that an anonymous donor has shown his support by making a sizeable donation to the cause. How much does a replacement wing mirror cost, I wonder? About a hundred Euros? One thousand three hundred Euros would be a great help to those well-meaning British ladies don't you think?'

Rafael grunted.

'Sorry, I've kept you from your dominoes. We're finished now, I think.'

I rejoined Pepito at the bar. 'What was that all about?' he asked.

'Nothing,' I said. 'Just a little misunderstanding, but it's sorted now.'

CHAPTER TWENTY-FOUR

The office was functional with harsh strip-lighting reflecting onto plain white walls devoid of any kind of embellishment apart from a calendar hanging at the side of the panelled door through which I had just entered. My back was beginning to ache after fifteen minutes confined to the straight-backed chair placed opposite the door to the inner office. A middle-aged secretary occupying the only desk in the room rose to draw a set of vertical blinds and eclipse the narrow shaft of early morning sunlight that was creeping across the floor. She returned to the desk and continued tapping on a keyboard, oblivious to my presence. She paused to sip a dainty cup of coffee – a courtesy that had not been extended to me.

The door of the inner office burst open and the corpulent figure of Colonel Antonio Cardells strode across the office, his rubber-soled shoes squeaking on the marble floor. I was directly in his eye-line but he seemed deliberately to ignore me as he approached the secretary's desk.

'That's fine, Faviola,' he said, depositing a sheath of papers on the desk. 'Just a few corrections and then you can send it off.'

Faviola, I thought. She was definitely not a Faviola. A Teresa or Maria maybe, but definitely not a Faviola.

Cardells turned on his heels, squeaking again and then, giving me only the briefest of glances, moved back towards the door. 'Come through, Michael,' he said brusquely.

I gathered the folder I had nursed on my knees and stood, straightening my tie as I followed him into the office. He rounded the mahogany desk and sat in the high-backed swivel chair to face me. 'Sit down.'

I obeyed, feeling the stickiness in my armpits as my shirt stuck to the skin beneath my jacket.

'This is a bad business,' he said with a sigh. 'I hope we can keep a lid on things when it comes to court. Abduction and murder are heinous crimes, but the tourist authorities are very twitchy about anything that affects the image of the Valencian region. It's bad enough with the European Parliament investigating complaints of human rights abuses over the so-called "land-grab" laws, but the economic downturn has only made matters worse. Tourism is in decline and the construction industry is already on its knees. Still, I'm sure we can leave it to the courts to handle the cases discreetly.'

He glanced in my direction, but I remained detached. I was sure he had lost weight since we last met.

'All the same, well done; a fine piece of detection. I never imagined when I gave you these cases that they would turn out to be linked. You and Sergeant Poquet have worked extremely well together. You have the makings of a productive partnership, wouldn't you agree?'

'Yes sir.' I left aside the question of how he already knew about the outcome of the investigation.

'So, Michael, how have you settled in Spain?' He opened the folder in front of him. 'I see your probationary period is due for review in a couple of months. Have you decided to stay in Parcent?'

'I'm not sure, sir.'

'Oh?'

'I heard this week that the agents have found a buyer for my apartment in Nottingham.'

'That's excellent.'

'I haven't accepted the offer yet.'

'Holding out for a better price, is that it?'

'No sir.'

'Then what's the problem? I can virtually guarantee your probation will be a formality and we can offer you a permanent post with the rank of Captain. You seem to have assimilated very well into the Spanish way of doing things.' There was a twinkle in his eye. 'Who knows what the future might hold?'

'There's something I need to clear up first.'

He gave me an inquiring look. 'Oh?'

I opened the flap of the folder and leant forward letting the contents slide out across his desk.

'What's this?' he asked with a hiss of annoyance.

I took a deep breath and swallowed hard.

'There's a document there from Tierra Nueva SL, a subsidiary company of Guardiola Property SA who submitted the development plans for Beniforell. It purports to give an explanation for a payment of a quarter of a million Euros to Juan-Jose Mora. There's also a receipt for the same amount, returned in cash to one of Salvador Guardiola's employees. The last document contains details of an account with the Gesteitling Bank in Zurich which contains a quarter of a million Euros. It's a numbered account, but I've included details of the access code, username and PIN.'

Cardells cast an eye over the documents without picking them up. His face was turning from red to crimson and his left cheek twitched as he reached forward to pick up the small device half the size of the smallest mobile phone.

'And what's this?' he said gruffly.

'It's a digital USB voice recorder. Very neat don't you think? And easy to hide,' I said, fidgeting with the red silk handkerchief protruding from the breast pocket of my jacket.

His nostrils flared and he glowered in my direction.

'It contains a recording of a conversation I had with Salvador Guardiola only last week. I'm sure you will find it revealing.' I met his eyes with a defiant stare.

'And what do you expect me to do with this information, Captain Fernandez?'

'That's entirely up to you, Colonel. There's something else there as well,' I said. 'It's a photograph of Salvador Guardiola. You might find the background interesting.' I rose from the chair and moved towards the door then turned. 'By the way, I've included a receipt for the voice recorder. I bought it in a local shop in Jalon. I guess I could have got it cheaper somewhere else, but I'm sure you'll be able to reimburse me.'

'Are there copies of this information, Captain Fernandez?' he said in a less than demanding tone.

'What do you think, sir?'

Mariela looked magnificent as she strode across the restaurant to join me at the table on the far side of the terrace at Restaurante La Pista in the centre of Jalon. I had never seen her in a dress before and the figure-hugging, calf-length white linen accentuated her curves perfectly and emphasised the contrast with her evenly tanned face and arms. Her normally straight blond hair bounced in soft curls, something else I had not seen before, and suggested she had made an extra effort for the dinner I had promised on several occasions. Her beaming smile was reflected in the brightness of her eyes as she reached the table. I stood to greet her and placed my arm around her waist, feeling a sharp twinge in my recovering shoulder. The pain subsided as our lips met and we exchanged a more than cursory kiss. Her subtly sensuous perfume filled my nostrils and acted like a kind of anaesthetic.

I lifted the chair away from the table and tucked it back as she sat and ran a hand through her hair. I took the seat opposite and felt a growing unease as I wondered if the dinner I had arranged was a good idea after all.

'You look very nice,' she said, before I could speak. 'I don't think I've seen you without a tie before. It suits you.'

'Thank you,' I said, not knowing what else to say and feeling butterflies flutter in my stomach. Mariela seemed to be waiting for me to say something else and, to be honest, I wanted to, but the doubts I was now having about the whole concept of the evening kept me silent.

Mariela must have noticed my agitation. 'Are you all right, Michael? Only you look anxious about something.'

I was wondering what to say, how to respond, when relief came as a figure approached the table behind Mariela. A frown narrowed Mariela's eyes as I stood to greet the new arrival and exchange kisses on each cheek.

'You know sergeant Poquet, I think. Mariela, you remember Dr Pilar Vidal, of course.'

It was at this stage I began to wonder if the idiom, *killing two birds with one stone* would translate sympathetically into Spanish.

The consternation I had felt during my meeting with Colonel Antonio Cardells just a few days before was as nothing compared to the trepidation I felt as I stood before Rosana's front door and lifted the heavy brass knocker.

Lightning Source UK Ltd.
Milton Keynes UK
06 December 2010

163960UK00001B/34/P